Sunday Morning Blues

Sunday Morning Blues

K.T. Richey

www.urbanchristianonline.com

Urban Books, LLC
97 N18th Street
Wyandanch, NY 11798

Sunday Morning Blues Copyright © 2013 K.T. Richey

ISBN 13: 978-1-60162-775-9
ISBN 10: 1-60162-775-0

First Printing December 2013
Printed in the United States of America

10 9 8 7 6 5 4 3 2 1

This is a work of fiction. Any references or similarities to actual events, real people, living or dead, or to real locales are intended to give the novel a sense of reality. Any similarity in other names, characters, places, and incidents is entirely coincidental.

Distributed by Kensington Corp.
Submit Wholesale Orders to:
Kensington Publishing Corp.
C/O Penguin Group (USA) Inc.
Attention: Order Processing
405 Murray Hill Parkway
East Rutherford, NJ 07073-2316
Phone: 1-800-526-0275
Fax: 1-800-227-9604

To

JMADP

Dedication

What an incredible journey this has been. I would like to thank God for the many blessings and adventures He has bestowed upon me throughout my life and for those in my future.

I dedicate this book to all the readers, book clubs, bloggers, churches, authors and the many people who have supported my ministry. You have been a wonderful inspiration to me. Thank you for your support.

To Joylynn M. Ross and the Urban Books family, I thank you for all that you have done for me and the knowledge and support you have given me.

To my family, I love you. You have been a tremendous source of inspiration, love, laughter and support for me throughout the years.

To all the first ladies who have been misunderstood, ignored, lied on, rejected and endured through it all, this book is especially for you. God has heard your prayers and will continue to bless you and your family.

Join me at Ktrichey.com, www.facebook.com/ktrichey, and on Twitter @AuthorKTRichey.

Peace and Love

All scriptures are from the King James Version.

1

"Mrs. Patrick, we will be taking off in about ten minutes," the flight attendant said as Shante sat back into the soft tan leather seat of her private Learjet. Never would she have thought that she would own a plane or be a best-selling author. She had come a long way from riding the bus with her baby, out searching for a job in an unfamiliar town. At that time, her face was loaded with so much makeup, she looked like RuPaul's cousin. She had to do something to cover the scars from the severe beating she received from her ex-husband. She didn't want people to look at her as if she had some dreaded disease they did not want to catch. That was a long time ago.

She closed her eyes and waited patiently as the engine of the plane revved up, preparing to take off. Her mind was filled with all the things she had to do when she got home. If only she could concentrate on how God used her to minister at Spirit Life Conference. She was told over fifty thousand people were there and all of them tried to jam the arena the night she preached. There was standing room only, even in the overflow room. Long gone are the days when no one wanted her to preach in their church. Those days were just a faint memory that seemed so distant and unfamiliar. Back then, she had to pay for her own transportation, hotel and meals to travel to cities to preach. She would leave with only a pat on the back and a "good job" coming from the mouths of the people who invited her. Now, one of the most prominent bishops in

America and his wife had invited her to speak. Bishop and First Lady LeBeuf were such gracious hosts. She was given the five-star treatment. She usually didn't preach conferences like these, but this was Bishop LeBeuf. Who would turn down the bishop?

She pressed the button on her seat belt, unleashing the restraint from her neck. She leaned back in the seat as the plane leveled off. Shante was so tired she could hardly see straight. If only this flight was longer than an hour she would have a little time to relax. This was her seventh conference in a two-week time span. Her body ached from the trek from South Carolina to Michigan, to Texas, to Atlanta, and now back to South Carolina. It was moments like these that made her long for the days when no one knew her and she could walk down the street without someone recognizing her. It didn't help to have graced the cover of *Ebony* magazine. Now, everywhere she went, someone recognized her.

"Mrs. Patrick, here is your water with lemon," the flight attendant, Joy, said as she handed her the cold glass. She knew exactly what Shante needed before she asked for it. She had been right by her side during this long trip, making sure the long and short flights were most comfortable. The tapping noise coming from the seat beside her interrupted her thoughts. She glanced to the seat across from her where her assistant, LaToya, was busy at work on her laptop. She had gone over their schedule, which never seemed to allow for a break, during this short trip home. As meticulous as she was, sometimes Shante thought LaToya liked the travel more than she did.

Shante had a longing in her belly for her husband Max and her children, especially her daughter, Camille. Since she moved to New York to work for Band Entertainment, they rarely saw each other. For years, it was only the two of them, a struggling single parent with a bright and happy child who looked at the world with so much optimism. Now, as she prepared for her wedding, Shante had to schedule her trip to New York to help pick out her daughter's wedding gown around her appearances on the morning talk shows and three book signings. Her heart ached sometimes when she thought about the many nights they sat in their small apartment, dreaming of the day when they wouldn't have to worry about anything and could go on fabulous vacations. Somehow, Camille's dream vacations always had something to do with an amusement park, while Shante's always included the sun and crystal blue water and people speaking with such strong accents that she wouldn't care what they were talking about.

Now, Shante lived in the big mansion that was only a dream so many years ago, and Camille was not there and only came for occasional visits when her busy schedule would allow. Yet, they managed to talk with each other almost every day. It was the highlight of Shante's day. If only their conversations were not cut short by their hectic lifestyles, she could enjoy them more. Shante wondered how Camille found the time to date this wonderful man she was engaged to. Aaron was a prominent music producer and Christian—the most important thing. He truly loved her and treated her well. He was everything a mother would want for her daughter; a saved, successful man of integrity that treated Camille with respect, dignity and unconditional love.

She was not the only one with the man of her dreams. Max was Shante's. When they met in college, he wasn't the type of guy she wanted to date at the time. Shante wasn't interested in nerdy, career-minded, goal-oriented men. She liked the pretty boys. Funny how time and life changed the outlook on things. It only took a few years after they left college for them to come back together after her nightmare of a marriage ended and the death of his first wife. It seemed as if they were destined to be together. Both of them were single parents and pastors of churches in Charlotte. When Shante picked up her daughter and left her abusive husband, with only the clothes on their backs, the Holy Spirit guided her directly to him.

Shante wished she could feel excited about seeing Max, but she was tired. He always greeted her like a soldier returning home from the battle. He prepared all the things any girl in her right mind would want; the perfect welcome home meal, a bubble bath, and a soothing massage to relax her mind. That might sound great, but it always ended with sex when all Shante wanted to do was sleep. However, she had been away two weeks, and she knew her man desired the nooky, and it was up to her to give him what he desired.

Then there were her boys, her stepsons, although she never called them that. She practically raised them. Their mother died when they were very young and as their godmother, Shante took care of them just like their own mother would. Her boys were a joy to her. Having a teenager and two preteens in the house was always challenging. Hopefully, when she got home, it would be peaceful as long as Jonathan, the oldest, had not been into it with his dad again.

Since he grew and became as tall as his dad, Jonathan wanted to challenge Max's authority and pushed them both to the limits. Shante wondered what happened to the mild-mannered son over the past few months. He was like a Jekyll and Hyde. Shante was fully aware that she and Max needed to spend more time with him and his brothers, but their ministries kept them busy. She closed her eyes and prayed for peace when she got home.

Shante shifted her hips from side to side, trying to find a comfortable spot on the cushioned seat, but she couldn't relax. There were so many things to do when she got home. As the first lady of Deliverance Temple, she had to complete the plans for the women's conference and make sure the Women's Fellowship was flowing in the way the Holy Spirit instructed her.

Max wanted the traditional first lady, but Shante was never the hat-wearing, sit-on-the-front-row-and-smile type of first lady. He was well aware that the church growth was due to Shante's ministry and not his. Many people attended their church in Columbia, South Carolina, in an effort to get closer to Shante. It pulled at his ego and had been a constant sore spot in their marriage. However, Shante had to learn to sit back and let him do what God instructed him to do at the church and be his behind-the-scenes advisor and confidante instead of Shante Patrick, the internationally renowned minister.

"Mrs. Patrick, we'll be landing in a few minutes," Joy said as Shante pulled her seat to the upright position and snapped her seat belt in preparation to land. Her forty-six-year-old body ached. She had to get in the gym more. She made a mental note to tell LaToya to schedule some time to work out. She used to work out all the time. Her schedule won't allow that now, and her body was feeling the results of her busy lifestyle of working all the time, eating on the run and sitting up all night on the computer trying to meet the next publishing deadline. Is this the lifestyle she prayed for?

There were days when she wanted to be the simple wife and first lady standing at Max's side. She tried to imagine what that would be like. It might be nice to sit on the front row looking like the best-dressed woman in the church saying, "Bless you, baby," to everyone who greeted her. But that wasn't Shante, and she knew it. On days like today, she wished the only thing she had to worry about was what she would wear to church next Sunday.

In addition to all she had to do, Max had thrown his hat in the political ring and was running for county council. He would make an excellent councilman, as he was passionate about the community and its needs. Shante sensed this was only the beginning, and somehow, she felt he aspired to hold a higher political office. Now she had to be the politician's wife and people were now going to watch everything she said and did more closely. It wasn't enough for her ministry to be scrutinized; now it's going to be her whole life. People had already asked about the missing money from her previous church which she didn't have anything to do with. Her ex-husband, Kevin, caused such a huge mess in her church. He planted seeds of corruption and scandal that had people questioning Shante's integrity and speculating that some wrongdoing was going on for both her and Max.

Max had been defending Shante on every hand. He even produced the private investigator's report showing Shante had nothing to do with the scandal and it was all a scheme devised by Kevin, her church secretary and members of the church board. However, the press won't let it go. They were still talking about it as if it happened yesterday instead of years ago. What some people would do to get elected as to stoop as low as this! It was beginning to have an affect on their children. They are the ones who were taking the brunt of the lies when the kids at school questioned and antagonized them.

The bump of the plane landing shook Shante back to reality. She took a long deep breath. The landscape surrounding the speeding plane rushed past her as it slowed to a stop. Shante didn't think she had ever been this tired returning from a trip. She needed a vacation. She promised herself she would give up her workaholic ways. As usual, she would stop for a short while, get bored and jump back on the wagon again. It didn't help that now she had agents, managers, editors and a host of other people who made demands of her time. All of this, in addition to her family and church responsibilities, had stretched her to the limits. How long could she hold up this schedule? She was called to preach the gospel, but at what expense? Her commitment said at all costs, but her body was saying, "slow down."

The plane slowly coasted down the small airstrip at the private airfield. She was back home. No five-star hotels or gourmet meals or people waiting on her hand and foot. She glanced at LaToya who was gathering her belongings, preparing to leave the plane. She looked so young, seemingly without a care—no husband, no children to go home to, only the peace and quiet of her apartment. There were times when Shante wished that was her life. But it was only a passing thought as the desire to see her family was overwhelming. She did miss them very much. It was back to reality now. She was no longer the celebrity preacher or *New York Times* bestselling author. She was Shante Patrick, wife, mother, minister of the Gospel and the first lady.

2

"Daddy, Daddy, Daddy," Deandrea's son screamed as he escaped from his towel and ran butt naked down the hall to greet his father. Jarrod had just arrived home from his long trip preaching and hosting a Christian talk show. Her twins, R. J. and Andrea, always managed to hear him when the door opened. Holding her daughter in the crook of her arm, Deandrea chased R. J. down the hallway holding the bath towel in her other hand. They had not seen their father in a week, and they delighted in his presence. Her plans were shot. She wanted to get the children bathed and in bed before her husband, Jarrod, returned home. It didn't work out this time. He arrived early. Now she was going to have to fight to get them into bed.

"Whoa, buddy. You got all your stuff hanging out," Jarrod said to R. J. This was his son. He looked just like him, even at three years old. Deandrea set the squirming child down and watched as she ran to greet her open-armed father. He picked both of them up in his arms and lifted them in the air smiling the entire time. Although he was smiling, his eyes were puffy and looked weak. However, he managed to get enough strength to lift two screaming children in the air. He glanced at Deandrea, winked, and gave a slight smile. He was happy to be at home. Deandrea was glad he was at home. She missed him so much when he travels. That was his calling, to preach the Gospel. He had to do it.

"R. J., you need to get your pajamas on," Deandrea said as she reached out and took his hand amid his loud protests. This child was just like his daddy, always wrecking her nerves. When they first met, Pastor Raymond Jarrod Fuller and Deandrea were archenemies. They could not stand being in the same room with each other. The seminary had sent Deandrea to his church to do an internship. It was an instant dislike, to say it mildly. They fought all the time. They even had an incident in his mother's kitchen. His mother, Miss Essie, had a fit when she came into the kitchen and saw they had torn it up with a food fight. To this day, she didn't let them eat at the small dining table in her kitchen, afraid they were going to get into another fight. She allowed the children to eat there but not the grown-ups. It always brought a smile to Deandrea's face, thinking about how they met and how far they had come.

"R. J., go put on your pajamas, and I'll come in your room and read you a story," Jarrod said. Instantly, the toddler stopped his protest and obeyed his father. Jarrod did not need to raise his voice or say anything in anger for this child to snap into obedience and run toward his room.

Deandrea sighed. He was going to have to teach her how to do that one day. Jarrod turned his attention to his daughter who was still squeezing his leg, afraid to let go, afraid he would leave again. She was a daddy's girl. She had his eyes, big and round, although not as tired as his, still deep brown and bright as the sun.

"How's my little girl? I have something for you," he said.

Deandrea turned and followed her son into his room to help him put on his pajamas. He always brought the children something back when he travels. If he had the time, he would bring back a toy. If not, he would pick up some candy in the airport or brought snacks from the plane. They loved it no matter what he gave them. Deandrea reached R. J.'s room in time to see that he had his Bob the Builder pajama shirt on backward. She sat on the bed and helped him put his pajamas on and watched as he ran out of the room toward his daddy.

Deandrea sat on the bed listening to the sounds of happy children and a tired husband who played in the hallway. She looked around the room of the house Jarrod purchased before they met. They were neighbors in the exclusive subdivision in the suburbs of Greenville, South Carolina, and had never met. When Deandrea found out that her enemy lived in her subdivision, in a house that was bigger than her own, she almost flipped. She would have never thought he could afford to live out there. He wore old outdated clothing with run-over shoes and drove this big goose of a car. He was nothing to look at or aspire to marry. He had a terrible attitude and a quick tongue. Combined with her quick tongue, it led to a lot of heated arguments, and they did not care who listened. Everybody kept telling them they were just alike. She did not see it, and neither did he. They almost hated each other and were willing to give up their dreams to get away from each other. What a difference a few days make.

"Hey, honey. I'm going to put the kids in bed." Jarrod walked into the room holding the children's hands while they sucked on the lollipops he'd purchased in the airport gift shop. The twins leaped onto the bed and leaned against him as he sat in the middle reading a book. He looked up at Deandrea and forced a smile.

Deandrea prayed for him as she walked down the hallway to their bedroom to wait for him to come in. She felt his tiredness in her spirit. She scheduled two weekends for him to spend with the family, one with the children and another with just her. She had to get him to relax.

She prayed he agreed to take the break. If it was anything like the other times, he won't. This didn't stop her from trying, though.

Deandrea could set her clock to how this evening would go. It was the same routine as always. After Jarrod left the children, he was going to come into the room, kiss her and talk about his trip. Tonight, Deandrea didn't want to hear about his trip. She saw him on television. She wanted to be with her husband. The world listened to him. Now, she wanted him to take a few minutes and listen to her.

Deandrea knew her life would change when they got married, but not like this. Some days she felt like a single parent. He traveled so much with his ministry, and she was left to take care of the kids, house and church. This was not what she gave up her successful psychological practice for. She was a board-certified clinical psychologist. She had her own practice and people working for her. She was very successful, even when she decided to go back to school and get another doctorate degree in theology. Her life was so together . . . until she met Jarrod and the bottom fell out.

In seminary, her college advisor, Professor Adabu, assigned her to do an internship at Star of David Baptist Church in a little town she never heard of called Snowhill, South Carolina. She thought he was crazy to assign her to a church so far from home. Deandrea waltzed into town with her arrogant and self-righteous ways and walked into Jarrod's office with an attitude that she was better than those country people. He picked up on it immediately. The first day they met was the same day they had their first argument. Even though it seemed like a negative memory, she smiled as she thought about how both of them have changed since that day, even physically.

He got LASIK eye surgery and no longer had to wear glasses. Deandrea, well, she had a little snoring problem that she took care of. They both had gained weight. When they met, Jarrod made all of the ministers in his church run six miles three or four times a week. As their friendship grew, they would run together on other days. Now, both of them were so busy they hardly had time to run or talk anymore. She missed those days.

"Both the kids are asleep. I put Drea in her bed. How are things at the church?" Jarrod asked as he pulled his necktie loose. He leaned into Deandrea and kissed her so lightly on the lips she hardly felt it.

What about me, Jarrod? Deandrea could not pretend she was happy. He asked about the church first. He didn't ask how she was doing or how everything went when he was away. He only cared about the church. She sat silently on the bed listening to him talk about all the things he had to do at the church.

Deandrea sighed and took his tie and jacket from the back of the flowered chair and walked into the large closet to hang them up. She never wanted to be a pastor. It was something Jarrod had suggested. He wanted the church to be in the hands of someone he trusted while he was away. He never asked her how she felt about it. He approached her saying the Lord told him to make her co-pastor. *News flash, He did not tell me.* She did it anyway. She was already an ordained elder in her church before she met him. She thought she would only have to preach a couple of sermons while he was away. Little did she know the responsibility of the position and that he would be gone all the time.

When they first met, Star of David was a small country church with a big membership. Now, years later, people were calling it a megachurch. They built a new, larger sanctuary and church growth had been outrageous with people driving from three states to get there every Sunday. Now the three thousand-seat sanctuary that they thought was too big at the time was so small. They had two services on Sunday morning, and Jarrod was considering adding a third. Deandrea didn't want her husband to work himself to death in the church. She wanted him around a long time. She wanted him to see their children grow up and their children too. But he was working too hard. Sometimes she wondered why.

"Hey, baby, I missed you. Come take a shower with me," Jarrod said as he wrapped his arms around her waist and kissed her on the back of her neck. As usual, his touch always made her forget, for a brief moment, her negative thoughts and gave her hope that everything would be fine. She turned to kiss him to let him know she was glad he was home.

"Come on," he whispered. Jarrod slid his hands down her arms and intertwined his fingers in hers. She followed him into the bathroom. He pulled the oversized tee shirt over her head, his eyes never leaving hers. It had been a long time since Deandrea had seen that look—one of wanting. Her husband was home, and he wanted to make love to her.

He reached down and turned knobs on the shower making the temperature exactly as Deandrea liked it. The warm spray heightened her mood as Jarrod moved closer to her. Deandrea ignored the familiar chime of his cell phone ringing. She reached out and took his arm as he looked in the direction of the phone sitting on the vanity.

"I've got to get that call," he spoke.

She thought, *Please, Jarrod, don't leave the shower. That phone call can wait.*

Her unspoken thoughts didn't keep him from answering the phone anymore than had she spoken the words out loud.

Deandrea slowly slid her wet body down the side of the shower and sat on the tiled floor wishing the spray of the water could drown how she was feeling.

She didn't have to know who was on the phone. It was his calling. But who took a phone to the shower? Did he really have to answer that call? It could have waited. She should have been the most important person at that time. Apparently, to her, something was more important.

She pushed open the shower door and wrapped herself in the soft towel hanging on the wall. She heard him talking about church business. Some days, Deandrea just wanted the church to leave them alone—let them be married sometime. It was taking a toll on their marriage. Jarrod was exhausted. She was exhausted and frustrated. He had just returned from a long trip. Couldn't they just let them have tonight?

Deandrea wiped the droplets of water from her body and reached for her silk gown. She slipped it over her head and drew back the covers on the bed. She eyed Jarrod sitting on the edge of the bed continuing his conversation. He hadn't acknowledged her entry into the room nor the sexy gown she had purchased for his return. She sighed. The same as always, and she slid under the comforter and pulled it over her head.

"I'm sorry. I forgot to turn it off. It's off now. Where were we?" Jarrod said as he crawled under the covers on their king-sized bed like he had not been on the phone for over an hour. Deandrea peered into his large brown eyes and could see his exhaustion. He snuggled into her and kissed her shoulder lightly. It was not the same, not like earlier. He didn't have the energy now. Deandrea knew the routine. It would only be a matter of minutes, seconds even, and he would drift off to sleep and she would be wide awake, trying to force herself to go to sleep.

When they first married, they could hardly keep their hands off each other. Sneaking around, searching for a place to make love was like a game to them. Now, as Deandrea gazed at his sleeping body beside her, she wondered if they would ever make love again . . . and not just because of his exhaustion.

Jarrod had a mistress, and she knew it. She had known it a long time, and her name was ministry. The sad part about the whole thing was that when he went off with his mistress, he left her to take care of the child he left behind at Star of David. Was she a fool to take care of this child? Her husband trusted her, and she trusted him. She was the only one he could trust with the child he had nurtured so many years.

Deandrea wanted to do the best work she could for him. But it was a long drive to Snowhill from their home, about two hours. She had been praying about that drive every day since Professor Adabu sent her down there the first time. The drive did not seem as long, but it was harder since she had two active children with her now. The light in the entire matter was that she could leave them at the plantation with Miss Essie, and she allowed them to run around until they passed out when they got in the car. She also fed them well, and Deandrea did not have to worry about cooking. Without her help, Deandrea did not know how she would do it without Jarrod there.

"I love you," Jarrod whispered.

Who is he talking to? His eyes were closed. He lifted his arm and wrapped it around Deandrea and pulled her close. She didn't feel loved. This was the longest conversation they had in weeks. They used to talk all the time. There were times when she wanted him to be silent. He was so funny, so animated. She laughed until her side hurt. He still talked, but not to her. It was all about his mistress. It was never about Deandrea or their relationship and how she felt or any of the silly stories unless it was about his mistress. His mistress, his mistress, his mistress . . . That was all Deandrea heard. There were times when she did not like his mistress and what she was doing to him. She had taken away his joy and the brightness of his eyes. Deandrea feared his mistress was killing him.

Deandrea placed her hands on his back and prayed for his strength, physical, mental, emotional and spiritual. She had to cover him with prayer. His mistress led him into all types of dangers and temptation each and every day. He had to know that of all the people he encounters every day, he can be assured that one person was keeping him covered in prayer.

"God, cover my husband and keep him safe from all danger. Keep him healthy and give him wisdom. Help him to resist temptation," she prayed. She asked God to help him resist temptation every day. She would be a fool not to think that temptation did not come his way.

Deandrea rolled away from her sleeping husband and asked God to teach her how to minister to him as his wife, his children's mother and the copastor of his church.

3

"Is she asleep?" Matthew asked as Misha sashayed into the bedroom disrobing as she entered. They loved when Courtney was asleep. It was their time to be alone. Their baby was eight months old, and she went to bed early. Thank goodness, she slept almost all night now. Now, it was playtime for her parents. Misha quickly pulled her robe over her body and backed away from Matthew as he walked toward her with his smooth swagger. The game of cat and mouse was one of their favorite.

"You know I'm going to catch you. I always do," he said playfully to her as she allowed him to pin her against the wall. Misha never thought she would be Mrs. Matthew Bernard Taylor. Every day she basked in the glory of being married to one of the most famous Gospel singers in the country. It was funny. Before they met, she had never heard of him, and she loved Gospel music. She thought she knew all the Gospel artists. Somehow, he slipped through the cracks.

Maybe, back then, she was too busy to even care about Gospel music or the artists that performed it. Misha was busy working in the church handling God's business. The Word of God said that single people cared for the things of the Lord. She was the poster child for that statement. She was involved in everything, missionaries, youth choir, hospitality group and so many other organizations it would make anyone tired to hear her talk about them. She was a successful teacher in Atlanta at Westdale High,

home of the Fighting Eagles. Then one day, she decided
to go into the ministry. One more job couldn't hurt, right?
That was where she was wrong.

"I want you," Matthew whispered in her ear and nibbled
on the lobe. The sensation made her weak in the knees,
and Misha pulled all the strength that she could muster
just to stand up.

Misha knew Matthew long before she met him. She
had waited all her life for Matthew, but Bernard showed
up instead. When she was a little girl, somehow she knew
her husband's name was Matthew. She did not know his
last name. All she knew was Matthew. There were times
when she forgot about him. But God had a way of bringing His word back to her memory at the chosen moment.
God allowed them to become friends long before she
found out his name was Matthew Bernard Taylor.

Matthew showed up at one of the worst times in her
life. She was a minister without a church. She was alone
and pregnant. Yes, she was pregnant when they met. In
the beginning, like most people, he had cast judgment
on her. He didn't say anything to her, but she could see
it in his eyes when he found out she was not married or
even in a relationship with her baby's daddy. She didn't
owe him an explanation. They had just met. It was none
of his business. Besides, meeting him was all about the
business of the kingdom of God. She was on assignment
to minister to him. Little did she know they were assigned
to minister to each other.

Misha's life had not been easy. All her life she had
always "known" things. She knew things about people's
lives that she should not have known. She knew when
people were going to die. She knew secrets that people
kept hidden from the light. She heard conversations
people were having miles away. Sometimes, she could
see their faces when they talked. How can this be? All

she could say is, it was a gift that was given to her by the Holy Spirit. Her grandmother told her that she was born with a veil—a thin layer of skin covering her face. She was told this was a sign of a prophetic anointing on her life. She still did not know whether to believe it. However, her daughter was also born with a veil over her face. She trembled at what her precious baby girl may have to deal with growing up. She didn't want her to go through what she had.

Misha grew up in Atlanta although she currently lived in Washington, D.C., with her husband and daughter. Growing up in Atlanta was not easy for her. Her brother, Justin, was the favored child even though he was the youngest. Her mother adored him. She let Misha know she didn't care much for her. They fought all the time. When Misha graduated from high school, she left Atlanta and headed to Howard on purpose to get away from her mom and Atlanta. She never planned on returning. But, after graduating with her bachelor's degree in secondary education, she returned to Atlanta because she had nowhere else to go. She got a teaching job at Westdale High and the rest, as one could say, was history.

"Ooooh, baby . . ." Matthew released a long, long soft moan as their bodies glided to the rhythm of each other. This man had brought so much healing in Misha's life. She thanked God every day for him. He helped heal the relationship between her and her mother. He helped her understand everything she had gone through and taught her how to forgive and build on each and every experience.

In the same way, he said, she had done the same for him. He was a man struggling with his identity. Misha was the only one who did not care if he was black or white. He could be himself around her. Life as a biracial child was tough for him. He experienced abuse unlike any she ever experienced. Misha did not understand how children and adults could make another child suffer like he had suffered. Misha believed God had put them together because they understood what it was like to grow up being abused and how to be victorious in spite of it all.

Misha ran her fingers through his short, curly blond hair. He no longer used brown hair dye or wore the brown contacts he wore when she first met him. For this, Misha was grateful. He had beautiful blue eyes, just like their daughter. Everyone always told him how much they looked alike. Their baby literally jumped out of Misha's arms when her daddy was around, and she was only eight months old. Misha was five months pregnant when they met. Each time he touched her, the baby inside moved. Matthew delighted in making her move. She was jumping for him in the womb, and she still jumped. There was such a spiritual connection between the two of them, like John the Baptist and Jesus. They had a connection so deep even Misha did not understand it.

"Don't go anywhere, I'll be right back," Matthew said as he leaped from the bed and walked into the bathroom. His creamy skin glistened in the soft light of the bathroom. Misha lay on the bed basking in the glow of their love. God is a healer. Before she got pregnant, she was diagnosed with cancer. She had two surgeries and was told by her doctor that it would be difficult to have children. Courtney showed up despite what the doctor said.

Misha slid over, trying to find a dry spot on the bed, smiling as she remembered the doctor telling her that she had had to remove the mucus membranes that lubricated Misha internally during sex. The doctor told her she would always have a problem with it. She had not seen the problem yet. God healed her and returned her body to normal functions. She had cried and prayed so hard for healing, and God blessed her. Matthew prayed for her complete healing numerous times before they got married, and God answered their prayers.

"Aw, girl, I'm glad I work out. Where do you get all that energy?" Matthew said. He rolled his body away from Misha's and lay his head on a pillow. To Misha, Matthew was the sexiest man alive, and she loved him deeply. But it was not easy being Bernard Taylor's wife, especially since *People* magazine named him one of their sexiest people. Some women thought that meant he was available. Misha had to let women know that they didn't go for that kind of stuff in Georgia. She had to control the urge to go "Decatur" on them. She was not always rich and hung out with celebrities. She was from the SWATS and she could go back to the neighborhood if she had to. He was her husband and she was not about to let any woman come in and take him.

The first time she visited his church, Misha noticed his church was overflowing with women. When he announced their engagement, someone screamed like she had just seen the Wolfman in an old horror show. After they got married, his membership drastically changed. The church emptied out. Now they were getting a new congregation of families and people really looking for change, spiritual healing and a place to worship instead of women looking for a husband.

Her life had changed in more ways than one since everybody found out that Misha knew him. Her mother had been christened the neighborhood celebrity because she was Bernard Taylor's mother-in-law, and he loved it. Some days, he boarded a plane and flew to Atlanta just to take her shopping—her favorite pastime. She got a thrill telling everybody her son-in-law was coming to town to take her this place and that. He also did a miniconcert at her church for their building fund. She was still asking him to come back and preach. Misha's dad was too cool to act like he was excited about Matthew. He was always the straight and quiet deacon. He was proud of his children, both of them. Then there was Bishop Moore.

Bishop Moore, Misha's so-called father in the ministry. She was his daughter until God revealed a deep secret of his to her. Instead of repenting, he decided to publicly kick Misha out of the church. He called her a witch and said she had a spirit of divination. He did not stop there. He attempted to destroy Misha's name all over Atlanta to get her black-balled from preaching. Little did he know he was pushing her into her ministry.

After going into the ministry, Misha went to Bishop Moore to speak with him about the gift. She did not understand it. She wanted to know why and how she was able to know things that she should not have known. She wanted to understand why she could see the future in some cases. She wanted to know how she could hear conversations between people who were not in the room with her. She wanted to understand why she could feel death or trouble. All Bishop did was belittle her and tried to destroy her until God revealed his secret in a big and public way.

Now that Bishop had lost his positions and most of his members, he kept calling Misha, asking her to preach at his church. This was the same church he had the deacons escort her out of and told her if she returned, he was going to call the police. Misha wasn't stupid. He did not want her. He was really after Bernard Taylor. Matthew would bring a lot of people to his church. Misha was well aware Bishop was trying to use her husband to build his membership back up.

Even her old boyfriend, Roger, had been calling trying to convince Misha to come to his church to preach. He told the church secretary that they were old friends, and she passed the phone call to Misha, who cringed when she heard his voice over the phone. He had some nerve calling her. She thought she had prayed him away.

They had dated for three years before Bishop Moore kicked her out of the church. Roger broke up with Misha because he thought hanging out with her would hurt his ministry.

Roger was just as evil as Bishop Moore. Somehow, he got a job at Misha's school as a youth counselor for the City Development League, and he began a determined attempt to destroy her name and get her fired. He convinced other staff members that she was a stalker and had mental problems. He accused Misha of so many things she forget them all. The harassment did not stop until she threatened to sue him, his employer, and the school for the hostile environment she was working in. Now, he had the nerve to call her as if he was Misha's best friend. She was not playing that game anymore.

Misha was learning who she could associate with and who to leave alone. A lot of people tried to use her to get next to her husband. There were women in the church who tried to become her so-called armor bearers, only to get next to her husband. Preachers who would not allow Misha to minister in their churches were calling her or her family members, trying to get Matthew to preach or sing at their church—for free.

It was so frustrating living in the shadow of a famous husband. Once, Misha had to preach at a local church. Without warning, the pastor asked Matthew to sing before she preached. Matthew was so sincere about his ministry. He agreed, and he gave a tremendous performance of an old hymn. The praise in the church was out of control until Misha stood to preach. She watched groups of people get up and walk out of the church. They were not there for the Word. They were there for Bernard Taylor. When Misha asked him not to do it again, they had their first argument. She wanted him there to support her. But he was a distraction to her ministry.

Although he was a distraction, he was more of a help to her. She gazed at his sleeping body and smiled. He once told her there were some advantages to being Bernard Taylor. Misha found this to be true. His name could get her into places ordinary people could not go. When God sent her places to deliver His Word, being Mrs. Bernard Taylor had gotten her into ministries where the congregants were not allowed to shake the pastor's hand. People did not know how to take her. Matthew was learning when Misha told him God wanted her to go somewhere, he did not question it. He had seen how God used her in the ministry. As a matter of fact, he was the one who helped her understand the call on her life. He did not make her feel stupid or crazy. Only her grandmother understood before Matthew came along.

Yet, being the first lady of Hope Tabernacle was not an easy job. Everybody expected Misha to be able to sing like her husband and were surprised when they found out she could not sing. Matthew was the preacher. Misha was the teacher. Matthew was charismatic and outgoing. Misha was shy and introverted. What a combination. Yet, she stood by her husband's side, trying to be the good wife, an excellent mother and the typical first lady.

4

"Shante, Pastor wants to know if you'll meet him downstairs to greet the visitors today," an usher asked Shante. She walked down the hallway to her office in the church. It was Sunday morning, and it seemed like the people in the church would see fit to call her Reverend Patrick or Pastor Shante or something other than just Shante. They called her by her first name. That was so disrespectful, seeing that she was an ordained pastor. With television and her books, she had become so common to them. She felt as if they no longer respected the anointing on her life. Even after she and Max corrected them, they continued to call her Shante.

Shante entered her office, moved around her desk, and sat down. She looked around the room, thankful of how far they had come. It only took a couple of years to build up this ministry after they moved from Charlotte to Columbia, South Carolina. They still had members from their Charlotte churches that travel to Columbia for services. They were delighted to see them join their new church. It made her and Max more comfortable in a new city. They really jumped in and helped build the ministry.

Rocking in her chair, Shante needed the escape of her own office to avoid the people who were calling on her. There were times when she sat in there and watched the services from the big digital monitor mounted on the wall in the corner. Those were the days when she was a distraction to her husband's ministry. People walked up to her as Max preached and asked for an autograph, prayer or even to take pictures. Not to interrupt the service, she would ask them to wait until after service. People acted as if they didn't know how to act in the house of God or at least when someone was speaking. Max said it didn't bother him. It did. Shante could tell because he seemed irritated and distant when it happened.

"Mama Tay, can I go over Devin's house after church? His mom said I could, but I had to ask you first." Joshua, her youngest son, rushed into the office interrupting Shante's thoughts. He ran across the room and eased onto her lap. Of all his brothers, he was the child who looked most like his father—only lighter-skinned. He didn't have the strong Asian features like his brothers. No one could tell his mother was Japanese. It's sad he never knew his mother. He was only a few months old when she died. Shante had raised him since his mother's death. She was the only mother he'd ever known. They were closer than Shante was with the older two boys. They had a bond that only God can give a mother and child. Shante loved him as if she had given birth to him. But today, he was not going to be pleased with her answer.

Joshua leaned his head on her chest and rubbed her back with his hand. The ploy was not going to make Shante say yes to his little proposal. He knew they always ate Sunday dinner together. It was their weekly family time.

"Josh, you know the rules. You have to eat dinner with us, and then you can go—"

"But Mama Tay—"

"Don't start. You knew the answer before you came in here. Now, if it is okay with Devin's mother, I will take you over to their house after dinner and you can stay no longer than an hour or two, understand?"

Joshua huffed and jumped off Shante's lap. He stomped his foot on the ground and placed his hands on his hips. He paced the floor and stopped in front of Shante, trying to decide the safest route to plead his case.

Shante smiled as she swung side to side in her chair, listening to his reasoning on how it would be easier on her and the entire family if he was allowed to go with Devin's parents at the end of service. It was funny. He looked and sounded like his daddy. Maybe he will grow up to be an attorney like his father. Shante fought hard not to laugh at him as she watched him pace the floor, giving his points one, two, and three—something he learned from his father. This was exactly the way Max explained things to them. Max even preached like that. At the conclusion of his rant, Joshua asked Shante what she thought. Shante hesitated.

"What did your daddy say?"

Joshua lowered his head in disappointment. Point one, he asked his father and he said no. Point two, he had not asked him at all. Point three, he already knew what his daddy was going to say, and it would be in agreement with Shante.

"Well?" Shante asked.

"He's only going to say no," he answered in a soft faint voice.

"Come here, Josh." Shante reached for him and hugged him tightly. He was disappointed. If she let him do this, the other two will want the same privilege, and that would be the beginning of the end of their Sunday family dinner. "Tell Devin's mom I'll drive you over after dinner."

Shante's heart hurt for him as she watched Josh walk out the door. She had to tell him no. She had to stand her ground and stick to the plan. It was one of the tough parts of being a parent.

The chime of the wall clock let her know it was time for morning prayer with the staff. Shante stood. Suddenly, she felt dizzy. She reached for the arm of her chair and quickly sat back down. She was so tired. She had not recouped from all of those conferences she preached a couple of weeks ago. Even with the children in school now, it seemed she couldn't get enough rest. Maybe she was anemic. She had to remind herself to have LaToya schedule a doctor's appointment to have her blood checked. She was over forty and had heard perimenopause could be worse than menopause.

"Hey, I'm glad I caught you before you left your office," Max said, walking into her office with a big smile on his face. He always got so excited on Sunday morning. He loved being a pastor. He loved ministry. He loved his congregation. Seems like he loved everything he did. His smile brightened Shante's attitude, and she returned the smile.

He was no longer the nerdy guy at Morehouse. He was all-man now; tall, dark chocolate with big lips. There was something about him that made Shante forget how exhausted she was. His energy was contagious. She braced herself on the desk and stood. Max reached for the lock on the door and turned it until he heard the familiar click, indicating it was properly locked. This gave Shante the needed time to regain her balance. They met each other in the center of the office.

"Oh, honey, God is good," Max said. He wrapped his arms around her as if she had just returned from another long trip.

Shante allowed her body to meld into his. She was so happy he stopped practicing law on a regular basis. Although he continued to take an occasional case and update his training, his full-time practice of law was over. This allowed her to minister and gave him more time to take care of the children when she was out of town.

"What happened? You were not acting like this before we left the house this morning. What's up?" Shante asked.

"Nothing. I was sitting at my desk and the Lord spoke to me and told me to come in here and give you a hug."

"Well, you better do what the Lord says," she replied.

Max leaned in and kissed her much like he did last night, passionately. Shante felt energized. He was transferring his positive energy to her. She could feel the tingle of his kiss all over her body. She was beginning to feel some kind of way. She pulled away from him.

"Max, are you trying to get something started in here? We're going to be late for prayer." Shante wiped the lipstick from his lips with her thumb.

"They will wait for us. How are you feeling?"

"I was tired until you showed up. I'm feeling much better now." Shante propped herself on the desk. "Your son just left here wanting to skip dinner to play with his friend."

"Jonathan? What is he trying to pull now?"

"No, not Jonathan, Josh. He wanted to go to Devin's house after church. I told him no."

"I don't see anything wrong with it."

Shante's eyebrow arched. "You don't see anything wrong? He'll miss Sunday dinner with us. Besides, if we let him miss dinner, then Jon and Jake will want to do the same thing. You know how much Sunday dinner means to me."

Max moved closer to Shante and leaned on the desk. "Honey, you should cut back on your schedule some. Then you will have more time to eat or do whatever with the kids."

"I'm trying. I told LaToya to only schedule me to minister one day a week now that the boys are in school. But I don't think she heard a word I said. This week alone, I'm preaching a three-day revival down in Charleston."

"That's today?" Max stood facing Shante.

"Not today. It starts Wednesday and continues until Friday."

"Friday? You're not going to be here Friday? What about the banquet at the Shrine Club?"

"Banquet? What banquet?" Shante walked away from Max and reached for a book on the shelf near the door. She could not bear seeing the disappointment in his face. LaToya was supposed to be on top of everything. She did not tell Shante about a banquet. With her, family always came first.

"Honey, I'll understand if you can't make it. I thought I told you about the banquet at the Shrine Club sponsored by the Women's Voters' League. They invited all the candidates."

Shante shoved the book back in its place on the shelf and turned to face Max. "Honey, I forgot to put it on my schedule. I want to be there for you. I'll have LaToya call the church and let them know that I will not be able to preach on Friday. They'll have to find someone else."

"No, you don't have to do that. I'll manage. I'll take the boys. I'm sure they'll love it."

"I'm sure they will." Both of them laughed, knowing the boys were going to moan and groan throughout the entire program. They hated those things as much as Shante did.

Although he was disappointed, Max had the biggest smile on his face. Shante embraced him again. His spirit was so peaceful and had a way of calming Shante's stressed personality. Whenever she was going through something, she knew she could depend on him for comfort and peace. He always had a way of letting her know everything was going to work out, even when he did not say a word. Shante felt so secure in his arms.

Max released her, and they walked hand-in-hand to the large conference room where the staff was gathered for prayer. They formed a circle and joined hands.

"Let us pray. Dear Lord . . ." Max started his prayer.

Shante couldn't put her finger on it, but she knew something was going on. Max was a little too happy this morning. Something was going on with him. He was praying a little too hard. Maybe it was this election. She closed her eyes and prayed for her husband. She was well aware that their staff prayed for Max. However, not a single one could pray for him as she did. She felt his spirit. She knew when he was tired or not feeling well. She knew when he was bothered by something. She even knew when he was happy about something, like today.

After prayer, Shante walked into the sanctuary and sat next to Joshua on the front pew of the church, observing worship service. The congregation was very vocal this morning. Max and Jake acted as a team in the ministry. Jake played the organ like a pro following rhythms of his dad's sermon. He seemed to know the right key to blend with his father's voice. Max called him his little musical preacher. He certainly acted like one. No one thought he could step in and play for the youth choir at such a young age. When he sat down at the keyboard, it was as if he was born to play this instrument. He had been playing the piano since he was five, so he had several years of lessons under his belt, and he was only in middle school. Shante often imagined what he was going to be like when he reached adulthood. By then, he would probably be directing the choir. He loved music. If he could only play his instruments—the piano, organ, drums, bass guitar and sax—he would not do anything else. He was such a focused child, unlike his older brother, Jonathan.

Shante gazed around the congregation in search of her oldest son. She prayed he was not getting into any mischief. He knew he was supposed to be down front sitting with her. As usual, he was testing them.

Shante quickly searched for that little girl that had been calling the house several times a day for Jonathan. If she found her, he was probably not far away. She spotted them in the balcony hugged up like they were in a dark movie theater. This would not sit well with his father. If Shante could see the spectacle, Max had already seen it from the pulpit. Jonathan did not hide. He was doing this out in the open, as if he wanted to be seen.

Shante resisted the urge to go snatch him up and drag him to the front pew. But she didn't want to create a scene. She would deal with it when she got home. Right now, she wanted to focus on worship and supporting Max as he preached.

Max walked the floor of the pulpit, preaching as the congregation rejoiced. Shante stood with them and watched as Max stepped out of the pulpit as he continued his sermon. His hands were all over the place, occasionally tapping the lapel microphone he wore. He loved that microphone; it allowed him to be more relaxed when he preached.

He walked down the center aisle preaching while people slapped him on the back with their hands, a program or handkerchief. Shante briefly glanced at Jonathan in the balcony with his arms wrapped around the girl as he whispered in her ear. The young girl smiled as if he was whispering sweet nothings only she could understand. Shante could not stand the sight. Jonathan was not raised to display such ignoble behavior.

She returned her focus to Max as he walked the aisle, preaching. He briefly stopped preaching and looked in the balcony. *Oh no.* Shante panicked. She crossed her hands on her chest. Max observed the same scene she had watched. Immediately, Max jumped back into his sermon, not missing a beat, and headed for the stairwell that led to the balcony. Still preaching, he climbed the

stairs toward Jonathan. Shante gazed around the sanctuary. The entire congregation looked at Max preach his
way up the stairs and move into the aisle where his son
sat, not noticing his father near him. Max motioned to
the people next to Jon to move. They got up and stood
against the wall. Max continued to preach as if this was
a planned part of the sermon. He stood over Jon and the
girl until they realized he was there and quickly separated
and sat upright in their seats.

Max motioned with his hand for the girl to move over
as he continued to preach. She picked up her purse and
moved to the next seat. Max sat in her now-vacant seat.
Jon was so busted. His cheeks were swollen in anger. The
congregation applauded.

We're not going to have a peaceful dinner today,
Shante thought.

Max continued his sermon sitting between the two
of them until he started his altar call. The associate
ministers moved to the altar for prayer. Max got up and
returned to the pulpit. The congregation clapped again
when he stepped into the pulpit. Shante turned toward
the balcony. Jonathan was gone. For a brief moment, she
was embarrassed for him. Maybe he learned his lesson
and would not do it again.

The service was coming to conclusion when Shante
stood for the benediction. Her head was spinning, and
she felt nauseated. She gripped the edge of the pew and
slowly sat down. She held her head down and took slow,
deep breaths and waited for the room to stop spinning.
She was definitely going to take some time off. She
was getting older and was not able to keep up her busy
schedule like she used to. Or, maybe she needed to get
back to the gym. Right now, she could not let Max see her
like this. He would demand she reduce her schedule. She

folded her hands as if she were praying and waited for the conclusion of the benediction hymn.

Shante busied herself in the kitchen preparing the Sunday meal when she heard loud voices coming from the family room. She wiped her hands on a towel and headed for the other room. She had hoped this argument would wait until after dinner. This was one morning she was thankful she and Max drove separate cars to church. She tried to talk to Jonathan to calm him down during their ride home, but he acted as if he did not hear her. She had talked to Max before she left the church, and he assured her he was over it and would not say anything. But now with the two of them together, the calm was about to change. Jonathan was not going to let his father have the last word.

"How can you embarrass me like that? You didn't have to sit down between us!" he shouted at Max.

"You know better than to sit all hugged up with that girl in church. You are grounded for two weeks, mister. You're lucky I didn't go upside your head," Max yelled as he pointed his finger at Jon.

"Here I am. Do what you have to do," Jon fired back, challenging his father, his arms outspread.

Shante ran between the two of them, who were standing face-to-face, and placed a hand on each of their chests. She felt their hearts beating fast, almost in sync. Jonathan balled his fists, his eyes never leaving his father.

"Max, calm down. Jon, go to the table. Dinner is almost ready," Shante said as calmly as she could. Her heart was racing too. Jonathan backed away, turned and walked into the dining room and sat down at the table.

"Honey, calm down." Shante reached for Max's hands.

"Did you see what he just did? He looked like he wanted to hit me. This is *my* house. He doesn't run the show here. I'm glad he had enough sense not to hit me."

"Baby, calm down. I'll talk to him after dinner." Shante caressed Max's back, trying hard to calm him down. "He's a teenager. He's testing you, or as Mother Thompson would say, 'He's smelling himself.' Neither of you can talk to each other now. Let's just get something to eat and we all will feel better."

Shante embraced him and caressed his back until she felt his body relax. "Baby, it's going to be all right. I'll talk to him. He's grounded for two weeks? How about one? He was embarrassed today. How would you feel if your dad did that to you? I know he was wrong, but the embarrassment should count for one week of punishment. What do you think?" Shante said. She leaned into his chest continuing to caress his back.

"Mama Tay, I finished setting the table. Can we eat now? I want to go to Devin's house," Joshua said, entering the room.

Shante glanced in the dining room and spotted Jacob and Jonathan sitting at the table in complete silence. Jacob's hands were folded as if he was praying. Jonathan's cheeks were puffed with an angry look. The air was thick with tension. Shante hated this. She did not like conflict, especially in her own house. She had come out of one abusive relationship. She promised herself this time her home was going to be happy. She was determined to make it happy.

"Hey, guys, go get the food and place it on the table. We'll be there in a minute," Shante asked the boys. They stood and walked into the kitchen. Shante took Max's hand and led him into his office that was to the left of the great room. She closed the door and embraced him. She had to minister to him now. She had to let him know she was on his side.

"Honey, are you all right?" she asked as she escorted him to the brown leather sofa near the window. She sat and patted the seat next to her. He sat and leaned his head on her shoulder. Shante stroked his head and said a brief prayer.

"I love you," Max said. He took her hands. "How are you feeling?"

"Me? I'm fine," Shante said puzzled. "You look tired. You preached really hard today. Is anything wrong?"

Max smiled. "Wrong? Naw, everything's great. How about you? You have been tired lately. I noticed at the end of service, you had this strange look on your face. Are you okay?"

"Strange look? What kind of strange look?" Shante pulled her hand away from his.

"Like you weren't feeling well."

Shante stood. She couldn't tell him she wasn't feeling up to par. He would overreact. There was enough drama going on in the house. She wasn't about to add to it.

"Max, I'm fine. I was praying for you and Jon. I knew this was going to happen. Cut him some slack . . . please . . . for me."

A wide smile spread across Max's face. There was a tap at the door. Joshua stood in the doorway.

"Can we eat so I can go?" he asked.

Shante and Max laughed. Everything was back to normal. Max stood and kissed her on the cheek. They walked hand-in-hand into the dining room where the other two boys sat silently at the table.

A strange silence filled the air as they ate their meal. Shante suddenly had a brilliant idea, or so she thought. She made eye contact with Max and nodded. He nodded, knowing what she wanted.

"Jon, your dad has something to say to you."

Max wiped his mouth with his napkin and placed it on the table. "Jon, I've been thinking. Maybe I was a little hard on you today. I should not have embarrassed you like that earlier."

"Yeah, you were sitting with that yucky girl," Joshua put his two cents in at the wrong time.

"Be quiet, Josh," Max told his youngest son, then he turned his attention back to Jonathan. "Look, Jon, I apologize. I shouldn't have done that. So I have been thinking about your punishment and decided that you are only grounded for a week."

Jonathan was unmoved. He sat with his head lowered, twirling his fork in his food. He had not eaten anything, still upset.

"Jon, your dad reduced your punishment. Is there anything you want to say to him?" Shante asked.

Jonathan looked up from his plate. He looked at Shante and turned to Max. "So what does he want, a medal?"

Max jumped from his chair and walked around the table toward Jonathan. Jonathan stood and boldly met his father halfway.

"You are grounded for *three* weeks now, buddy. This is my house, and you will respect me in my house." Max pointed an angry finger at his son.

Jonathan turned and ran up the staircase toward his room. Max followed him. Shante followed them. Jonathan made it to his room before Max reached him and slammed the door. Max shoved the door open. He had already taken off the lock from a previous incident.

Shante finally reached the top of the stairs. Max and Jon's voices permeated the top floor of their house. A loud crash arose from the room. Shante picked up her pace and ran into the room. She stopped, seeing Max on top of Jonathan. Max had his teen's arms pinned under him and his face was pressed into the floor.

"Max, stop! Don't do this. Oh my God. Jon, stop. Don't fight your dad. Max, please let him go," Shante said. She ran into the room and tugged on Max's arm.

"This child tried to hit me. He doesn't run the show around here. I'm not going to have him in my house trying to take over."

Shante pulled Max. "Max, you're hurting him. Please let him go. He's not going to do anything. Let him go," Shante heard the faint sound of crying behind her. She turned to see Jacob and Joshua standing in the doorway. Joshua was crying. She turned to Max and Jonathan. "Both of you are scaring everybody. This is not how we handle things in this house. Max, let him go. We need to pray."

Max cautiously released one hand from Jonathan. Jonathan's eyes were stretched in terror. Max slowly stood, never taking his eyes off of his son, his body stiff, prepared to fight him again, if needed. Jonathan pulled himself onto the bed. Shante sat next to him.

"Honey, are you okay?" she asked.

Jonathan nodded his head as a tear flowed down his face.

All this over a girl? Something more has got to be going on with this child. Shante took her hand and moved Jonathan's head against her shoulder. She reached up and took Max's hand. "Baby, are you okay?" He too replied with a head nod. She eyed the two children still standing in the doorway, the look of fear on their faces.

"Josh, Jake, come in here. Everything's going to be fine. Come on. We're going to pray."

Joshua ran across the room, stepping on the clothing that littered the floor. Max used to get on Jon all the time about cleaning his room. But he finally gave up. There were a lot of things he let the boys get away with now that he never would have done a couple of short years ago. But what happened today, he would never let go.

Joshua squeezed his small body next to Shante and hugged her waist. Jacob walked to Max and hugged his father. Max returned the hug, his eyes never leaving Jonathan's.

"We're going to pray as a family. I don't know what the enemy is trying to do, but he does not have power in this house. We love each other. We will not let the enemy rule here. I'm going to pray," Shante said boldly.

"No, Mama Tay. I want to pray," Jacob said as he released his grip from Max.

Shante and Max did not object. This is one child who could pray. They heard him pray before he went to sleep. There were times when his prayers brought Shante to tears. If anyone could pray the devil away, it was Jacob.

Jacob prayed, "In the name of Jesus, I take authority in this place right now. I command the spirit of confusion to leave this place. You do not have dominion over this house. As for me and my house, we will serve the Lord, and you can not dwell here."

Shante couldn't believe what she was hearing. It was a mature prayer for a preteen to pray. She opened her eyes and saw him with his eyes closed praying for peace, wisdom, understanding and the ability to communicate. Then he asked God for something that made Shante gasp.

"God, help us to love one another in peace. God, if this girl is causing all the confusion in our home, she is not of you. I ask you to separate her from my brother and help him to understand that it is for his good and send him a girlfriend that loves you and will love him for the rest of his life, even into his old age."

His old age? Shante thought, raising an eyebrow. *Did I just hear my son pray that God sends his brother a wife? Does he realize his brother is just fifteen years old? He is not even old enough to date.*

Max opened his eyes and smiled at Shante. He leaned his head in Jacob's direction and gave a proud grin. He was so sure Jake was going to be preaching before he turned eighteen. If Shante could have her way, if he got the call, he would be in ministry training until he finished college. He needed to grow up first. That was only her opinion, not the Lord's. But, the way he was praying today, it was only a matter of time.

After the prayer, Shante released her son. "Jon, we are going to give you a few minutes to calm down while your dad takes Josh to Devin's house."

"Mama Tay, I don't want to go to Devin's house anymore. Can I play my video game?" Josh asked. He had a fearful look in his eyes, a line of dried tears stretched from his eyes to his chin.

"Honey, you can still go."

"No. I just want to play my game."

How could Shante assure her baby boy that everything was okay in their now calm house? Feeling emotionally drained herself, she said, "Go ahead." Joshua ran out of the room. Jacob followed him.

She turned to Jonathan, "Are you going to be okay?" He nodded. "I'm going to talk with your dad." She ran her fingers through his thick black hair and hugged him. "We'll talk later." She kissed his forehead and stood. Then she entwined her fingers with Max's and led him out of the room, down the hallway and into their bedroom.

Max walked into the bedroom. He was still upset about having to restrain Jon. He didn't want to hit any of his children, and it upset him that he had a child who would try to hit him.

"Are you feeling better?" Shante asked.

"Yeah, I guess. What is wrong with that child?" Max took a deep breath and rubbed his hand over his head.

"I think he'll be okay. We'll let him calm down, and then try to talk to him." Shante kicked off her shoes. "I think I'm going to take a nap. All this drama has me drained."

Max pulled Shante closer to him. "How are you feeling? Are you sick?"

"What's up with you, Max? Why do you keep asking me if I'm okay?" She stepped back.

Max's lips curved to a wide smile, and he released his grip on her shoulders. "Oh, I was only concerned."

"Mom, Dad, can I talk to you a minute?"

Both Shante and Max turned to face the doorway where Jon stood stiffly. Max motioned for him to come into the room. He closed the door behind him. His head hung low as he walked toward them. He stood in front of Max.

"I wanted to apologize to you for pushing you. I was mad. I didn't mean it," Jonathan said.

"Your apology is accepted. I hope I didn't hurt you when I held you down on the floor."

"No, you didn't hurt me. I was wrong. I should not have been in the balcony with Marshay."

Shante moved to Max's side. "Jon, you know we want you to sit with me, as a family supporting your dad while he ministers. If you want, you can invite her to sit with us." He smiled at them. "But, not until your punishment ends. You're still grounded," she added firmly.

"Your mom and I talked about it earlier," Max interjected. "I did embarrass you today. That should count for something. So what I'm going to do is reduce your punishment back to one week, and if Marshay wants to sit with you, your mother and your brothers next Sunday, it is okay with me. Is it all right with you, honey?"

"I don't see anything wrong with it." Shante was pleased with the peace offering. It lifted a burden off her shoulders.

Max excused himself to take a shower. It had been a long day for both of them. The exhaustion was overwhelming. Shante's head was spinning. She reached to steady herself against Jonathan but fell onto the bed instead.

"Jon, go get your father. Tell him to come here quick."

5

"Copastor, someone has requested you sing a song for them this morning," the minister of music told Deandrea as he handed her a piece of paper with some words scribbled on it.

Usually, she would sing a special request, but this morning, she did not feel like singing. She looked at the note and saw it was one of those "I'm going through something" songs. Somebody else had the Sunday morning blues. She just couldn't sing anything depressing today. She needed cheering up herself. She hadn't seen her husband all morning. He was up early and at the church before anyone else as usual. He was such a micromanager with everything except their family.

The twins were extrahyper this morning. Since Jarrod was not there, Deandrea had to get them dressed and feed them. Then she had to pack all the survival tools she needed to keep them happy in the car and drive two hours to Snowhill. The DVD player in the car kept them quiet on that long ride to church. In addition to that, she had to stop by Miss Essie's house to help her get ready for church. Deandrea loved her mother-in-law. She was one of the first people she met when she came to Snowhill. Every Sunday, she prepared breakfast for them. This gave the two of them the opportunity to talk. As the curator of the Snowhill Plantation and Museum, Miss Essie knew everything about the history of this small town in South Carolina. She knew all its secrets, and quite possibly everyone who lived there. She was old now. Her movements were slow. But, her mind was still strong. This morning, however, when Deandrea walked into her home, she looked pale.

"Miss Essie, are you feeling well this morning?"

"Lawd, child, yes. Can't wait to get to church this morning. Y'all come on in. I made some biscuits," Miss Essie said. She turned and walked toward the kitchen. The twins rushed past her and ran to the old yellow chrome table and chairs that stood in the kitchen.

Deandrea followed her but did not believe she was okay. Miss Essie's movements were slower as she braced herself with her hands against the wall on her way to the kitchen.

Miss Essie was a proud woman, and she wouldn't tell anyone if she was sick. She served them as if nothing was wrong. After they ate, the children found a program on television to watch while Deandrea removed the pink hair rollers from Miss Essie's silver hair. As usual, Miss Essie told stories of raising nine children in the small farmhouse. She was proud of the fact that out of the nine, eight went to college, five were in ministry, and two were pastors. Yet, no matter what the subject, she always managed to talk about how Deandrea and Jarrod met. It seemed to lighten her spirit to laugh about all the silliness they had.

It was those moments Deandrea enjoyed most. She didn't know if it were the stories or the fact that Miss Essie was one of the few people that call her Deandrea, or, on most days, Dee. Most people called her copastor, not doctor or Mrs. Fuller. To them, it was as if her life began when she married Jarrod. It annoyed her when she went into the mall, hair salon, grocery store, restaurant or anywhere in town and no one seemed to know her name—only Copastor. Who was that? Did they really know her? Deandrea often thought if they did, they wouldn't send her these silly notes like the one she held in her hand.

"Good morning, baby," Jarrod bounced into her office full of energy and quickly walked to Deandrea and kissed her on the cheek. "How's my baby this morning?"

Baby? Baby? Well, for one, your baby could use a little morning loving. Deandrea turned her head and allowed his lips to meet her cheek. She wasn't excited to see him this morning, even if he did look fantastic in the gray suit she purchased for him. The tie and shirt she laid out for him on the settee in their bedroom matched perfectly.

When they first met, he would wear clothes with the tags still on them. He was so country then. The funny thing was, he did not know he was country. Maybe it was not that he was country, but single. He needed a good woman to help his lack of fashion sense. He got Deandrea, a good woman. Now, he looked great, and she felt neglected.

"Baby, I see you blocked off my calendar for next weekend," he whispered in her ear. His strong hands glided up and down the center of her back. He kissed her softly on her lips.

Deandrea wanted desperately to spend time alone with her husband—no church, no meetings, no emergencies, just the two of them alone on the beach. She had already arranged for someone else to take the emergency calls to the church and asked Charlene, her assistant, to step in to preach. She was ready to be alone with this man to revive their stagnant marriage.

"Baby . . ." He paused and kissed her again.

Deandrea moved away from him. She locked the door.

"What'cha doing that for?" he asked.

"Well, I want to give you a little preview of the trip that I planned for us." She reached for him and pulled him close to her body. Their lips met, and it felt like the first time. The memory of that night engulfed Deandrea. He had invited her to the church Christmas dance in Snowhill. They had planned to stay at Miss Essie's house after the dance, in separate rooms, of course. They sat up all night talking. He turned on some music. They held each other closely as they danced around the room. She didn't remember who made the first move. She only remembered feeling that she wanted to be with him for the rest of her life.

"Baby, next weekend, I have a meeting with the association. I have to attend."

Deandrea backed up. Her lips pursed. She almost cussed. He had some nerve. He loved those people more than he loved her. He spent more time with them than her and his children. She couldn't believe he was doing this . . . again. This was the fourth vacation he cancelled on her. Why did she even try? She held her breath, trying to hold back the vile words she was thinking. She took a deep breath, letting it out slowly before she spoke.

"Can't you find someone else to be in charge of the meeting? Don't you have a vice president? What good is Harold if you don't use him?" She placed her hands on her hips.

"Baby, you know we are working on that project with the community center. I have to be there. There are a lot of important things we need to go over."

Deandrea turned away from him. She couldn't look at him. She didn't even want to hear his lame excuses. She felt him wrap his arms around her. His touch felt like sandpaper, edging away the bare essentials of her emotions, leaving her raw and empty.

"The meeting will probably be over by three. We can have an early dinner and spend some time alone before I have to study for my sermon on Sunday."

"You don't get it do you, Jarrod?" She turned to face him, hoping he could see the only emotion she had left for him—anger—in her eyes. Her eyes filled with unshed tears. "I made plans for us this weekend. I arranged for Mom to take care of the kids. Charlene is prepared to preach on Sunday. I made reservations. You cancelled the time with the kids last week, and I had to take them to Chuck E. Cheese all by myself. Do you know how hard it is trying to keep up with two kids alone?" He did not respond. "Of course you don't. You're never around." Deandrea moved around him and reached for the note on her desk. "I've got to practice this song someone requested I sing this morning. Do whatever you want to do."

Deandrea raced to the ladies' room to release the flood of tears she so desperately tried to hold back. How could he do this to her again? She could not remember the last time they were alone together or even made love. "God, I don't know what to do," she prayed.

Today, she couldn't stand the sight of him. Didn't he know his first ministry was to his family? Yet, he neglected his family to take care of his mistress and all her children, leaving his family an empty shell of loneliness desperately seeking any smidgen of life in a lifeless relationship.

Deandrea sat at the piano watching the congregation praising God all over the sanctuary. She sang that song. She felt that song. She felt some relief freely shedding the well of tears. The congregation may have thought it was the anointing, but it wasn't. It was tears of sadness; the kind one sheds at a funeral. She looked into the choir loft and saw people praising God, knocking over chairs. She eyed the large video screens on each side of the pulpit.

The images were jumping from one person praising to another. Dee wondered if they were praising for the same reason as she. Were they shouting for victory, past, present or future? Or, were they praising because the music sounded good? She didn't know. She couldn't think about that now. She couldn't feel anything for them now. She was too jealous. These were the people her husband was having an affair with.

She couldn't take it anymore. She stood from the piano and quickly walked out of the sanctuary through the side door and down the hall to her office. She locked the door. She didn't want to be bothered with anyone trying to minister to her. How could they be effective when they didn't even know her issues? She didn't want to hear any blank scriptures coming from people who lacked understanding. If they understood, they would know that what she truly wanted was her husband and her family to be together. She was well aware ministry was his calling. She couldn't overrule God. She wouldn't even try. Maybe she was being selfish. She wiped the tears from her eyes and looked into a mirror that was hanging on the wall beside her desk.

There was a knock on the door. Deandrea furiously wiped the tears from her face. She did a quick check of her makeup and opened the door. Charlene rushed into the office closing the door behind her.

"Copastor, I came to see if you needed any help," she said with a concerned look on her face.

Deandrea loved Charlene. She saved Dee from a group of racist men who were harassing her in a convenience store where Charlene worked. They became friends. Charlene and her family visited the church and later joined it. They were the first white members. She was now one of the associate ministers, and Deandrea could always count on her when she needed her. Outside of

Miss Essie, she was the only one in the church that really knew her. Deandrea had to be strong, or Charlene would know something was wrong.

"I'm feeling a little weak," Deandrea answered. She walked around her desk, taking a small key from her pocket. She unlocked a large drawer and removed her purse. "I think I'm tired. Can you do me a favor?" She searched her purse frantically for her keys. "I'm going home. Can you let Pastor know? Tell him he'll have to get the twins from the nursery and bring them home. Make sure he doesn't forget them for me. You know how busy he is."

"Okay. You can count on me. Are you sure you're fine? I mean . . . You don't look so good. You need a Tylenol or something?"

"No, I'll be fine. I think I'm going home to lie down for a few minutes. Thank you. Please don't let Pastor forget the kids."

Deandrea raced past Charlene, leaving her standing alone in the office. She had to get out of that place. It was suffocating her. She ran to her car that was parked in her reserved space near the back door of the church. Tossing her purse in the passenger seat, she turned the car on and tore out of the parking lot.

She didn't want to go home. There was nothing there but emptiness and loneliness, and she was tired of dealing with those two. If she drove quickly, she may be able to reach Columbia and attend Shante's church before service ends. She needed to talk to her.

Driving down the two-lane highway that led to Columbia, Deandrea felt guilty about leaving her children. She slowed and pulled her car to the side of the road and began to weep. She felt pain in her chest. Her breathing was labored.

"God, I need your help. I don't know what to do. I want my husband back. I want Dee back," she prayed.

It felt as if her world were crashing in on her as she sat alone in her car with the engine still running. She glanced at the clock on her dash. She would never make it to Shante's church in time. Besides, she couldn't put her burdens on Shante. She checked for traffic and made a U-turn and pulled over on the other side of the road. She was surrounded by trees. She felt like getting out of the car and running through the woods. She now understood why Forrest Gump ran. She could feel the sadness, loneliness and frustration that would make a person want to run away from everything.

She pulled onto the road and headed home. The drive seemed longer than usual. But, she was glad to arrive home. She climbed the stairs of her home and headed to her bedroom. She fell across the bed and cried herself to sleep.

"Mommy, Mommy." The distant and familiar sound of her children stomping on the hardwood floors and screaming her name woke Deandrea from her restless sleep. She was so tense, her body ached. She did not feel like moving. She wiped the dried tears from her face and rolled over. If she lay there for a while, Jarrod would take care of the children. He should. Today was his turn.

Why did she give up her practice? If she had known this was how her life would become, she would have continued practicing psychology. She had a good staff and a steady patient flow. She had income coming in—her own money. It was a lot more than she was getting now as copastor. Even though she made a few extra dollars preaching on special programs in the community, like women's day or ushers' anniversary, those were few and far between.

"Copastor, are you here?"

Deandrea sat up. Who was that? It sounded like Charlene. Did she bring her children home? She gathered the energy to jump out of the bed. She reached for her robe and headed downstairs. The twins met her midway on the stairs with Charlene trailing behind them. *That Negro could not even bring his own children home.*

"Charlene, I didn't expect to see you here." Deandrea wrapped the belt of her robe around her.

"Well, Pastor said he had to preach at Walter's church at four. So I volunteered to bring them home."

"You drove two hours. You didn't have to go out of your way to do that for me. You could have left them at Ms. Essie's house and called me. I would have picked them up." She bent to hug each child. They held out their toys so Dee could get a better look. The toys looked as if they came out of a fast-food child's meal.

Noticing Deandrea looking at the toys Charlene said, "I took them to McDonald's."

"Thank you. How much do I owe you?" Dee asked as she continued her descent down the stairs. Charlene allowed her to pass and followed her.

"Nothing. Are you feeling better?"

"Yeah, I'm fine. Come on in and have a seat."

They walked to the small table that stood in the breakfast nook near the bay window in the kitchen. Charlene pulled out a chair and sat down while Deandrea turned on the television in the adjoining family room and pressed the remote until she saw children's cartoons. The twins sat quietly, gazing at the screen. Deandrea walked to the table and sat down.

"Where are your children?" Deandrea asked.

"At home with their daddy. I dropped them off on the way."

"Excuse my manners, can I get you something to drink or eat? I know I got something in here." Deandrea stood and rounded the kitchen island and opened the refrigerator. "Let's see I have some juice, milk, bottled water—"

"Water will be fine." Charlene stood and walked toward the island. "Dee, what's wrong?"

Deandrea held the door open, hoping it blocked the way she was feeling that was written all over her face. She reached for the bottled water, took a deep breath, and planted a fake smile on her face. She rounded the island and returned to the table.

"That's the first time in a long time anyone has called me Dee." She took a sip of water. "Hey, thanks again for bringing the kids home. Did Pastor say what time he will be home?"

"Pastor?"

Deandrea sighed. She called her husband Pastor in their home. The only time she called Jarrod Pastor was at the church and other religious functions, not her own house. Charlene's eyebrow arched, puzzled at the formality.

"Jarrod. Did he say what time he would . . ." Deandrea quickly tried to change her words.

"I'm going to be straight with you. Are you two having problems?" Charlene said as she set her water bottle on the table.

Deandrea looked toward the children to be sure they were watching television. They were lying on their stomachs on the floor looking up at the screen. They looked content. She focused on Charlene, her hazel-eyed sister. Before joining their church and going into the ministry, she looked plain and homely. Now she had a complete transformation. Her dark brown hair was cut into a short flip. Her makeup was perfect. Her clothing was very stylish and classy. She had learned that it was okay to be a woman of God, sexy and supplicated at the same time. She looked like a suburban housewife.

"Well?" Charlene asked.

"Well what?"

"Don't avoid the subject, Dee. I have been watching the two of you the past few months. You guys look so distant. Not like when you first got married."

"Nobody stays the way they were when they get married. Everything's fine. Jarrod is busy with ministry."

"And how does that make you feel?"

I know she is not using the counseling technique I taught all the associate ministers at the church on me. "I don't need counseling, Charlene," Deandrea sighed.

"You can't be an effective counselor if you are afraid of receiving counseling." Dee said the words along with her. Charlene sat patiently waiting for an answer to her question. "How does Jarrod's ministry make you feel?" Charlene rephrased the question.

Deandrea decided to tell her just enough to satisfy her curiosity and convince her everything was fine.

"Well, sometimes it's frustrating having him gone a lot. I manage. Today, I did not manage too well. I'll be okay."

"What do you mean by 'manage'? I don't understand."

Deandrea needed to end this now. "Look, I know what you're doing, and I appreciate it. I can't do this today," she said. She stood and leaned against the counter.

"Dee, you've got friends. If you need help, you can call me. I may not have all the answers, but I can listen."

Deandrea's eyes watered. She fought to hold back the tears. There were some things a pastor did not need to share with anyone in the church. Some things must remain private.

"I love my husband very much," Dee said, trying to convince herself of this truth.

"I know that. I also know he loves you very much too. It's going to be all right. God will work it out. I better go unless you need me to stay."

"You have a long drive back home. Thanks again for bringing the kids." Deandrea looked at her children who were now asleep on the floor. Anger replaced tears as Dee looked at her children. Jarrod didn't have the decency to take his children with him. She took the children with her when she had to preach, even if he was not with her. He was rarely there when she preached. It made her feel as if he did not think her ministry was as important as his. She was tired of making up excuses for him.

Deandrea tried to make her children's evening as normal as possible. When they awakened from their nap, she read them a book and got them ready for bed. She played games with them until they were too tired to go on. After placing them in the bed, she showered and slipped into her bed. She picked up her Bible from the nightstand and began reading. However, too many things were on her mind to concentrate.

She heard the garage door open. She turned the light off and pulled the covers over her head. She listened as he closed the door when he entered the house and walked up the stairs and into their room.

"Baby, are you asleep?" Jarrod kissed Deandrea on her forehead.

She did not open her eyes. She adjusted her body slightly. She didn't want to talk to him. She was too angry. She didn't want to hear his excuses. But, she couldn't resist when she heard his cell phone chime, once again.

Jarrod reached into his jacket pocket for his phone. Deandrea stretched as if the sound of the phone awakened her. With the phone to his ear, Jarrod used his other hand to loosen his tie. Deandrea hesitated to help him, because she was afraid she wouldn't be able to explain to the police how she managed to tighten his tie so much his head popped off. It was his mistress on the phone again. She didn't want to argue with him. But, tonight,

Deandrea couldn't help herself. The longer he talked, the angrier she got.

She sat on the edge of the bed and continued to stare at him. Jarrod continued his conversation as he walked into the bathroom. Today it was the community center. What will it be the next time? Deandrea had to get this man off the phone.

"Jarrod, are you going to be long? We need to talk."

After a few minutes, he finished his conversation and jumped on the bed. He pressed his lips against Deandrea's cheek. If he sensed her anger and was trying to calm her down, it wasn't working.

"Baby, I feel good," A wide smile spread across his face. "I think we got all the funding for the center. That was Pickett on the phone. He said the State is going to give us a four hundred thousand dollar grant. Now all we need to raise is another three-fifty. Do you think Aunt Jean would give us a donation?"

Deandrea's eyes widened. "Aunt Jean?" She couldn't believe he had the audacity to ask her aunt for money for his mistress. She had already paid off the church. Well, Dee thought, she was the one who paid off the church. She never admitted to it. After she won all that money in the lotto, somehow the four million dollar loan on the church got paid off. Now Jarrod wanted to ask her for more money. Dee was not asking her aunt for money. "Why didn't you tell me you had to preach this afternoon?" She purposely changed the subject.

"I thought you knew. I always preach Walter's anniversary."

She put her hand over her mouth. How could she forget their good friend's pastoral anniversary? They always attended the program together. However, she was not letting him get off that easy. "Why didn't you take the children with you? I'm sure you could have asked someone to watch them for you. Charlene drove an hour past her house to bring the kids here."

"I didn't think about that. She volunteered. She said you were sick. How are you feeling?"

She eased to the edge of the bed. "Don't change the subject. When I have to preach somewhere, I take them with me. They're not a problem."

Jarrod rose from the bed as Deandrea scolded him. He sat beside her and placed his arm around her.

"I know they are no trouble. She volunteered. I didn't think anything about it. If I had known you were feeling that bad, I would have taken them to Mama's house to give you more time to rest."

"You don't get it." Deandrea stormed into the bathroom. She pulled a towel off the shelf, turned on the water in the sink and allowed it to soak into the towel. She placed the warm towel on her face. As she lowered the towel she noticed her reflection in the mirror and saw her swollen eyes. It looked as if she had been crying all day. She couldn't believe Jarrod didn't see it.

"Dee, what's wrong? I'm sorry. I didn't know you were feeling that bad. What can I do to make you feel better?" Jarrod said as he wrapped his arms around her waist.

Deandrea shook his arms away from her. She walked back into the bedroom. As soon as she climbed into the bed, his phone rang again. He answered it but quickly got off the phone. He climbed into the bed fully clothed, next to her. He wrapped his arms around her. When she wanted to be touched he would not do it. Now, all of a sudden, he wanted to touch her? She couldn't take much more of this.

Jarrod prayed for Dee, but her heart was cold to his words. It was not like before. Then, when he prayed, she could feel all his love being transferred to her. This made her love him even more. But tonight, she wanted him to get his hands off her. The very touch was scratching at her soul, erasing any hint of caring whether or not he prayed for her.

"I love you, baby. I appreciate everything you do for me. It will get better. I promise."

Deandrea didn't believe him. She knew she had to start taking care of herself. It was time to cut back on her duties at the church and open another counseling practice. She needed another outlet, another focus other than church.

6

"Good morning, First Lady," Brenda, the church secretary, greeted Misha as she walked through the back door of the church from the private garage where she parked her car. "And look at Courtney this morning. Hey, little Courtney. How's my girl doing this morning?" she said and reached for Courtney, taking her from Misha's arms.

Misha adjusted the diaper bag over her shoulder and switched her purse and Bible to her other hand. They walked into the office with Brenda holding Courtney. Misha placed her bags on the desk and watched as Brenda played with the laughing baby. It was another Sunday morning, and she had to get into the right mind-set for the service. She was still getting used to being the first lady of this growing urban church. Each Sunday was a challenge for her. However, Matthew brightened her day and helped her start it with a smile.

"Brenda, where's Pastor?"

"He's in the choir room rehearsing a song with Jamal. You want me to get him for you?"

"No, that's okay. How's Sunday School going?"

"There are a few people here, more than last week. It's growing," Brenda said as she stood up from the chair she was sitting in and placed Courtney in the playpen that sat in the corner of the office. "Well, I better get back to the office. You know how the phone is on Sunday morning. You got a fax. I put it on your desk."

Misha rummaged through the papers on her desk locating the fax when she heard Courtney whimper. She placed the papers on the desk and walked to the playpen. She bent over to pick up Courtney when Matthew walked into the room.

"Now you know you can't bend over like that in front of me. If we were at home . . ." he said in his low sexy voice.

"But we're at the church." She smiled and walked to him with the squirming baby in her arms. Courtney stretched to reach Matthew. "Here, your child wants you." Misha handed the child to him. "Are you singing this morning?"

"I might."

"Well, try not to stress your vocal chords too much. You know you have two concerts this week." Misha returned to her desk.

"Yes, Mother."

"I'm not your mama. But I'm concerned about you. You've been a little hoarse lately. I think you should cut back on your schedule, for a little while at least. Let your voice rest."

Matthew walked to a large chair in front of the desk and sat. "How's daddy's little girl? Did Mama take the long way to church this morning?" Matthew asked Courtney as he held her above his head.

Misha watched the scene being played out in front of her. Courtney pursed her lips and cooed in an attempt to talk to her daddy. Matthew seemed to know what she was saying. Misha laughed at the mock conversation they were having. They were wearing the matching clothes she laid out for both of them this morning. Matthew had on his blue suit and French cuffed shirt with sapphire cuff links as he danced on the chair talking to Courtney who was wearing her light blue lacy dress and blue ribboned bows in her hair.

Misha turned and lifted the paper on her desk and read it. Her smile left her. "He has some nerve," she huffed.

"Who?"

"Bishop Moore. He sent me a fax asking me to preach at his church. He's really got some nerve."

Matthew stood with baby in tow and walked to Misha. "Let me see it." He passed Courtney to her and took the paper from her hand. Courtney released the loudest ear-piercing scream as she fought to get to Matthew. He looked up from the paper and laughed. Courtney kicked with her head thrown back and tears rolled down her face. He reached under her arms and took the baby from Misha. Courtney gave a twisted satisfied smile.

Misha sighed. Courtney only protested like that with Matthew. Misha could not remember one time when Courtney screamed for her. Could it be that Matthew was always playing with her and she did the everyday mundane things that were needed to take care of a growing baby? Or, did Courtney love Matthew more? Misha allowed her insecurities to flood her mind. She shook them loose and said, "You got her spoiled. She didn't act like that until you got here."

"You should go," Matthew said and handed her the paper.

"Go where?"

"To Bishop's church."

"Bishop doesn't want me. He wants you. You know that."

"It doesn't matter. You should go."

Misha could not believe her husband was telling her to return to the church where Bishop embarrassed her in front of the entire congregation. He wanted her to go back to the church where the deacons threw her out and threatened to call the police on her if she did not leave. The thought of that day still held a painful spot in her heart. It was the turning point of her ministry. She barely knew who she was in Christ when she went into the ministry. Then, to have someone toss her out of the church without helping her identify her ministry was even tougher. If it had not been for her grandmother who taught her about ministry and spiritual gifts, she would have never known her purpose in ministry.

Now the same bishop wanted her to come back to his church. He had tried to call her since she and Matthew got married. Misha never returned his calls. She thought he would get the message. Apparently he didn't.

"You should think about going." Matthew bounced the baby on his knee.

"Matthew . . ."

"Wait. Think about it. If you go back, it will show everybody that you did not fail or die like they expected you to. You can show them how God got the glory in the situation."

"Mama said a lot of people left the church. He's trying to build up his membership. He's trying to use you . . . us, to regain his credibility. I'm not playing that game with him. Besides, he never apologized to me."

"How do you know he won't apologize to you at the church?"

Misha's mouth clamped shut. Matthew waited for an answer. It was getting close to service time, and Misha didn't want to discuss the matter anymore. She walked to him and pulled the resistant baby from his arms.

"You better get ready for service. We'll talk about this later," she said and walked away from him. She placed the baby in the playpen.

"Honey, think about it. That's all I ask." Matthew stood and walked toward the door.

"I'll think about it."

Matthew walked out of the office. Misha picked up Courtney and took her to the nursery. She moved to her seat on the front row in the sanctuary and waited for service to start. Matthew walked into the pulpit as service started.

Matthew stood when the choir stood to sing their first selection. Instead of a hymn, he sang a song off his new CD. Based on the applause from the congregation, he had another hit on his hands. Misha sat on the front pew with a proud smile on her face. Her husband was anointed to write music and sing. He was a living example of a psalmist.

When he first approached her in Atlanta, she thought he was trying to pick her up. He didn't tell her he was a superstar Gospel artist, and she wasn't about to go out with some random man she met at a barbeque restaurant. She wasn't even attracted to him. Now, she couldn't take her eyes off of him. He was so gorgeous.

Her smile widened when Matthew winked at her from the pulpit. He had a way of flirting with her. They had only known each other since she was six months pregnant, but it seemed as if they had known each other all their lives.

Misha perused the sanctuary of their small church that was quickly filling up and spotted a new face, a woman, sitting on the other side of the room on the front row. Misha could spot a woman after her husband the minute they showed up. It was late September, and she sat on the front row with her skirt too short and her breasts waving at Matthew. Hadn't she heard Bernard Taylor was married? Since being married, Misha had found out some women didn't care.

The woman glanced at Misha and smirked, as if she knew who Misha was. Then she looked at Matthew and crossed her legs suggestively. Misha motioned for an usher to give the woman a lap cloth to cover her legs.

The woman refused the cloth. The usher walked down the aisle holding the cloth in her hand. Misha prayed this woman would not distract Matthew as he preached.

Service went by quickly. Misha walked down the hall on the way to the nursery to get Courtney when she heard voices coming from Matthew's office, one a female. Matthew was asking the woman to leave. The door was open. Misha walked in and spotted the front-pew woman confronting Matthew.

"You know one day, we can get together and—" the woman said as she inched toward Matthew.

"You heard what he said. I advise you to leave this office now," Misha said as calmly as she knew how to, although she was so mad she could have punched her. Matthew smiled in relief at his wife's interference.

"Hold on, sister. You don't know who you are talking to." The woman held her hand out to Misha. She was bold and had a lot of nerve. Misha was bolder. The woman stepped to Misha in her too tight, too short, and too revealing dress, threatening her.

"Woman, I don't know who you are, but I'm from Decatur, Georgia," Misha replied. "Don't let the Southern accent fool you. There is a reason why they call it the 'Dirty South.' Do you want to find out? Now, my husband asked you to leave." Misha stepped closer to the woman.

"Wait, baby," Matthew rushed to separate them.

Misha was not backing down. She was going to let this woman know she did not intimidate her.

"Miss, please leave," Matthew asked the woman just as a deacon walked into the room. "Deacon Patton, would you do me a favor and escort this young lady to her car?" Matthew asked the tall man.

"Sorry, Pastor. I don't know how she got back here. It won't happen again," Deacon Patton whispered.

"Don't worry about it," the woman huffed and exited the room on her own accord.

Misha was so mad her palms were sweating. She rubbed them on her skirt, relived the woman didn't hit her. She learned a long time ago how to fake toughness. It worked every time. Fighting, on the other hand, was another story. Matthew laughed as he closed the door.

"What's so funny?" Misha asked as if she didn't know.

"I don't need to hire bodyguards as long as I have you around," he said and started to imitate her. "Don't let the Southern accent fool you. I'm from Decata, Jawja." He bent over in laughter.

Misha laughed at his antics. It must have been real funny, two women standing toe-to-toe getting ready to fight in the church.

"Girl, I didn't know you rolled like that. Where were you when I first got started? I sure could have used you." He loosened his tie and hugged her. "I married the right woman. But, honey, you can't jump up in everybody's face like that. You've got a little thug in you."

"That woman shouldn't have been in your office. I wanted her to know she wasn't playing with a fool. You're my husband, and I'm not going to let another woman come in my house. I don't think so."

"I don't think so," Matthew imitated her. They both laughed.

There was no laughter in Misha's life when Matthew showed up. He showed up at one of the worst times in her life. He breezed in like a breath of fresh air. She was six months pregnant and had no one to talk to. They felt so comfortable with each other. It was as if she knew what he was going to say before he said it, and he did the same with her. They were meant for each other. So if any woman thought she was going to come into Misha's house and easily take her husband, she had another think coming. Misha wasn't an easy kill. If she went down, she was going down fighting.

***

"I'll put Courtney in her bed." Matthew reached for the sleeping baby as they walked into their custom-built home in the gated community. Misha held onto her. She didn't want to disturb her anymore than she already had getting her out of the car seat. It had been a long day. She was tired. Matthew was tired. They couldn't wait to take a quick nap while Courtney slept.

Misha headed up the stairs with the sleeping child when the doorbell rang. She placed Courtney in her crib and headed back downstairs. She approached Matthew who was fixated on some papers he held in his hands.

"Hey, honey, who was that at the door?" she asked. He leaned on the doorjamb reading the papers.

"Baby, sit down."

"Why? What's that?" Misha took the papers from his hands and scanned them. She gasped at the heading on the legal documents. OBJECTION TO ADOPTION.

"Who could be objecting to you adopting Courtney? Her biological father is dead. He certainly can't object from the grave," Misha said as she ruffled through the documents.

"Honey, it's going to be okay," Matthew said. He wrapped his arm around Misha.

"Who are these people? Heckler's parents? I never met them," She waved the papers in the air. "I didn't think they knew he fathered a child. Rick said it was routine to put that notice in the paper. He said no one would object. How can they do this?"

"Don't get upset. We'll call Rick tomorrow and talk to him. I'm sure he got a copy of these papers too."

"No, I'm calling him today. I can't wait until tomorrow. These people are asking for custody or visitation with my child. I'm not going to let my baby near those people. Where's the phone?"

7

"Shante Patrick . . ." the nurse shouted when she walked into Shante's examination room at the ER. She then looked at the electronic medical chart she held in her hand and looked back at Shante. "Oh my goodness. I was just reading your book."

Shante had been in the emergency room a couple of hours. She was feeling much better now, but Max wouldn't let her leave until all the test results were back. He sat watching the nurse check the IV that was pinching the vein in Shante's hand. She was told by another nurse that she was a little dehydrated. Couldn't she just drink some water instead of having this bag of fluids pumped into her body?

Nevertheless, she had to sit in the cold room until the doctor released her. She tried to rest, but the emergency room staff just changed shifts and her new nurse was going on and on about how her ministry has helped her. Shante was glad to be of assistance. But, right now, she was the one in need of assistance.

"Miss, do you know how long it's going to be before we find out anything?" Shante asked her, wanting to end the glowing reviews of her work. It was beginning to get on her nerves, or maybe it was just being in the cold sterile room.

Why did she allow Max to talk her into coming here? It was probably just a twenty-four hour flu or something. Max babied her too much.

"You've been here awhile. It shouldn't take much longer. I don't know if I should ask you this, but . . . could you autograph my book?" the nurse asked.

"Miss, this is not—" Max jumped in trying to be the great protector.

"No, Max. It's okay." Shante adjusted herself in the bed.

It was obvious the nurse was a supporter of Shante's ministry. It was the least she could do.

"Thank you," the nurse said. She walked out of the room.

"You're in the hospital. Can't people leave you alone? She's supposed to be your nurse; instead, she is acting like a fan."

"Max, she only wanted an autograph. She did her work without acting all crazy. You've got to give her credit for seizing the opportunity and supporting my ministry."

Max stood and threw his arms in the air for a full stretch. Even he was getting a little impatient. "I'm going to check on the boys. You want something while I'm out?" he asked.

"No. I only want to go home."

Max kissed her forehead before leaving the room. The nurse returned holding her book in her hand. She passed it and a pen to Shante.

Shante looked at the title, *Silence Is Not Golden: Tales of Abuse in the Pulpit*. She opened the book and flipped through the pages. There were many passages highlighted and notes were written in the margins of the book. Deciding not to push her for information, Shante signed the book and handed it back to her.

"Thank you for writing this book," the nurse said to Shante. "I've experienced some of the things you put in here. For a while, I had turned my back on the church and God because of some of the things you talked about.

I thought just because one minister abused me and others, all ministers were like that. I learned it was okay to talk about it to other people. I'm not keeping it a secret anymore. I share my testimony with other people who have dealt with the same thing. Now, I have repented and returned to the church. Not the one I was going to but another one. My whole life is changing. I feel God healed me with the help of your book, and I want to thank you." She held the book to her chest.

"It's not me, it's God."

"I know. But you allowed yourself to be used by God to bring healing to others. It's an awesome thing you do. I pray God continues to bless you as you walk in obedience to bring healing to me and other people like me."

"Well, thank you . . . What's your name?"

"I'm sorry. My name is Libby." She held out her name tag so Shante could get a better look at it. "Well, I better go check on my other patients. Thank you for signing the book for me. The doctor should be in here shortly with your test results."

She walked out of the room just as Max was walking back in. He was holding his briefcase that he had left in the car.

"Have you heard anything?" he asked. He sat in the chair beside Shante's bed.

"No, hopefully, the doctor will be in here soon. How are the kids?"

"They are worried about you. I told them you would be okay, and we were waiting for the results of some tests."

"Well, looks like everything is okay." A short slightly balding man walked into the room. "I'm Dr. Phillips. I'm taking over for Dr. West." He shook Max and Shante's hand. "We got the results of your tests. Everything looks fine. You were a little dehydrated. We've given you a bag of fluids. I think we can take the IV out now. How are you feeling?"

"Much better. Thank you, Doctor," Shante replied.

"Doctor, why did she get so dizzy? She almost passed out twice today. What is it, a virus?"

"Well, it could be the pregnancy."

"Pregnancy!" Max and Shante yelled at the same time. Instantly, Shante's body propelled itself upward on the bed.

"Pregnancy? Doctor, I'm not pregnant," Shante shook her head.

"I knew it! I *knew* it." Max leaped from his chair as if he just saw his favorite team score a touchdown.

"Well, Mrs. . . . . Patrick. Your lab tests showed you are pregnant, about twelve weeks. You didn't know?"

"That can't be right. I've had my period on a regular basis," *I think*. She had been too busy to keep up with that sort of thing. She pled her case as if it was going to change the results of the tests. "Doctor, do you know how old I am? How could I be pregnant?"

"You seem rather surprised. I see you're in your late forties. Is this your first child?"

"No, we have four other children," Max chimed in. His face bore a wide smile. Shante, on the other hand, was stunned. She lay her head on the pillow. She couldn't seem to talk anymore. All of a sudden she didn't feel so good.

As she lay on the bed, Max and the doctor continued their conversation. How could she be pregnant? This couldn't be happening to her now. Her career had taken off. Her daughter was grown. Her sons would be out of the house in a few years. She didn't have time to take care of a baby. She barely had time to take care of herself.

Everything was a blur. Shante didn't remember the nurse removing the IV from her hand or the drive back home. She sat in the car, frozen on the word "pregnant."

The boys rushed out of the house into the garage to the car as soon as they pulled in. They opened Shante's door and waited for her to exit.

"Mama Tay, are you okay?" Josh asked.

She couldn't speak. She nodded and forced her body out of the car. She walked to the family room and plopped onto the sofa. The boys followed her and stood in front of her, staring as if she were on her last breath.

"Mama Tay?" Josh inched to her with a worried look in his eyes. Shante reached for him.

"I was dehydrated. They gave me some fluids. I feel much better. After a good night's rest, I will be back in top shape. Come here." She opened her arms and allowed all the boys to gather in her embrace. "Now, you guys go get ready for bed. You have to get up early for school in the morning."

Max dropped onto the sofa beside Shante. His mouth stretched in a silly grin. His chest was swollen like a proud lion. He propped a pillow behind Shante's back. Then he reached for the blanket on the back of the sofa, covered Shante and snuggled into her. She moved away.

"Can I get you something?" he asked her.

"No."

"We need to tell the kids."

Shante had not come to grips with it yet. She was forty-six years old. She couldn't be pregnant. Camille was supposed to be calling her, telling her she's pregnant— not the other way around. What was she going to do? The doctor got it all wrong.

Shante jumped off the sofa, flinging the blanket through the air. She reached for her purse and keys on the coffee table and headed for the door. She reached her car before Max realized what was going on, then she tore out of the driveway.

About ten minutes later, Shante pulled into the parking lot of the twenty-four-hour discount store. It was late, and hopefully no one would recognize her there. She sat in her car trying to get up the nerve to go into the store. She pulled out her calendar to check to see when she last had her period. It had been a couple of months. She didn't even think about it. Besides, she was glad she didn't have a period. She thought it was perimenopause. She had read all the books that told her about the hot flashes, mood swings and irregular periods. Not one said anything about getting pregnant. As a matter of fact, most of them said it was unlikely that a woman's body could produce eggs that were vital for pregnancy at her age. Somebody lied.

Finally, after a few minutes, she ignored Max's constant calls to her cell phone and got up enough nerve to walk into the store. She walked past the line of cash registers, headed to the pharmacy. She stopped briefly to look at her books being prominently displayed near the books and magazines section. Her last four books were there. She picked up one she wrote a few years ago and the last one she wrote. She turned them over to see her picture on the back. She had changed through the years. On the earlier cover, she looked so much younger, confident and full of life. Where did that woman go? On the other cover, even with the touch-ups, she looked older and tired. Her smile seemed forced. Even now, she felt as if she had lost control of everything. She had asked her doctor to give her birth control, but he said there would be too many hormones for a woman her age. They should have used something else. She returned the books to their stand and continued to the pharmacy area.

She reached the aisle she was looking for and quickly glanced around to see if anyone was watching, then she picked up one of each type of home pregnancy test, shielding them with her purse. She felt like a teenager, hoping her indiscretions did not catch up with her. After listening to unsolicited advice from the cashier about the most accurate test, she rushed home to take every one of them. That doctor cannot be right.

"Hey, honey, where have you been? I've been calling you," Max asked as she entered the house.

Without answering, Shante rushed past him toward their master bathroom. She reached the bathroom and locked the door before Max caught up with her. Ignoring his knocking she pulled the tests out of the bag and carefully read the directions on each box. Plus or minus, pink or blue, pregnant or not pregnant, one line or two, each one had a different indicator.

Well, here goes nothing. She took all the tests at once.

The first one showed the word *pregnant* immediately. She didn't have to wait the allotted time. She sat on the edge of the spa tub, holding the stick in her hand. She looked at the other tests which showed positive results. Finally, she sank to the floor and admitted defeat. This was an interruption to her life that she did not need. They only had another ten years and Joshua would be out of the house and she and Max could travel and be alone for once. A baby would change that schedule by another eighteen years at least. How was she going to keep her schedule pregnant? She was booked up for a year.

Shante opened the door and saw Max sitting on the edge of the bed. She held out the multiple pregnancy tests and started crying.

He walked to her and wrapped his arms around her. "Baby, it's going to be okay," he assured her.

Shante hoped it would. At her age, it would not be easy being pregnant.

Either way, what was going to happen to her ministry? There were people like Libby that needed to be ministered to. What was going to happen to them? Why did this have to happen now?

"We need to tell the boys," Max said.

Shante groaned. How were they going to react to a baby in the house? Joshua was so used to being the baby. Jonathan was wrestling with his teenage hormones. She didn't think they had to worry about Jacob. As gifted as he was, he probably already knew she was pregnant. She had to tell Camille. How was she going to react to her mother being pregnant? She was getting married in a few months. Would she be embarrassed being escorted down the aisle by her very pregnant, nearly fifty-year-old mother? How was she going to react to a having a sibling over twenty years younger than she? That was going to be a big adjustment for her. She had three younger stepbrothers, but they had always been there. They essentially grew up together. It wouldn't be the same. Would she get to know this child as a sibling? She lived so far away. How was this going to affect their relationship?

Max called the boys to come into their room. The boys gathered around them. "Your mom and I have some news." He looked at Shante. "You want to tell them?" he asked her. She shook her head. Max waited, then looked at the boys. "Well, tonight at the hospital, we found out your mom's pregnant. You guys are going to have a little sister or brother."

Jonathan walked out of the room. Max stepped up to follow him.

"Wait, Max . . . later," Shante said. Max returned to Shante's side.

"Congratulations," Jacob said and walked out of the room.

"I'm going to be a big brother?" Joshua asked. "That's great. Now I can have somebody to boss around." He hugged Shante, then Max, and left the room.

The boys' reactions troubled Shante as she tried to get some sleep. She tossed and turned. So many questions filled her head. Why was the sky blue? Why was grass green? Why was yellow, well, yellow? The questions fought for space in her head. She was so upset she couldn't pray. All she could do was ask God why. He had a plan for her life, but right now, she couldn't see it. Was she being selfish? No matter what celebrities say, there was nothing cute about an old pregnant lady. With the way she felt, she didn't believe she would have enough energy to keep up with a baby.

The house was quiet. She looked beside her. Max had already gotten up. The sun shined bright outside her window. She groaned and rolled over.

"Honey, can I get you anything before I go to work?" Max peeped his head in the bedroom door.

"No, I'm fine." She pulled the blanket up around her as she stretched out, pretending to still be sleepy.

"Are you going to call LaToya today and let her know you are going to have to change your schedule?"

"I'll call her."

"Okay. If you need anything, I'll be home at lunch. I'll bring you something back. I love you." Max kissed her forehead.

After he left, Shante propped herself up on the pillows. It was time to make a doctor's appointment. She lifted the phone and punched in LaToya's number and waited for her to answer.

"Hi, boss lady. It's a beautiful morning. What can I do for you?" LaToya sang.

Shante rolled her eyes. It was a little too much cheer for her this morning. "Good morning, LaToya." She switched the phone to her other ear. "Do not schedule any new appointments for me. Plus, I need you to cancel all my appointments for the next month. I will let you know about the other engagements already scheduled."

"Are you sure you want me to cancel all your appointments?" LaToya's voice rang out over the phone. She wasn't sure if Shante was serious or not.

Shante did not offer an explanation, just a simple "yes," and ended the call. Afterward, she walked around her big empty house. It was quiet now that Max and the boys were gone. There were no sounds of Jonathan on the phone, Jacob on the piano or Joshua playing video games; only numbing silence. Her new book was complete. She didn't have any sermons to prepare. She remembered she needed an article for her Web site. She rushed to her computer to begin working on it when she heard her phone ring. She raced to pick it up. "Hello," she answered.

"Shante, what's wrong? LaToya said you cancelled your appointments. Are you sick?" Gia, her agent asked. There was concern in her voice. Shante never cancelled engagements, even when she was sick.

"I'm fine. Just tired and I need to get some rest," Shante tried to convince herself. She didn't think Gia believed her.

"We can't cancel the events in New York next week. You are scheduled to be on the morning talk shows. We worked hard to get that. You have to go. Since you will be in the city anyway, you should do the book signings too. We need this so your new book will be another bestseller."

Shante sat in the cushioned arm chair. "I'll let you know how I'm feeling next week. Right now, it looks as if we may have to cancel."

"Okay. Let me know. We scheduled these to coincide with your plans with Camille. I really need you to go."

Shante still had not told Camille about the pregnancy. She ended the call with Gia and stared at the phone in her hand. She could not bring herself to punch in the numbers to call Camille.

She walked to the large bay window in her bedroom and looked out at her tree-lined backyard. The trees had already lost their leaves and the early-fall wind was blowing small loose leaves across the yard. She always imagined she would be happy in a big house like this. Now, it felt so empty.

When she and Max purchased this house, they imagined all types of family gatherings. They danced in every room. They were thrilled at every possibility opened to them. It had turned into a glorious hotel. Now the only time they came together as a family was after Sunday morning service for dinner. Then they spread out to their corners only to speak to say good night. Where did they go wrong? What happened to the dreams they had? Where was the vision? Shante wrapped her arms around her waist and hung her head. "God, help me to deal with this," she prayed. Her phone rang.

She looked at the caller ID. It was LaToya. She pressed the speaker. "Hello, LaToya."

"Hi, Shante. You're not going to like this. I called the people at Shining Light Ministries. They said they won't be able to find another speaker in a week. They even threatened me with the contract you signed," LaToya warned. "I tried to reschedule you for another event at their church. But they said they had already spent a lot of money on advertising that you would be there. I even told them you were ill. That didn't help. What would you like for me to do?"

Shante knew LaToya tried everything. That was the type of assistant she was, and she always got the job done . . . until now. "Where is the conference?"

"Philadelphia."

"What night do I have to preach?" Shante asked.

"Friday."

"Just one night? That's good. How long is the conference?"

"It starts on Wednesday and ends on Saturday. It's a first ladies' conference."

"Oooh, that's the conference you're talking about? I wanted to do that one. I believe God gave me a word for first ladies. Call them and tell them I'll do it and complete the arrangements with them. I will be coming from New York."

"New York?"

"Yes. Gia reminded me that I couldn't cancel the book signings or the interviews in New York. You don't have to make hotel arrangements. I'm staying with Camille. I'll leave New York and go to Philadelphia. I won't need the plane going to Philadelphia. I'll take the train. It's a short ride. Can you take care of everything else?"

"I'll take care of it. Anything else?"

"Well, I'll be with Camille so you don't have to go with me on this trip. If something comes up, I'll call you."

"You sure about that?"

"Yes. Camille will help me."

"Okay. I will call them back and take care of everything."

Shante hung up the phone. Now that Shante had something to look forward to, she regained some of her energy. She headed for her office to start working on her pitch for the television shows. She stopped in the hallway. How was she going to convince Max she was able to go? He seemed to have made up his mind and made the decision for her. He expected her to stop everything until after the baby's born. He was not going to like that she was leaving Monday and wouldn't be back until Saturday afternoon. He would not go for it, especially after she fainted twice. Someone other than LaToya needed to go with her. It had to be someone Max trusted like family. LaToya was fine, but Max still considered her an employee. Camille wouldn't do. She would spend her time shopping. She needed someone else. She thought for a minute. She picked up her phone and punched in her friend Patrice's number who lived in Atlanta.

After a conversation with Patrice, she informed Shante she wouldn't be able to travel with her on such short notice. Her second choice, her friend Gwen in Charlotte, couldn't make it. She had to preach a conference the same weekend. Who could go with her? She sat in her chair at the desk. *There has to be someone else,* she thought. Just then, a name popped in her head.

Dee.

She punched in Deandrea's number. Once Dee was on the line, she told her about her dilemma.

"A conference in Philadelphia? I don't know. Jarrod may have something going on."

"Come on, Dee. It'll be fun."

"What kind of a conference is it?"

"It's for first ladies. I only need to be at the conference Friday night when I speak. We can do some of the tourists things . . . eat cheesesteaks. We don't have to attend all the events. Come on. I'll pay all your expenses."

"You know that's not it. I'll talk to Jarrod, and I'll get back with you. When do you need to know?"

"Well, I've got to go to New York to do some interviews and go shopping with Camille for her wedding. Then I'm going to Philadelphia. So, as soon as possible."

"I'll check Jarrod's schedule to be sure he can take care of the kids. I'll let you know soon."

"Thanks, Dee. I appreciate it."

Okay, a possibility. Shante prayed Dee would be able to go with her. She took a deep breath and realized she had not taken a bath today. She walked to the bathroom to shower before Max came home for lunch. She was feeling better. It was going to take some time to get used to being pregnant.

After her shower, Shante quickly dressed and headed downstairs when she heard Max's car pull into the garage. She opened the refrigerator door and reached for the pitcher of sweet tea on the top shelf. Max stepped into the room carrying bags filled with sub sandwiches for their lunch. He kissed Shante lightly on the lips and asked, "Are you feeling better now?"

"I think I need prayer. I'm not young. I want to have a smooth pregnancy."

Max set the bags down on the granite countertop. He placed his hands on her belly and began to pray. "Heavenly Father, we are in awe of your goodness. We thank you for the miracle you have entrusted us with. Father, I love this woman I am holding, and I know she loves you. We ask that we have a smooth pregnancy without any complications. We pray our baby is healthy and strong. We will teach this child to love you as we have taught our other children. We will glory in your goodness, grace and mercy and give you all the honor. In Jesus' name we pray. Amen."

Shante could feel the power of the Holy Ghost all over her like a cooling wind. She loved when Max prayed for her. When they were just friends, he would pray for her whenever she had to travel or whenever he thought about it. He had a sixth sense that made him call whenever she was going through something, and he would pray for her as no one else has. He always knew the right words to say.

They sat at the table in the breakfast nook. Shante lifted her sandwich and took a bite. "Honey, I have a doctor's appointment Wednesday," she told him.

"Good. I'm going with you." Max took a bite of his sandwich.

"You don't have to."

"I know. I want to. I'm going to all your appointments. I'm not going to miss anything," he said with a big smile on his face. "We're having our first child together."

"First?"

Max gulped, trying to keep the water he just drank from spewing out of his mouth. He laughed loudly. He reached for her hand and squeezed it. "Yes, dear, our first." He laughed again and took a big bite out of his sandwich.

There was a good vibe in the room. It seemed like the right time to tell him about the trip next week. "I talked to LaToya," Shante said.

"What did she say when you told her you were pregnant?"

"I didn't tell her."

"Why not?" He set his sandwich on his plate.

"Well, I haven't told Camille or the church yet. I thought I would wait until I at least tell Camille."

"Oh, okay."

Shante twirled the sandwich in her hands trying to find a spot to take her next bite or to say what she needed to say. "You know I was supposed to help Camille pick out her wedding dress next week. I think I'll tell her then. I need to be face-to-face with her."

"Why don't you just use FaceTime or Skype?"

"I need to tell her in person. Besides, I have those book signings and interviews in New York next week. It will be after the doctor's appointment, and I can tell her everything then. You know she will want all the details."

"You're going to New York to work?" He set his sandwich on the plate and leaned back in his chair.

"Max, I thought since I have to be there anyway, I might as well do it. Besides, Gia said that I might not be able to reschedule anything. We need this to coincide with the book release. Camille will be there with me, and Dee may come along. I won't overwork myself. I promise."

He took a deep breath. Shante recognized the intense look on his face. He was trying to figure out what to say next. He stood and took his plate to the sink.

"LaToya also said I could not cancel on the first ladies' conference I'm scheduled to preach next week in Philadelphia. They said it was too late for them to find another speaker. They made special arrangements for me. I have to go."

Max leaned against the countertop, sipping on his bottle of water. The smile he had on his face only a few minutes ago was gone.

"What are you thinking?" Shante turned to him.

"I thought we agreed that you were coming off the road."

"You agreed. I didn't say anything."

"We agreed that you were going to take it easy now."

"We never discussed it. You decided that. I'm just coming to terms with being pregnant. This was totally unexpected."

"You sound like you don't want this baby."

"I didn't say that, Max. I'm under contract. I can't break these engagements. It could cost me if I don't show up."

"At what cost to your family?"

"What do you mean?" Shante walked to him. "That was a low blow, Max. You know I love my family. I would do anything for you. What are you talking about?"

"Well, you always seem to put your ministry first. Do you really know what goes on in this house when you're gone? Even when you're here, you're working. You never have time for us."

"You knew I was a minister when you married me. You knew I spoke at conferences and traveled a lot before you married me. Now you want me to stop my whole life just because I'm pregnant? I'm only a few weeks pregnant. I'll be okay."

"You do what you want to. I've got to get back to work."
He set the water bottle on the counter and walked toward
the door.

"So you're going to walk out without talking to me
about this?"

"You seemed to have made up your mind. Do whatever
you want." He flung his hand, and then walked out the
door.

Max did not understand that she couldn't be the type
of wife he wanted her to be. She was not a stay-at-home
mom and front-row first lady. Shante always thought he
loved her because of her passion, commitment and drive.
Now, it seemed to be tearing them apart.

Her family came first. This was not worth losing her
family over. She would rather lose the money, fame and
fans than lose her family. But she gave her word.

She returned to the table and placed her hands on her
face and prayed. "God, what should I do? My family is
sick. My entire household is sick, and I need to stay at
home and take care of it before it gets any worse. Help
me."

8

"Copastor, do you want to go out to lunch with us?" Eleanor, the church secretary, asked Deandrea as she walked into her office.

Deandrea had been going over budgets and had been in staff meetings all morning. The last thing she wanted to do right now was go to lunch with them. She passed on lunch. The only thing they talk about is church business and how anointed she and Jarrod are. Today, she didn't feel so anointed. She missed her husband. Not because he was away on another trip, but because she had lost him to his mistress and didn't know how to get him back. She couldn't do this anymore today. She was tired of people calling her copastor and tired of taking care of Jarrod's baby. She should have gone to the conference with Shante. She couldn't because Jarrod was scheduled to be out of town, again. He wouldn't be back until tomorrow.

She walked out of the church and hopped into her Volvo station wagon. She stopped at the driveway entrance and spotted the old church across the street. The church held so many good memories for her. Now, it sat idle until someone needed it. Then, they used it for weddings or funerals. This was where she met Jarrod. This was where they had their first argument. This was where they fell in love.

She got in her car and drove down the road toward town. Deandrea recalled the days when she traveled down the long tree-lined road to this church that she thought was so country back then. She couldn't understand why her school would send her so far away to do an internship. There were so many other churches she could have gone to. However, her advisor, Professor Adabu, insisted she come here. She didn't realize then how much her life was about to change.

Now the street was no longer filled with trees. Instead, it was filled with the signs of economic development that a prosperous church brought. She drove past fast-food restaurants, businesses, and subdivisions and into the center of town. She pulled into the small strip mall the church owned. It hadn't changed much since she arrived in Snowhill. Miss Nelly's restaurant was still there. She pulled into an empty parking space in front of the restaurant. A good meal might be good for her soul right now.

Miss Nelly's restaurant was the same except the table-cloths. She changed with the season. Today, they were deep fall colors of burgundy, brown and yellow. Other than that, everything was the same, the same old wobbly tables with mix-matched chairs and a color of yellow on the walls so covered with the grease and grime that Sherman Williams could never duplicate it. The food was still delicious.

A loud scream came from behind the counter when Deandrea walked in. It was Miss Nelly's familiar greeting. She barreled around the counter, wiping her hands on her apron and wrapped her arms around Deandrea so tightly, she couldn't breathe.

"Copastor, the Lord told me you was coming by here today. Sit down. I got your plate already on the way out."

Deandrea walked through the restaurant, politely speaking to members of her church along the way. She planted a fake smile and acted like the adoring, happy first lady when she knew, deep down inside, she was hurting. She sat at a table with her back toward the door. If luck was on her side, no one would come to talk to her.

Unfortunately, a couple of people stopped by her table to talk. Finally, after a few minutes, Miss Nelly arrived with her plate of food and tea. Miss Nelly made the best sweet tea Deandrea had ever tasted. She picked up the chilled glass and lightly sipped the fresh brewed treat. However, the taste gave her little comfort and no satisfaction today.

"Dee, what's wrong?" Miss Nelly asked as she slid into the chair across from Deandrea.

"Why do you think something's wrong?" Deandrea forced her lips into a smile.

Miss Nelly could see right through her. Dee tried not to look into her eyes. Her strong age lines etched in her light skin tone showed the seriousness of her concern. Dee used to think she was nosey. However, she found out Miss Nelly was truly a woman of God. Besides, she was one of the few people who still called her Dee in private.

"I have been praying for you and Jarrod all morning. What's wrong?"

"Nothing's wrong. He's out of town at the Baptist Convention. He'll be back tomorrow. He'll teach Bible Study tomorrow night. How are David and Rhonda? I've been meaning to call her. I keep forgetting about the time difference between here and California."

Deandrea missed her best friend Rhonda. She married David, Miss Nelly's son. David used to be the town cop. Now he was a successful entertainment attorney. His first client was his daughter, Jaden. After she won the Apollo kids competition, she got a record deal and they moved to California so she could pursue her career in the entertainment business. His son, David Jr., was a freshman at South Carolina State University. He came to the church from time to time when he was home on break. David and Rhonda have a new baby girl. Deandrea was her godmother but hasn't even held her yet.

"Dee . . ." Miss Nelly calling her name interrupted her thoughts. "God's going to work it out."

"What?" Deandrea looked around the restaurant.

"I don't know. Whatever it is, He's got it under control. You don't smile anymore unless you're giving people that fake smile you flashed around here a minute ago."

"I'm just tired. I miss my husband."

"He loves you."

Deandrea couldn't even respond to that. She wanted to believe he loved her. She felt like nothing more than a glorified babysitter for him. Yet, she had to remember Jarrod's purpose and why he does what he does. She had to think of all the lives that have been changed because of his ministry.

Jarrod was working so hard to make life better for so many people. Deandrea tried not to be jealous. She was and didn't know how to stop the jealousy, anger and the guilt for feeling the way she did. She was a minister too. She understood what it was like to have passion for ministry. However, she learned to balance family and ministry. She didn't want her children growing up being the stereotypical preacher's kids. She wanted them to feel and know they were loved. This was something Jarrod had to work on. He placed his family second—no—last.

"Dee, you know you can talk to me," Miss Nelly continued.

"Everything's fine."

"Then why are you crying?"

Deandrea placed her hands on her cheeks and felt the small stream of water coming down her face. She tried to wipe the tears away without drawing attention to them from the other people in the restaurant. Miss Nelly took her hand and pulled her toward her small office in the back of the restaurant and closed the door. She hugged her and began to pray. Her strong, deep voice, that no one would ever imagine coming out of such a small woman, prayed so powerfully for her and Jarrod.

"It's going to be okay. I know it's hard being a preacher's wife. You've got friends. We're praying for you. Don't let the enemy fill your mind up with foolishness. Jarrod loves you, and you love him. It's going to be all right."

"I wish I knew that." Deandrea pulled a tissue out of the box on the desk and wiped her face.

"Listen to me. Sit down here, child."

Deandrea sat in an old torn chair in front of Miss Nelly's small brown desk.

"Don't you let the enemy mess with your mind. He will tell you all kinds of things, like Jarrod's doing all sorts of things. Don't listen to him. Your husband loves you and would do anything for you and them babies of yours. You've got to believe it. I've known that boy all his life. He is loyal. He would never do anything to hurt you."

"I know he loves me." Deandrea wanted to believe it as Miss Nelly tried to comfort her. However, nothing was getting through. She had built up a wall so thick nothing could penetrate it.

Deandrea left the restaurant feeling more depressed than when she walked in. Miss Nelly did her best to cheer her up. One thing Dee had realized was how she felt inside was now showing up on her face and she could no longer hide it. Not wanting to go back to the church, she headed for the peace and quiet of the plantation.

The groundskeeper, Darrin, and his helpers, were blowing leaves along the long driveway that led to the Snowhill plantation. David introduced her to Snowhill Plantation, home of Colonel Beauregard Snowhill and the site of the famous slave revolt. The home was full of many artifacts defining the history of the town and home of several slave cabins. It was the first time Dee had ever seen a real slave cabin. Although Colonel Snowhill had a reputation of being a ruthless slave owner, somehow Dee always found peace there.

There were times when Dee would visit the plantation just to take a nap in one of the private bedrooms Miss Essie did not allow the public to see. She used the bedrooms when she babysat her many grandchildren and great-grandchildren. This allowed them to take a nap or play while she worked.

Deandrea pulled into a parking space and walked onto the massive covered porch. She opened the door and spotted Miss Essie's assistant, Shannon, at the front desk on the phone.

"Hey, Copastor. How are you? Miss Essie's in the kitchen," Shannon said. She held the phone to her ear and continued her conversation, barely looking at Deandrea as she walked past her toward the kitchen. Shannon was there to help Miss Essie because Jarrod didn't want his mother to be out there alone at her age.

Deandrea walked past the pre-Civil War displays that had not changed much over the years. The picture of Colonel Snowhill and his family still hung over the fireplace. The slave tags and shields were still in the enclosed glass cases throughout the house. The colonel's clothing embraced the mannequins that were strategically placed in the house. Miss Essie walked out of the kitchen toward Dee with a plate in her hands. She had a slight limp. She limped when her knees were aching. In spite of being in pain, her lips curved to a bright smile when she spotted Deandrea walking toward her.

"Dee, I didn't expect you here today." She set the plate of food down and hugged Dee tightly. She looked at Dee with the concern only a mother can give. "What's wrong, baby?"

"I miss my husband."

She peeped into the front room and saw Shannon leaning on the desk talking on the phone. "Come on, we'll talk in the kitchen."

Miss Essie's face grimaced as they walked into the kitchen. She held onto Deandrea's elbow as they entered the kitchen and sat at the wooden island stationed in the middle of the room.

"Miss Essie, you should stay off your feet when your knees are hurting like that," Deandrea said.

"I'm all right. We just gonna get some rain in here. That's all. You want something to eat?"

"I ate at Miss Nelly's." At least she *tried* to eat at Miss Nelly's. Right now, she was void of emotion. Food was the last thing on her mind. Maybe she should fast and pray. Yes, it was time to fast. It was like Miss Nelly said, the enemy was trying to take over her mind. Dee couldn't let that happen. She had to be strong for her children.

"I don't know why y'all keep going over to Nelly's. She puts too much salt in her food. You have to be careful with all that salt," Miss Essie said. She picked up the sandwich on her plate and took a tiny bite. "Now tell me what's wrong."

"Nothing really. Jarrod's out of town again. I guess I was feeling a little lonely."

"Have you talked to him today?"

"He called last night—talked to the kids. He couldn't talk long. He was getting together with some of the officers for a meeting."

"Did you talk to him?"

"Briefly."

"I told that boy he shouldn't work so hard. He's got a family now. Some of that stuff he's doing somebody else can do." She took another bite of her sandwich.

"You know he's passionate about his ministry."

"I don't know if it's passion or what. He's got to be involved in everything. He's been like that all his life." Miss Essie wiped her mouth with a paper napkin and laughed. "When y'all were dating, you were the only thing Jarrod would slow down for. Lawd, child, he was so smitten with you, he went out and bought him some new clothes," Miss Essie laughed loudly.

Deandrea remembered those days. Jarrod did try hard to get her to see him as something other than her instructor. But she disliked him so much, her only goal was finishing her internship and getting out of Snowhill. Little did she know she was going to be attached to this small town the rest of her life . . . or at least until now.

After talking with Miss Essie for about an hour, she decided to go back to the church. It was almost time for the final meeting of the day, and she had to be there. The chime on her cell phone blared. She looked at the caller ID. It was Jarrod. She didn't feel like talking to him now. She didn't want to hear about the conference. She didn't want to hear him give her another assignment to do, like she was his personal gofer. So, she let the voice mail pick up the call.

She turned into the parking lot and noticed Jarrod's car in his reserved space. He didn't tell her he was getting his car serviced while he was away. She pulled in beside it and dragged herself into the church.

She turned the corner toward the executive suite and stopped at the sight of Jarrod leaning against the wall outside her office.

"Hey, honey, surprise," Jarrod said. Smiling, he rushed toward her. He leaned in for a kiss. Deandrea turned her head. It didn't seem to bother him as he planted his face on her neck. It was not often she saw him casually dressed in jeans and a sweater at the church. He pulled her into the office, wrapped his arms around her waist and began pulling her into his slow dance. They hadn't danced in a long time. They danced on their first date. Now, the only time they danced together was at the Christmas party, and they only do it because it was what people expected them to do.

However, today, Jarrod was swinging her around in his arms and doing a bad cha-cha. Deandrea finally broke away from him because with all his smiles and dancing she knew it was not because of her. She wished it were.

"I didn't expect you back today."

"I missed you, and I wanted to come home and play with my wife," He took her arm and pulled her back to him.

Deandrea had been there before, and today, she couldn't play the game. She pushed away from him. "I've got a meeting in five minutes."

"No, you don't. I cancelled it." She tried to move away from him but he held onto her.

"You cancelled it? Why didn't you tell me? I was at the plantation. I could have picked up the kids early and drove home."

"I tried to call you. You didn't pick up your phone. How's Mama?"

"She's got rainy knees again. She said she was okay. I wish you hadn't cancelled the meeting. I have an agenda to discuss."

"That can wait. I want to be with my wife. I kept thinking about you. So, I dumped those boring preachers and caught the first flight I could get just to be with you."

He wrapped his arms around her waist and began dancing again. Why was she not excited? Could it be she heard this all before? There was a time when just the mention of him wanting to be with her was all it took to get her clothes off, and it didn't matter where they were. Their love life was so passionate. Now, the passion was gone, at least for Deandrea. She did not want him touching her. She knew Jarrod. He was happy about something other than their marriage.

"I called Aunt Jean, and she's going to watch the kids for us. I'm taking you out to dinner and dancing. Wear something sexy," he whispered in her ear.

"I've got a lot of work to do here." The truth was she didn't want to go out with him. It was only a matter of time before he told her why he was so happy. He had yet to ask her how her day was going.

"Come on. It will be fun," Jarrod sang.

Deandrea gave in to his request and walked to the day care to pick up the children. She loaded them and all their gear into the car and headed home.

Deandrea arrived home before Jarrod. She fed the children and packed their bag with toys and snacks. She took them the short distance to her aunt's house. The twins ran through the house with their cousins. They loved it at Aunt Jean's. She let them run wild until they passed out.

She returned home and showered. She slipped on her jogging suit and waited for Jarrod to return home. Two hours passed and Jarrod had not arrived. She placed the simple black dress she had planned to wear across her bed in case Jarrod arrived home to actually take her out.

There was no need calling him. Deandrea knew exactly where he was and what he was doing. She curled up on the sofa and pressed the remote control, searching for something to grab her attention on the television. The creak of the garage door opening let her know Jarrod was at home. She eyed the wall clock.

He was three hours late.

"You're not dressed?" he asked when he walked into the room.

"I've been home over two hours. I didn't think you were coming to take me anywhere." Deandrea did not take her eyes off the television.

All of a sudden Jarrod leaped in front of the television and pulled a bouquet of roses from behind his back.

"Ta-da," he smiled as if he had just presented her with the Hope diamond.

She was not impressed. Did he think a few flowers were going to make up for the months he had not shown the least bit of attention toward her?

"I can't see the television," Deandrea said coldly.

He turned to look at the television and back at her. He fell to his knees and wrapped his arms around her. "I'm sorry, honey. I got caught up at the church." Deandrea rolled her eyes. It was always something at the church. "I got dinner . . . Luigi's. It's your favorite," he said playfully.

Deandrea swung her legs off the sofa. She did not have an appetite. Jarrod sat beside her.

"I'm sorry, baby. Here, I got these for you." He offered her the roses.

He seemed so proud of them. Deandrea took the flowers from him and walked to the kitchen just to get away from him. Instead of putting them in the garbage can like she wanted, she walked in the pantry, took out a vase and placed the flowers in it.

Jarrod walked into the kitchen holding the bag of food from Luigi's. He was singing as he placed the bags on the table and walked to the cabinet to retrieve some plates and silverware. Deandrea leaned on the counter near the sink watching his display.

After setting up the tableware, he danced toward Dee and wrapped his arms around her waist.

"Go get dressed," he said.

"I thought we're eating here."

"We are. I promised you dinner and dancing, and I'm going to give it to you. Now, go get dressed." He twirled her around.

For a brief moment, she smiled, thinking maybe it wouldn't be so bad. He did come home to be with her. He brought dinner and flowers. He hadn't done that in a while. He arranged for Aunt Jean to take care of the kids, and they could spend the night with her if needed. There was some light in this situation.

She walked upstairs and put on the dress and shoes she had selected and headed downstairs. At the bottom of the stairwell she saw the lit candles around the dining room. The lights were low and soft music was playing. Jarrod was still singing while he finished placing the food on the table. He looked up and spotted her standing on the bottom step. He stretched out his hand. She walked to him and took his hand.

He pulled out the chair at the head of the table for her to sit. Then he leaned down and kissed her lips. Now, she felt her husband. Was he being real tonight? Her body relaxed with his simple touch. Jarrod moved around her and sat in the neighboring chair. He moved his chair closer to her and leaned in to kiss her again.

He forked the antipasto and lifted it to Deandrea's mouth. She reached to catch the tangy juice dripping from the fork as she accepted the bite.

"Mmm. Delicious," she commented.

Jarrod smiled and placed a forkful of the treat into his mouth. He leaned in and kissed her again. The food was filled with spices and vinegar, but it was delicious to her. She placed her hands on his cheeks. It wasn't the food she wanted. It was her husband.

As he reached for another forkful of food, he talked about the convention and election in which his candidate won. He had to ruin the moment. Deandrea completely zoned him out. She didn't hear anything he said until the phone rang. Jarrod leaped and ran to his phone.

"I will only be a minute," he whispered to Deandrea as he walked out of the room.

A minute turned into minutes, minutes to an hour. He didn't even notice her leaving the house. She drove the half mile to her aunt's house and picked up the children. She arrived home and put them to bed. Jarrod was still on the phone in his office.

Deandrea blew out the melting candles and put the food away. She went to her bedroom and pulled the tight dress over her head.

"Hey, what are you doing?" Jarrod asked.

"I'm getting ready for bed."

"I thought we were spending some time together? Remember, it's our night."

Why did he say that? Dee did not know what was happening to her. It felt as if her body exploded. Her heart was beating fast. Her hands were shaking. That was the final straw.

"Our night? *Our* night, Jarrod?" she screamed.

"We were having a good time."

"We? There hasn't been a *we* in a long time."

"What are you talking about?"

"Did you notice I left the house and picked up the kids? They're in their rooms asleep," she continued. She stood in front of him dressed in her bra and panties. She was so mad, she was determined not to hold anything back. Right now, she did not like this man in front of her. Nor did she like what he had done to her and their family.

"You picked up the kids? Why?"

She walked into her closet and reached for her light blue warm-up suit. She slipped on the pants, pulled a T-shirt over her head and put on the jacket. Then she reached for her suitcase and threw it on the bed.

"Where are you going?" Jarrod followed her around the room.

"To Philadelphia," Deandrea answered. She rushed into the closet, grabbed an armful of clothes, not paying attention to what she had in her hands, and threw them in the suitcase.

"Philadelphia? What's in Philadelphia?"

"You . . ." She stopped and pointed her finger in his direction. "You are not in Philadelphia. I can't be around you right now."

Jarrod caught Deandrea's arm as she rushed past him trying to get to the bathroom. She stopped and the fiery glare she gave him caused him to release her arm. She continued to the bathroom with Jarrod following her.

"You can't take the children out this time of night."

"I'm not. You're taking care of them."

"I can't do that. I have a lot of things to do."

He had to go there. "You don't get it. You just don't get it, Jarrod. It's all about you and what you have to do. Did you even bother to ask me about my day today? I'll answer that for you—no. You don't care about me or what I do anymore. When was the last time we went on vacation, just the two of us? A *real* vacation, not one where you had to preach or we were attending some convention. When was the last time we made love? Can't remember? Me either. We never spend any time together anymore. When was the last time you went somewhere with me when I had to preach? I know you don't remember. Neither do I. You're always gone, and even when you are here, you're not here, like tonight. Everything was going fine until you got on that phone and you forgot about me. You didn't even notice I left the house. I can't take this anymore. Get out of my way."

She pushed past him and threw her toiletries in the suitcase. Jarrod stood back watching her slam the suitcase and zip it. Deandrea stomped into the bathroom. She picked up a brush and brushed her hair back and secured it in place with two gold barrettes.

"What's really in Philadelphia?"

"Shante invited me to go to a first ladies' conference with her last week. I told her no because your schedule did not allow me to be out of town. But you're here now. So I'm going."

She lifted the large bag off the bed and headed for the door. Jarrod followed her down the stairs and through the kitchen. The wheels of the luggage clicked as she passed through the mudroom and out to the garage.

"You got a flight this late at night?"

"No. I'm driving the Mercedes. You can take the Volvo for a change," she said. She pressed the key for the Mercedes. The lights on the car flickered on. Deandrea opened the door and threw the suitcase on the backseat. Slamming that door, she reached for the front door.

"You can't drive to Philadelphia this late at night by yourself. What about the kids? Who's going to take care of them?" Jarrod asked.

"They are your children, Jarrod. You seemed to have forgotten your first ministry is to your family. You take care of them. You'll be all right."

"When are you coming back?"

She opened the door and tossed her purse into the car. She dipped into the driver's seat, started the engine and slammed the door. She pressed the garage door opener and waited for the door to rise. Finally, she looked at Jarrod standing near the front door waiting for an answer and said, "I'll be back when I get back."

9

Misha and Matthew sat in their attorney's office discussing their case with their lawyer. "Rick, I thought you said the notice in the paper was routine and nothing would come of it," Matthew said. He was furious. He sat on the edge of his chair talking to the plump man.

Misha was so upset she could barely say a word. She didn't understand how a stranger could walk into her life and try to take her baby. Courtney was Misha's baby. She was Matthew's daughter. Her natural father was dead. Matthew was the only father she had ever known. Their families were her only family. Misha had not slept since all this started last Sunday. It was difficult to wait several days until Rick returned from a trip to discuss the objection to the adoption they received. How could anyone dare to object to Matthew adopting Courtney? Maybe it was the money. Since Matthew was a celebrity, someone was always trying to sue him. Now they were using their baby to extort money from them.

Misha wasn't having it. She was a fighter. She would fight them with fasting and prayer. She would fight them even if she had to go to Nebraska to confront them. They were not taking her baby from her.

Misha eyed Matthew talking to Rick. He did not get any sleep last night. They had gotten up about two in the morning to pray. An hour after that, she overheard him downstairs praying again by himself.

"I have already answered the objection. Misha, are you sure you never met these people? Tell me about your relationship with Courtney's father."

Misha couldn't believe Rick was asking her that question. There was *no* relationship with Courtney's biological father. Her father worked at the school where she taught. He was a consultant hired by the district to evaluate the school. She never went out with him even though he had asked her numerous times. The only reason she knew he was from Nebraska was because he told her in passing conversation. She was surprised she remembered it. She never met his family.

Rick was Matthew's attorney. He took this case because he thought it would be simple. Now, he was referring them to an attorney that practiced adoption law. Misha prayed this case didn't hit the papers. The media loved to tear down preachers.

Misha and Matthew left the attorney's office not feeling any better than before they went in. They both passed on lunch and headed home. On any typical day, they would have delighted in an afternoon of intimacy. But today, neither felt like it. The atmosphere held a nervous tension.

"I have to go over to the church for a little while. I'll pick up Courtney on the way back," Matthew said. Sitting around the house was driving him crazy.

"No. I'll go get her now. Will you be home for dinner?"

"Yes." Matthew walked toward Misha and embraced her. "It's going to be okay. This will pass quickly. We don't have anything to worry about."

Misha wished she could be as confident as her husband. Her faith was being tested. Could God be chastising her for even considering having an abortion when she found out she was pregnant? She repented of that a long time ago. She loved Courtney so much she couldn't see how she considered it. Courtney and Matthew were the two biggest blessings she had ever received in her life, and she almost walked away from both of them.

Misha walked into the laundry room and opened the dryer. She reached in for the dry baby blanket inside. Laying the unfolded blanket on top of the dryer, she began to pray.

"God, I honor you for your awesome power and your love, grace and mercy that is new every day. Forgive me of my sins, especially of the thought of having an abortion. I thank you for my child. She is a most precious gift. I know this situation is under your control. Give me peace and guidance. Show me what you would have me to do. In Jesus' name. Amen."

Misha needed to vent to someone about her legal woes. After picking up Courtney from day care, she stopped by her mother-in-law's medical office to see if she had some free time to talk. She had always found her mother-in-law easy to talk to, more than her own mom.

She needed to talk to someone about this other than Matthew. He was as troubled about it as she was. Sometimes, Misha thought he had some questions about her relationship, if you can call it that, with Courtney's father. She explained everything to him and thought he understood. Hopefully, deep inside, he knew there was nothing more to it.

"Ooooh, look at little Courtney. How's my baby doing?" Misha's mother-in-law, Dr. Lauren Taylor, said as she spotted Misha and Courtney walking down the hallway in her office. She set the folder she was holding down on a small table tucked inside a cutout in the wall and ran to get Courtney. Misha handed over the stretching baby to her. They had her so spoiled. She took Courtney in her arms and hugged Misha at the same time.

"Who is this cute little girl?" one of her patients asked.

"Mr. Goodwin, this is my granddaughter."

Courtney twisted her lips. She babbled as she talked to the man. The man's laughter made Courtney squeal in delight. He walked away leaving her with the swarm of Dr. Lauren's employees who were passing Courtney among them. The baby squealed with all the attention. She was so much like Matthew it was crazy. She was not even one year old yet, and she was already an entertainer.

After a few minutes, Dr. Lauren collected Courtney in her arms, and they walked to her office. Misha sat in the beautifully decorated office filled with her mother-in-law's many degrees and accreditations and a small display of African American art. It was nice having a dermatologist in the family. Misha's skin had never looked so good. She was even more grateful she could get along with her in-laws. At first, she was afraid they would think she was with Matthew for his money and they would be suspicious of her. However, they accepted her like family.

"Matthew called and told me what Rick said today. I don't think you have anything to worry about. He'll straighten it out," Dr. Lauren said as she bounced Courtney on her knee to the delight of the baby. "This is Grandma's little girl, and no big bad man is going to take her away." Courtney screamed with delight as she tried to talk with her grandmother.

"I keep telling myself it's going to work out. Besides, anybody can file anything in court and nothing happens to it, right?" Misha said as Courtney's loud chatter filled the room. Courtney's blue eyes sparkled as her grandmother played with her nose. Her long ponytails swayed with every bounce. "Do you think God is punishing me?"

Dr. Lauren sat Courtney in her lap. She opened the top drawer in her desk and pulled out a small rattle and handed it to Courtney. "Punishing you for what?"

"You know . . . about the abortion."

"Don't ever think that. It was a tough time for you. Anybody would have thought about having an abortion. I told Matthew those people want money. Watch, it's just a matter of time and they're going to ask you for money." She took a tissue and wiped the long line of saliva from Courtney's mouth and put the rattle in it. "Where are you going after you leave here?"

"Well, I need to go home and start dinner. Matthew will be home soon."

"Call him and tell him I'm going to take y'all out to dinner. I've got two more patients in the office to see. Call Matt's office for me and tell him to meet us at the Main Course restaurant."

That was the best offer Misha heard all day. She didn't feel like cooking. The reality of the day was she did not really feel like eating. She cradled Courtney in her arms. She couldn't bear the thought of losing her.

Misha joined the group at the restaurant after stopping by the store to pick up food for Courtney. Matthew had already ordered for her when she arrived at the table holding the baby in her arms. Her father-in-law, Dr. Matt, stood and reached for the squirming baby. He lightly kissed Misha's cheek. Matthew grabbed the strap of the diaper bag off Misha's shoulder and placed it in a chair beside him.

The meal was quickly delivered to the table. Misha only picked at her food. She hardly participated in the dinner conversation. She could only think of what might happen. How would she handle it? How would Matthew take it? What kind of impact would this trial have on their marriage? The sound of her name snapped her back to the conversation going on around her.

"You hardly ate anything. Don't let these people upset you so much you can't eat," Dr. Matt said to her.

Misha glanced at Matthew. He was scrapping the last of his risotto from his plate. Apparently he hadn't lost his appetite. She looked around the table and wondered how she ended up here. She and Matthew were raised so differently. His parents were doctors. His father was a neurosurgeon. Her parents were no less honorable. Her mother has worked for the hospital almost thirty years. Her father recently retired from driving long-distance trucks for a company. She was just a girl out of SWATS. Now, she was in a world she never imagined being in.

Courtney wailed at the top of her lungs, demanding everyone's attention. Misha reached for her as the baby flung her head in protest. At least this took the attention off her plate. People in the restaurant stared at them. Misha reached into the bag and pulled out some strained carrots. Matthew pulled Courtney from her. Misha twisted the cap and dipped a spoon in it. She placed the carrots on Courtney's tightly closed lips. The baby shook her head, refusing the food.

Dr. Matt took the crying baby and bounced her on his leg. Nothing they did stopped the crying or the tears that ran down her face. Dr. Matt took some mashed potatoes off his plate and placed it on her lips. Courtney licked the food from her mouth and reached toward the potatoes on the plate. Dr. Matt spooned more potatoes into the mouth of the now satisfied baby.

Somehow, Misha knew that was the problem. Matthew fed Courtney from his plate all the time. She had now acquired a taste for table food, and she demanded it. Her pediatrician told them to watch her weight. She was a chubby baby. Suddenly, everyone was feeding her from their plates. Misha would like them to be around when she got up in the middle of the night with a baby whose stomach was hurting.

"Y'all need to stop feeding her that food," Misha demanded.

They laughed at the expressions the baby had on her face when she gobbled up the tiny assortment of foods they took turns giving her.

Misha eyed her baby sitting comfortably in her grandfather's lap. She was so amazed by their resemblance. He was white, and his blue eyes stood out in the crowd. She could understand the attraction. Even at his age, he was still a very handsome man, with good skin. Matthew looked like his father, only darker skinned. They had the same features. Both of them were tall and slim. They talked alike and had the same mannerisms. They even acted the same way when they sang. Matthew often joked he had more soul than his father.

"Honey, when is the court date? I need to take that day off so I can go with you. I want to see these people for myself," Dr. Lauren asked Matthew.

"We don't have a court date yet. We should know something by the time Misha gets back from Philadelphia."

"Philadelphia? Why are you going to Philadelphia?" She directed her question to Misha.

In all the commotion, she had forgotten about Philadelphia. "I was going. I don't think I'll go now."

"Why not? You've been looking forward to the conference," Matthew questioned her.

"What conference?" Dr. Lauren repeated.

"It's a conference for first ladies of churches," Matthew responded for his wife. "I found out about it a couple of months ago and suggested Misha go. I already made all the arrangements. She has been looking forward to it since one of her favorite preachers will be there."

"Who's that?" Dr. Lauren asked as she wiped Courtney's mouth with a napkin.

"Shante Patrick," Matthew answered.

"I'm not going now." How could she go to a conference when someone was trying to take her baby away from her? Matthew had lost his mind if he thought she was leaving her baby for one minute.

"Misha, I think you should go. Courtney will be fine. I'll help Matthew out if he needs me," Dr. Lauren suggested.

"No. I don't feel it's the right time to go. There will be other conferences. Right now, I want to stay on top of things. Besides, I won't be able to focus on the workshops or sermons with all this mess going on."

"Misha, that's the main reason why you *should* go. It will take your mind off everything for a little while. Who knows, you may get something out of it that will help you with everything that's going on. When is the conference anyway?" Dr. Matt asked her.

"It starts tomorrow and continues throughout the weekend. I'll be gone for too many days." Misha felt they had ganged up on her, giving her multiple reasons why she should go to Philadelphia. She was too troubled. What if something happens while she was away? It would be the first time she left Courtney for more than a few hours. She had no doubt Matthew would take good care of her. It was still hard to leave her, especially now. She didn't know if she could do it.

The dinner had been a good diversion for Misha and Matthew this evening. Her in-laws never let her focus on the hearing too long.

She sat on the bed dressed in her silk pajamas reading her Bible. She tried to find a verse that sent comfort to her restless soul. Matthew had volunteered to bathe Courtney and put her in the bed.

"Courtney's asleep," Matthew said as he walked into the bedroom. Noticing the Bible in her lap he asked, "What are you reading?" He sat on the bed beside her.

"Psalm Thirty-four."

"Let me see." Matthew took the Bible from her hand and leaned on the contemporary headboard of the bed and began reading. Misha placed her head on his chest and listened to him.

Go to Philadelphia.

The familiar voice in her spirit spoke to her. Misha knew it was the Holy Spirit telling her to go to the conference. How could she? She looked around their large master bedroom suite. The colors, the furniture, the curtains, everything seemed new to her. Where had she been all this time? She didn't even like paisley, and there were paisley curtains hanging in the room.

Matthew tried hard to comfort her. What was she worried about? There was no way these people could take their child.

Matthew closed the Bible and held Misha. He closed his eyes and began singing, "'Tis So Sweet to Trust in Jesus." Misha knew the only time Matthew sang hymns was when he was troubled. This was the first real test in their marriage, and they were both struggling with it.

Tell him nothing happened between you and Heckler. The Holy Spirit spoke to her again. She obeyed the voice in her spirit.

"Honey, nothing happened between me and Courtney's dad. There were no feelings between us."

"I know." He kissed her forehead. Misha felt his tense body relax. They lay on the bed in silence. "You know you should go to Philadelphia."

"How can I go now?"

Matthew sat up and looked her in the eye. "You *need* to go now. Daddy was right when he said you might get something you need out of it. I believe this conference is something you need."

"I don't know." Misha caressed his chest.

"Think about it. How many people are you close to here other than my family?"

He had a point. She wasn't close to anyone other than his family. The couple of people she thought were her friends were only using her to get next to him. On Sunday morning, the people attending church only wanted to talk to him. As they stood side by side, people spoke to him but completely ignored her. Some had pushed her aside to take pictures with him. She didn't trust anyone outside of family. She was not going to talk to anyone about her marriage or church business. She did have days when she wished she had someone to go shopping with or just talk to about things other than church stuff. Courtney had more friends than she had. She was already being invited to parties, and she was not even one year old yet.

It would be nice to have someone other than her family call her and ask her how she was doing. She prayed God sent someone to be her real friend. Matthew's friends were celebrities and so arrogant. Many times being around his friends sent her into sensory overload. There were times when she didn't like being around them because of what God had shown her about them in the spirit. When they had them over to their house, they only wanted to talk to him. Misha usually ended up acting like their servant, serving food and drinks. They made her feel unwelcomed, like an outsider in her own house. Even on her birthday, they didn't pretend to be happy for her. She was pushed out of her own party and ended up playing with Courtney in her room until they left the house.

"What can we do now but wait? So, while you wait, you can be receiving a word from God and allowing Him to minister to you about being a first lady. Baby, I see you and what you have endured. I know it's not easy being my wife. At the conference, you'll meet other women who understand what it's like being in your position."

Misha sat quietly listening to the many reasons she should go to the conference. But she felt she needed to keep her child close.

Go to Philadelphia.

The voice in her spirit was relentless in pushing her to go to the conference. She had to obey the voice of the Lord. For whatever reason, the Lord wanted her to go. Maybe there was someone there she had to minister to. She had to remember she was a minister of the Gospel, a prophetess. He would show her who needed ministry when she got there.

"Okay, I'll go." Misha gave in.

Matthew's lips widened into a smile. He jumped off the bed and ran into the closet and returned, pulling some paper out of an envelope.

"Here," he handed her the papers. "I printed your boarding passes earlier. Your flight leaves at ten."

"You were so sure I was going." Misha reached for the envelope.

"I needed you to go."

"What? You're trying to get rid of me?"

"No, I'm trying to prevent you from going to jail."

"Jail? I don't get it."

"I'm hoping you can find other ways of dealing with all the women at the church. I know they are there. I don't pay them any attention, but you do. I know it bothers you. You can't keep jumping up in every woman's face, talking about you're from Georgia and threatening to cut them. I'm scared you're going to end up in jail, and I can't get any until visitation day." He started to laugh.

Misha jumped off the bed and placed her hands on her hips. He was only joking, but two could play that game. "You say that like you're going to get some tonight."

"Well, you are going away for a few days. You've got to put something in storage." He slowly approached her.

Misha backed away from him and circled the bed. She stopped at the other side not wanting to play this game tonight. Tonight, she needed to be with her husband.

10

Wednesday morning Shante hugged her daughter, Camille, before stepping in line to board the train in New York. She wondered if she would ever get used to being so tired. It had been a whirlwind week. Along with the interviews and book signings, she spent two exhausting hours in the bridal shop with Camille. She looked forward to the brief rest she would get when she arrived in Philadelphia.

"Bye, Mom. Call me when you get to Philadelphia," Camille said. She bent down and placed her head against Shante's belly. "Bye, my little boo-boo. Take care of Mom."

Camille's reaction to the pregnancy shocked Shante. She had thought Camille would be upset because it would be embarrassing. It was the total opposite. She thought it was funny. When she was a child, she used to pray for a sibling. She was thrilled God finally answered her prayers. She loved her brothers, but to her, it wasn't the same. She explained to Shante her brothers were not her biological brothers and now she had a biological sibling that she could claim all her own.

She was so happy, she told everyone she met Shante was pregnant. Shante was embarrassed by it. She didn't know why. There were many older women having babies these days. It could have been the way some people thought it was a joke. They looked at how old she was and thought Camille was playing with them. Camille's fiancé, Aaron, did not know what to say. He made jokes about it once he saw they were okay with it.

Shante sank into her seat on the train. She was thoroughly exhausted. She had spent the last few days looking at wedding dresses, tasting myriad cakes and looking at some of the most beautiful flowers she had ever seen. With a budget of a hundred and fifty thousand dollars, Camille was going all out. Shante personally thought it was too much money to spend. She could have used that money to buy herself a house or condo. Real estate was very expensive in New York. They didn't have to worry about paying for a honeymoon. Max and Shante had already gifted that to them. But they had yet another special surprise for them. They planned to present them with it at the reception.

The wedding planner, Tatiana, was shipping flowers in from all over the world for this event. She seemed very knowledgeable about the resources in and around New York City. Shante felt she was being overcharged for some services because of the budget and because of who she was. Who needed to pay five thousand dollars for a wedding cake? It was ridiculous. She and Max only spent about thirty thousand on their entire wedding, including the dresses, tuxedos, flowers, reception and honeymoon. They had two churches of people to feed and managed to do it with a small budget. Now, Camille was having flowers and cakes shipped to South Carolina for her "destination wedding."

"Ma'am, your ticket," the train attendant held out his hand as Shante handed him her ticket. She could feel the gentle shake of the train. She leaned her head back on the headrest. She didn't have to leave New York early, but one more day and she would have passed out again. It wouldn't hurt to have a couple of days to rest in Philadelphia before she had to preach on Friday. With all that had happened, she didn't know if she should preach the sermon she had planned. The twenty-first-century

wife was going to be such a good message, a twist on the
virtuous woman.

Shante saw herself as the twenty-first-century virtuous
woman. She was a woman who had it all. She had a
successful career, wonderful husband and family and an
effective ministry. She was able to balance it all at one
time.

Now, when she looked back, she could see the subtle
signs of trouble. Her teenage son was acting out. Her
second son was more withdrawn in his own world. Her
youngest son's only friend in the house seemed to be his
video games. Her workaholic pastor husband was as busy
as she was. The only difference was, he did not travel
as much as she did and the whole world didn't know
him. None of them had time for one another. Their busy
lifestyles were beginning to wear on their family.

Shante didn't know what to do. She had been called
to preach. God had opened all sorts of doors for her.
Who would have thought she would be such a successful
writer? At first, she did not even think of writing as a
ministry. However, people had written her and told her
how her books had brought deliverance in their lives.
With this type of ministry came obligations, ones she had
to abide by in order to get the Gospel out to the world. She
didn't know why Max didn't understand that.

She took a deep breath and slowly released the air so no
one would notice her frustration. Max had hardly spoken
to her in the last few days. He didn't even pray for her when
she left. She had to drive herself to the airport. He said he
was too busy. Max had never been this mad at her before.
Shante thought he was trying to control her. They never
sat down and discussed her career or ministry. He wanted
to make all the decisions and demanded she lived by them.
He didn't understand why she had to do this conference.
Yes, she promised him she would ease up on her schedule

and not travel as much, but she kept getting invitations to preach. Shante still remembered what it felt like when no one wanted to hear her preach. Now it seemed as if everyone wanted her. She had to go . . . didn't she?

Shante looked out the window at the city landscape; no cows, horses or farmland. She watched the gray, brown and blacks of the city speed past the window. She wondered if she should call Bishop and Mother Thompson? She needed to tell them she was pregnant. She didn't want them to hear it from anyone but her.

Bishop and Mother became her surrogate parents when she moved to Charlotte with Camille after she left her ex-husband Kevin. They rescued her from the women's shelter and allowed Shante and Camille to stay with them rent-free while her body healed from the beating Kevin did to her, and even after she was able to get a job.

She missed them so much. They always seemed to know what was going on in her life just by looking at her face. She couldn't hide anything from them. They could minister to her in a way no one had, even Max. It was a different type of ministry, like parent-child. That was something she missed from her own parents who died when she was in college.

Max was there for her the entire time. Shante thought she could always count on Max to minister to her. But now they had separate lives. They had become each other's trophy spouse. She was his internationally famous preacher-writer-wife, and he was her successful renowned attorney-pastor-politician-husband. They were two over-achievers striving to acquire more and more. She couldn't forget their four beautiful trophy children who were successful in their own right.

"Philadelphia," the train attendant cried out as the train slowed to approach the Thirtieth Street Station.

Shante pulled her carry-on from the overhead compartment and shuffled toward the door. She was looking forward to not having anything to do but pray for her situation at home. She and Max were going to have to find some balance. It was getting to the point that they no longer knew each other. God called her to preach the Gospel. How was she supposed to do it without sacrificing her family?

She stepped off the train and walked into the magnificent Thirtieth Street Station. The loud sound of busy travelers filled the air. She asked for directions to the taxi station to get a ride to the Omni Hotel. If the stars were aligned right, she would make it out of the terminal without anyone recognizing her.

A young lady ran up to her and grabbed the handle of her suitcase. Shante pulled it back.

"Excuse me, Rev. Patrick. I apologize. I'm late," she said. "Pastor Edmunds told me only about thirty minutes ago that I had to come and pick you up."

"Pastor Edmunds?"

The lady released Shante's bag and held out her hand to shake Shante's.

"Hi, I'm Monica from Shining Light Ministries."

Shante's eyes stretched. How did they know she was going to be there today? She only told Camille and LaToya. *LaToya.* There goes her peace and quiet. She forgot to tell LaToya she wanted to be alone.

The lady picked up Shante's bag and began walking. Shante picked up her step to walk alongside her.

"We were able to change your arrangements, and we got you a suite at the Marriott at the Convention Center where the conference is taking place. It will be easier on you. You can just walk to your room whenever you want to."

They exited the station and got into a waiting SUV. Shante sat in the front seat of the vehicle, trying hard not to show her displeasure. She was going to have to contact LaToya as soon as she got to the hotel. LaToya needed to work her magic so she could get some rest.

"First Lady Edmunds has arranged for you to have lunch with them on Thursday after the first session. She also wants to know if you can do a book signing today or tomorrow. We received all the materials you sent us for your table."

A book signing was not on the agenda. This was going to be one of those conferences where they wanted all the extras without asking first. They probably announced she would be signing books. Shante almost regretted not having LaToya come along on this trip. She could have handled all the extras.

The young lady handed Shante a folder filled with information about the conference. She opened it to find a schedule of events. It looked pretty full.

"My cell number is in there too. If you need anything, I will be the one to assist you."

Shante twisted her arm to get a glimpse of her watch. It was only 9:30 in the morning. The conference did not start until this evening at seven. She had several hours she could rest and pray. Depending on how she felt, she may go to the opening service tonight.

Monica escorted her to her suite and handed her the key. "I'll be back here to escort you backstage about six," she said.

"It won't be necessary. I may not attend tonight's service."

"Oh. I'll inform Pastor. If you need anything give me a call."

Shante watched Monica walk away before she entered her room. She closed the door behind her and rolled her luggage into the room and set it next to the minibar. One thing she loved about these conferences was the fact she got fantastic rooms. She was pleased with the two-bedroom suite they reserved for her.

Her phone chimed. She sighed and reached into her purse. She took out her cell phone and noticed Deandrea's number on the caller ID.

"Dee. How are you this morning?"

"Are you in Philadelphia yet?"

"I just got here. Why?"

"I'm on my way there. Can you see if you can get me a room in your hotel? I don't have reservations. It was sort of a last-minute decision to go to the conference."

"You can stay with me. I'm at the Marriott at the Convention Center. I have a two-bedroom suite. You can stay in the other room. What time will your plane arrive? I'll have somebody pick you up."

Shante leaped with joy inside. God does work wonders. He sent someone she could talk to. Dee was such a good listener and understanding. It was probably the psychologist in her. Shante laughed at herself. God sent her a psychologist. She guessed she was in more trouble than she thought.

"I'm driving," Dee said.

"Driving? By yourself?"

"It's a long story. Can you give me the address of the hotel so I can put it in my navigational system?"

Shante walked to the desk and found the hotel stationary. She gave the address to Deandrea. Shante leaned on the dresser.Was she reading too much into the quiver in Deandrea's voice? She sounded a little upset. Shante said a quick prayer for Deandrea's safe travel. She punched Monica's number in her cell and informed the young lady that she would definitely not be attending evening services. Then she punched in Max's number. They hadn't spoken much since she had been away. Now was a good time to call before Deandrea arrived.

"Max, hey, it's me. How are you?" she said into the phone.

"Okay, I guess. How's the baby?"

"The baby's fine."

"Camille called me this morning. She sounded excited about the baby."

"She is. I'm in Philadelphia now. I'm staying at the Marriott at the Convention Center. The church changed my reservations. I'm not going to do anything today. I think I'll lounge around the hotel until tomorrow. Dee will be here this afternoon."

"Dee?"

"Yes. She changed her mind about attending the conference at the last minute. She's on her way here now. How are the boys?" Shante looked out the window at the view of downtown Philadelphia.

"They're at school," he said dryly.

"Max, are you okay?"

"I'm worried about you."

"I'm fine. A little tired. Today is my rest day. I'm not doing anything." Shante checked the minibar for something to eat. "You don't have to be worry about me. I'm taking my vitamins and trying not to do too much. Max, this is my last conference. I promise. I'm coming off the road. I need to be at home and not because I'm pregnant. I . . . I just need to be at home."

"Don't make promises you can't keep."

Shante searched for the words to say to Max. It had never been so difficult to talk to him before. She couldn't allow a wall to be built up between them. She had to keep the lines of communication open. Her experience being a pastor had shown her that once that wall was built it was difficult to tear it down. The wall blocked trust, love and respect, leaving only negative emotions that made the couple's heads hurt as they banged them against the wall, trying to reach each other. She didn't want that happening to them.

"Shante, I didn't pray for you before you left. Can I pray for you now?"

Shante was happy and relieved as she listened to Max's prayer. The wall was just her imagination. She and Max would be okay.

She had just ended her conversation with Max when her phone chimed again. She did not recognize the number but answered it anyway.

"Pastor Patrick?"

"Yes."

"This is Pastor Edmunds. I wanted to welcome you to Philadelphia. I hope the accommodations we arranged for you meet your needs."

"Everything's wonderful, Pastor Edmunds."

"We look forward to worshipping with you tonight. We have a powerful speaker. The Lord is going to show up in a mighty way. We expect the blessing of the Lord to rain down on us. We're going to set the atmosphere for the rest of the week."

Shante knew exactly what he was doing. He wanted her to show up tonight at the conference. Monica must have called him and told him she wasn't going. She had to make sure he knew today she was resting. But, he was real churchy. She needed to talk to him in his language.

"Pastor Edmunds, I'm sure the Lord has great things for all of us this week."

"I was wondering if you could do an offertory appeal for us this evening."

People paid two hundred and fifty dollars to attend the conference because of all of the big names he brought on, and he's asking for an offering? Conferences can be expensive, especially one like this one that had ministers coming from across the country. But, if God told them to do it, wouldn't He also provide?

Shante shook her head and said, "Pastor, I had not planned on attending tonight. I was going to stay in and work on my sermon. I've been away from my home all week, and I need time to go before the Lord tonight."

"Well, I understand. We are looking for a mighty word from the Lord. Well, if you need anything, please feel free to call me and order whatever you need from room service. I will see you tomorrow at lunch."

"Thank you. Bye-bye." Shante ended the call, mumbling to herself, "This guy won't quit." Good thing she will have Deandrea to go with her to the luncheon. It was always better having someone she knew attending these functions with her. It should be Max. With him there, it would show everybody they had a solid marriage and he supported her ministry.

Shante looked out of the hotel window at the Philadelphia skyline and sighed. It would be great to look out into the crowd and see her husband's face. It had been awhile since he traveled with her. This trip would have been the perfect time since she was carrying his child.

She walked into the bedroom and pulled off the slacks she wore on the train. She caught a glimpse of her body in the mirror. A small pooch sat amid the fat on her stomach. She had gained some weight. She was going to gain a lot more. What in the world was Deandrea going to say once she found out? She would understand. She was almost forty when she had the twins. *God, I am so glad you're sending Dee to Philadelphia.* She had to thank her Lord just one more time.

Shante lay across the bed and wondered if the linen had been changed. She reached for the phone and called the front desk. She was relieved when she was informed they did it before she arrived at the request of the church. She set the phone in its cradle and pulled back the sheets, then she climbed into the bed and melted into its softness. She yawned, and then took a deep breath, trying to relax. She had to believe God had this thing already worked out. She had to trust Him.

11

"Welcome to Maryland" the sign on the highway read as Deandrea sped down the highway. She placed her hand over her mouth and yawned. She had been on the road for hours. The journey had not been easy. She stopped in Charlotte, North Carolina, and got a hotel room. Then she awoke early and got back on the road for the remainder of her ten-hour trip. She had been on the road for four hours before she hit stalled traffic in Washington, D.C. This part of her drive was tedious. It was bumper-to-bumper traffic going into Washington. She had to fight sleep, anger and guilt for leaving her children, all at the same time. The guilt saddened her. The anger kept her foot on the gas pedal. Should she go back and admit defeat and go through life doing the same humdrum things every day? She couldn't go back now. She had already told Shante she was on her way.

She pulled into the Maryland state welcoming center and sat in her car. The thought of going back home made her head hurt. If she returned, it would only be for her children. How could she leave her children like that? Was she a bad mother to just run away from home and not consider how her children were going to be taken care of? Only sorry moms walked out on their children. That settled it. She was going back home. She picked up her phone and punched in Jarrod's number.

How could she leave her children with Jarrod? Yes, he was their father, but he didn't know them. All he was to them was a man who occasionally lived with them and brought them gifts whenever he showed up. He wasn't involved in anything in their lives. He only thought about ministry, not his children. He had only been a father to them in a biological way, not in relationship.

"Dee, baby, I'm glad you called. I've been worried," Jarrod said.

Deandrea didn't believe him. If he was so concerned he would have called. The sound of his voice made her angry all over again. He didn't know or care how she felt. He let her leave in the middle of the night and didn't even try to stop her.

"The children were looking for you. I told them you went on a trip like me and would be back in a few days."

"Let me speak to them," Deandrea said angrily.

The sound of her children on the phone broke Deandrea's heart. A tear ran down her cheek as she listened to their loud chatter. They sounded upset that she was gone. She could not understand everything they were saying, but she was positive they were telling her their father did not know what he was doing.

Andrea cried when she heard Deandrea was not coming home now. She hated to say good-bye to them, even if it was temporary.

"Drea said something about cereal. Did you feed them this morning?" Deandrea asked Jarrod once he was back on the phone.

"I gave her cereal. She got mad and threw it across the table. I don't know what she wants. I tried to give her pancakes, and she kept crying. She won't eat anything."

"She likes oatmeal. Cook her some oatmeal. There is some instant oatmeal in the pantry. She'll eat that. Don't forget R. J. doesn't eat eggs. I don't allow them to watch all those violent children's shows. So if they ask, don't let them. They have to play with their flash cards and go over the alphabet, numbers and colors. I try to pick them up from the day care by three. Don't forget."

"I won't. Dee, we need to talk. I'm sorry. I didn't realize—"

"I don't want to talk right now. I'll call you when I get to Philadelphia." Deandrea ended her call. She didn't want to hear what he had to say. Sorry. Yes, he was sorry. Sorry for leaving his family for his mistress. Sorry for neglecting his duties when it came to his wife. Sorry for not thinking it was important to take care of his family. Sorry for letting her take this long ride by herself. Sorry for not even knowing his daughter liked oatmeal for breakfast. Sorry? Yes, he was sorry. If she had known he was going to be this sorry, she would have never married him.

She sat in the parking lot at the welcome center. She still had a couple of hours of driving ahead of her. Somewhere along the way she was going to have to buy something to wear. She was so mad when she left the house, she didn't realize she only packed blouses and underwear. He saw her packing. Why didn't he say something? *Sorry.* She didn't even notice until she stopped at the hotel last night and opened the suitcase to get her pajamas, and they were not there. All she could do was cry. She had been doing a lot of that lately. She felt like a dead man walking—empty, lifeless and alone. She pushed aside the thought of returning home. Jarrod needed to figure everything out. She needed this time for her sanity. She would be no help to the children or herself with her head messed up. She started the car and entered the highway.

"Coming up in the next hour, Marvin Sapp, Mississippi Mass Choir and that new one everybody's talking about from Bernard Taylor." The announcer on the radio was the only friend she seemed to have right now. He kept her awake and gave her a small spark of hope in this situation. The warning light on the gas gauge shined. She needed to get gas soon. She was hungry too. She hadn't felt hungry in a long time. Her stomach was actually growling. She hadn't had anything to eat since Jarrod fed her those two forkfuls of food last night. The evening was messed up.

Deandrea swept across two lanes of traffic to take the next exit off the highway. She pulled into the gas station, swiped her card and began filling her tank. Gas was forty cents a gallon higher than it was in South Carolina. She had no choice. It was either pay or walk. The latter was not an option.

Deandrea had never done anything so stupid in her life. How could she just up and leave her family? What was wrong with her? Jarrod was called to minister the Gospel. Why was she jealous of it? God could not possibly be pleased with her right now. She was not pleased with herself. She had a great husband and two beautiful children. She had earned two doctorate degrees and had all the material things she could ever want. Why was she not happy?

After eating a fast-food meal of chicken and french fries, Deandrea felt energized. Just being separated from Jarrod for a few hours made her feel a little better. She loved her husband. She promised to live with him forever. She couldn't live with him like this, however. There was going to have to be some compromise. She could not be miserable all her life. She wanted her children to grow up in a happy home with loving parents. She gave them a hundred percent and more. Jarrod gave them candy whenever he showed up. Nevertheless, right now, she had to take care of herself.

Her cell phone rang. She didn't want to talk to Jarrod, but he could be calling about the children. She took a deep breath and answered the phone.

"Hi, honey. Where are you?" Jarrod tried to sound cheerful.

"Is there anything wrong with the kids?"

"No. I was thinking about you and . . . everything."

"Jarrod, I don't have time for this. I'm in the middle of traffic, and I have to pay attention to the road. I shouldn't be on the phone while I'm driving."

"Dee, don't hang up. Please talk to me. Why didn't you tell me about the conference?"

So now he was turning the tables on her and acting as if this was her fault. He was the one who had been gone the last two years. She barely saw him two days out of the week, and he had the nerve to question her? She couldn't go there with him, especially while she was driving.

"Dee, please talk to me."

"What do you want me to say?"

"Why didn't you tell me about the conference? I would have changed my schedule."

"Would you? Would you *really,* Jarrod? You couldn't even change your life to spend an hour alone with me. How were you planning to change three or four days?" Deandrea pressed the speaker on her cell and set it in the cup holder next to her.

"I'm sorry. I was wrong. It won't happen again. I promise."

What is this? The one hundred sixty-seventh time she had heard the same promise. Each time it turned out to be an empty promise or just a flat-out lie. Did he even realize what he was saying when it was coming out of his mouth? Did he *listen* to himself? Deandrea used to believe him. Now she didn't listen to it anymore. Her emotions were blank. She could not get mad at him. She didn't care what he did as long as it didn't hurt her children.

"Say something." Jarrod sounded sad. Deandrea tried hard not to fall for it. "If it meant so much to you, you should have said something."

"You don't get it, do you? It's not about the conference. It's everything." He was beginning to touch a nerve. "Look, Jarrod, if there is something wrong with the children, call me. If not, leave me alone. I can't talk about this with you now."

She pressed the END button on her phone before he had time to answer. "God, where did the love go?" She prayed. She didn't care if he was upset or remorseful or truly sorry for what he had done to them. She had a lot of thinking to do when she got to Philadelphia. Shante would be there. Deandrea needed her godly advice. It would help her in the decision she had to make.

The drive was far longer than Deandrea thought. She didn't get much sleep last night. She was emotionally, physically and spiritually drained. Could it be that God ordained her to go to this conference? No. If it were God's plan, she wouldn't have all this drama. She pulled off the highway toward a rest area. Her phone rang again. It was Jarrod.

"What!" she yelled into the receiver.

"Hey, honey, I was calling to see if you were in Philadelphia yet."

"Is there something wrong with the kids?"

"No. They're in the den playing."

"They didn't go to day care?"

"No. I decided to take the day off. They are here at home with me. Where are you?"

So *now* he decided to take the day off and stay at home. He should have done that last week, last month or last year. No, he waited until she left to take the day off. He couldn't even take the evening off for her. Yet, he could take a whole day off when she was not there.

"Dee, where are you?" Jarrod repeated.

"I'm in Delaware at a rest area. I'm getting ready to get back on the highway."

"You're only in Delaware? You left last night."

"I got a hotel room. Anything else? I've got to get back on the road. Shante is expecting me."

"Who's sponsoring the conference? I know a few people there. I can call them and tell them to look out for you."

She didn't know. She never asked Shante. The only thing she knew was Shante was going to preach on Friday. She should have asked just in case someone needed to get in touch with her. Right now her only mission was to get Jarrod off the phone without having to hang up on him again.

"I'm not interested in meeting any of your friends."

"I'm worried about you. You haven't been this mad at me since we first met."

He succeeded in getting a slight smile out of her. He was right. She did the same thing she was doing today, taking a long drive to get away from him. Back then, she took many long drives to get away from him. She couldn't stand him, sort of like what she was feeling now. Is that where she went wrong? Was it the Lord telling her then he was the wrong guy?

When they first met, everybody seemed to think they were perfect for each other. They couldn't stop arguing. His sister, Step, told her it was part of the process because she and Jarrod were so much alike. She said the same thing happened to her and her husband. They've been married almost twenty years now and have a whole bunch of children. They seemed happy. Step's husband was not like Jarrod. He took care of his family. Jarrod was never around to enjoy his.

Deandrea ended her call with Jarrod and got back onto the highway. After a couple of hours, she was finally in Philadelphia. She steered through the traffic toward the Marriott.

She was so happy to be at the hotel, she tipped the valet plentifully. She placed her suitcase beside her as she stood in the lobby, then she picked up the hotel courtesy phone and punched in Shante's room number. "I'm here," she exclaimed.

"I'll be right down to help you with your luggage," Shante said.

Deandrea perked up at the sound of Shante's voice. She couldn't wait to lay eyes on her. Deandrea still looked a mess. Her hair was not combed. She was wearing the same warm-up suit she had on yesterday. She didn't have on any makeup, and she had big black circles under her eyes. There was really nothing she could do to fix herself up before her friend laid eyes on her. She brushed back her hair while she waited.

Within minutes Shante stepped off the elevator. Dee dropped her bags and ran to greet her. She wrapped her arms around Shante. She didn't want to let her go. It had been a long time since she felt someone sincerely hug her and was glad to see her.

"I'm so glad you changed your mind. Let me help you with your bags." Shante reached down and lifted the handle on the overnight bag.

"I need to be here. I wish I had flown. That was a long drive," Deandrea said.

"Why did you drive?"

"Girl, it's a long story. I'll tell you when we get to the room."

They punched the elevator key and stepped in when the door opened. Deandrea was silent until they reached the room. As soon as she entered the room, she flopped on the floor and cried. Shante sat beside her and listened to her saga.

"So you just left?" Shante asked.

"Jarrod made me so mad I couldn't stand to be in the same house with him."

Shante hugged her and prayed. Dee couldn't stop the tears and snot. Shante handed her a tissue. Strangely, Deandrea felt relieved. She felt free.

"Well, did you throw any food at him?" Shante asked with a laugh.

Why does everyone continue to bring that up? It was a long time ago when she threw eggs in Jarrod's face and started the food fight that people can't seem to forget. Deandrea laughed. Shante always had a way of making her laugh.

"No. I should have. I didn't think about it at the time. He would have deserved it."

"It's going to be all right. You're only overwhelmed right now. It's good for you to be away for a few days. It will help clear your mind. Hey, Bishop Jones is preaching tomorrow. I wanted to go to that service. You feel like going?"

"Yeah, I'll go hear him preach. I need to hear the Word. But I've got to do something first."

"What's that?"

"Last night, I was so mad I only packed blouses and panties. I need to buy something to wear. All I have is this warm-up suit I'm wearing."

Shante's loud laughter filled the room. "All that luggage and you don't have a skirt or pair of jeans?"

"Not even a pair of shoes."

Shante continued laughing. "You're in luck. There is a mall attached to the convention center. We can go shopping there." Shante stood and stretched out her hand to help Dee from the floor. "Go wash your face while I put on some different shoes. We'll go shopping and find you a couple of items to wear."

Deandrea was pleased. God had a way of working things out. She was feeling better already.

12

Matthew set Misha's luggage inside the trunk of the car and walked inside the house. "I got your list, and I know what to do. If I have any questions, I'll call Mom. Now, hurry. You're going to miss your flight," he cried out to Misha. He walked to Courtney's playpen and lifted her out of it.

Misha was still not too keen on leaving Courtney for a few days, especially at a time like this. Yet, everything in her being was pulling her toward the conference. She had to go. It was her ministry. Someone there needed her.

Misha headed for the door holding her travel documents in her hand. Matthew was bent over, locking Courtney into her carrier. He was good with her, and she loved her daddy. She was definitely a daddy's girl. He was looking forward to taking care of her on his own. His mother assured Misha she would keep an eye on them. That didn't change Misha's feelings about leaving them. She still wanted to stay, just in case something happens with the adoption case.

They walked to the car, and Matthew locked the car seat into the car. Then he started the engine and headed for the beltway.

Misha thought she had at least ten minutes before she had to leave for the airport. Stuck in the slow beltway traffic, she had to admit Matthew was right. They should have left earlier. The bumper-to-bumper traffic headed toward Dulles Airport was brutal. She could have hopped onto the metro and caught her flight at Reagan National Airport. But Matthew insisted on driving her.

They made it to the airport with a few minutes to spare. Matthew parked and escorted Misha into the airport. A screeching yell startled Courtney.

"Oh my God, Bernard Taylor!" a lady screamed.

Someone had spotted Matthew and was running fast toward them. Misha took Courtney from his arms so he could greet his fans. A small crowd surrounded him, asking for autographs and taking pictures with their cell phones.

Misha looked at Matthew who was neatly but casually dressed in designer jeans and an oxford shirt. He looked nice today. The first time they met, he was dressed in old baggy jeans and worn-out tennis shoes. If it weren't for Misha, he would still be dressing this way. She made sure Matthew was dressed well when he left the house. He was a celebrity, and they never knew when someone was going to take a picture of him. It was important that he looked good. If he didn't, Misha thought it reflected on her.

Matthew had pulled some strings at the airport, and he was allowed to wait for her flight to board. They entered the VIP club room at the terminal. Misha did not even know they had those rooms until she met Matthew. She found a cushioned chair and sat down, holding Courtney in her lap. Courtney giggled at the faces she made at her. Her aqua-colored eyes sparkled. How did God do it? No one would ever know she was not Matthew's biological child unless they told them.

"Matthew, don't forget, if you can't do her hair, let your mother or your sister do it. Don't let her go around with wild hair."

Matthew sat next to her.

"I got it. I can handle it. You better go. Your flight is boarding."

Misha kissed her husband and daughter good-bye and stepped into the boarding line. She gave the flight attendant her boarding pass and entered the plane. In a few short minutes, she would be in Philadelphia. It was a short one-hour flight. Misha took her seat in the small commuter plane, fastened her seat belt and waited for the plane to take off.

In a matter of minutes, the plane landed in Philadelphia. Misha called Matthew on her way to the luggage claims.

"Honey, I'm here. I'm waiting on my bag. How's Courtney?"

"You just left her. She's playing in the playpen while I work on some music. Relax. Have a good time and I'll see you on Saturday." Misha ended her call and looked at the carousel waiting for her bag.

Her leg twisted nervously. How could she relax? She left her baby for the first time. She was having first-time mommy jitters bad. She spotted her luggage and fought the crowd to get it before it circled again.

Misha rolled her bags toward the taxi stand and saw someone standing with a sign that read M. Taylor. Did Matthew arrange for a car to pick her up? She asked the man, and he confirmed she was the one he was waiting for to take to the Marriott Convention Center. He reached for Misha's luggage, and she followed him to a black stretch limousine. She smiled as she stepped into the car and saw the dozen long-stem red roses Matthew had arranged to be in the car. It was a wonderful surprise. Misha was thankful she did not have to get a taxi. She didn't feel like taking a tour of Philadelphia today. With her Southern accent, the driver probably would have circled the city twice before taking her to the hotel.

Misha entered the hotel and headed for the front desk. The hotel was full of people milling in and out of the various areas in the lobby. After getting her room key, a bellman escorted her to her suite and placed her bag and flowers in her room.

Matthew always got the best hotel rooms. Misha walked to the large bouquet of flowers on the table near the window. Beside it was a large bowl of fresh fruit. A card in front of it had Misha's name on it. Inside was a note from Matthew. He was so romantic. She had to call him.

"Now you know better than to start something you can't finish," Misha said.

"I can finish it. Don't make me drive to Philadelphia tonight."

Magazines had said Matthew was one of the sexiest men alive. If only they knew he was much more than anything they ever said about him. He was her blessing. He was loving and kind. He had integrity and was funny. His appearance was only a small part of who he was.

Misha looked at the clock. It was after twelve. The conference information showed registration would begin at three. She had some time to kill, and she was hungry. She picked up the phone and called the concierge, seeking a good restaurant. He recommended she visit the Reading Terminal Market just across the street from the hotel. Misha slipped her purse over her shoulder and left the room.

The Reading Terminal Market was just as the concierge described. It was a smorgasbord for the eye. Misha strolled in and out of the many vendors located there. She tasted homemade ice cream and pastries. She sampled slices of fruit and fudge. She watched sushi being made from fresh fish. With all the sampling, she was still hungry. She spotted a family-style restaurant and decided to eat there.

Misha sat at the table looking at her menu when she heard a familiar voice. "Misha? Misha Holloway? Oh my goodness. How have you been?"

She looked up and was shocked to see First Lady Moore, her former pastor's wife, standing in front of her.

"First Lady, it's so good to see you." Misha set the menu on the table and stood to greet her. "Look at you, always sharp. I told you, I want to be like you when I grow up."

First Lady could dress. She always had. Today, she was dressed casually in a blue jean skirt and matching jacket with a white blouse underneath. Her gold earrings matched the thick necklace she wore around her neck. Even at a size twenty and over sixty years old she looked fabulous.

"Have a seat. Are you by yourself?" Misha asked.

"No. I came up with a group from Atlanta. Everybody's spread out in here. Look at you. Marriage looks good on you. How's Bernard?"

"He's great, and Courtney's growing each and every day. Have you ordered yet? The food here looks good."

First Lady pulled out a seat and sat. She seemed happy. Misha didn't know what to say to her. So much had happened since they last spoke. Bishop was hit with a paternity suit and was forced to pay child support for the two children he fathered outside his marriage. He had to give his paramour the house she shared with her children. There was so much talk going on about Bishop, Misha didn't know how much of it to believe. She only hoped First Lady did not say anything about her coming to preach at the church.

"I didn't expect it to be so cool up here. It's only October, and the temperature has already dropped. It's still hot in Atlanta." First Lady began the conversation after ordering her food.

"It gets cool up here before it does in Atlanta. You would think I would be used to it since I went to Howard."

"I forgot you moved to Washington. Are you working?"

"Not yet. I'm helping Matthew with his ministry."

"Matthew? Who's that?"

"My husband." Misha suddenly remembered the world calls him Bernard Taylor. "I'm sorry. His name is Matthew Bernard Taylor. He uses his middle name for business. Everybody in his family calls him Matthew. How's Bishop doing?"

"He's doing fine," First Lady said as she turned to look around the restaurant.

"I wonder if there's somewhere to shop around here," Misha changed the subject.

"Somebody told me there's a mall around here somewhere. The bus is taking us to an outlet park this afternoon. You want to come along? There were a few empty seats on the bus coming up. I'm sure no one would mind you riding with us."

Go shopping with a bunch of first ladies from Atlanta? That was the *last* thing Misha wanted to do. The waitress set their food on the table and walked away. Misha prayed and lifted her fork to eat.

"I think I'll hang around the hotel today. Registration starts at three. I want to check out some of the vendors before everything gets picked over. Thanks for the invitation, though."

"Where are you staying?" First Lady asked.

"Here at the convention center, at the Marriott."

"We're at the Crowne Plaza."

Thank you, Lord. "That's a nice hotel. I think Matthew wanted me to stay close to the conference in case I get tired and want to go to my room. Let me show you a picture of Courtney. I just had some taken." Misha opened her purse and pulled out her cell phone to show her the pictures of Courtney stored in it.

"She's beautiful. She looks just like Bernard."

"That's what everybody says."

This had to be the most uncomfortable lunch Misha had ever had. They searched for things to talk about while trying to avoid the subject of Bishop. First Lady put on a good front. She looked happy, but Misha sensed sadness. She didn't know what it was. She was sure it was not her imagination. She loved First Lady. She was always kind to her in spite of her relationship with Bishop. First Lady supported her ministry, even when Bishop tried the stop it.

Now she understood why the Holy Spirit wanted her to come to this conference. This was her assignment. She was sent here for First Lady. Before she ministered to her, she would have to pray for God's direction first. This was not the time or place to talk with her about it.

A group of women walked up to the table. "There you are. We've been looking for you all over the place. It's time for us to go to the bus," a lady interrupted their conversation. Misha recognized the woman from Atlanta, however, she could not remember her name. First Lady introduced Misha to the woman as Bernard Taylor's wife. The woman was not impressed.

Misha offered to pay for their meal. She hugged First Lady before she left with the group of women. Misha watched them walk away. First Lady's sadness weighed heavily on her heart. She sat quietly looking at the dessert menu when she noticed two ladies at the next table trying to get her attention.

"Excuse me, miss. Did I hear that lady say you're Bernard Taylor's wife?" one of the women asked.

"Yes. He's my husband."

The lady did the Bernard Taylor scream and asked if they could take a picture together. Surprised, Misha agreed. This was the first time this had happened to her. Somebody actually wanted to take a picture of her and not Bernard. Misha stood between the two women and smiled as the waitress took their picture.

"Are you famous?" the waitress asked after the ladies left.

Misha laughed. "No. I'm not famous. My husband is."

"Your husband? What's his name?"

"Bernard Taylor."

"Bernard Taylor? I never heard of him. What sport does he play?"

Misha laughed again. She couldn't be insulted. She had the same thought the first time someone told her about him. She had never heard of Bernard Taylor or one of his songs when he approached her at the restaurant. He looked as if he had just left a homeless shelter. He did not make a good first impression with two goons following him. Turned out his "associates," Antonio and Bruce, were good guys. No matter what he said, they were still bodyguards.

Philadelphia had such a diverse mix of people; Misha was entertained by them as she walked the downtown street. She had to do something to keep from calling home again. She had to trust God and believe nothing would happen while she was away. Misha shook her head. If she was acting like this now, what was going to happen when she went to school? She was going to be a mess.

Misha walked back to her hotel and decided to take a nap before registration started. The quietness in the room caused her to doze off quickly.

Misha leaped from the bed when she realized she had slept longer than expected. It was after four, and she was late for registration. She walked into the bathroom and washed her face. Her natural twists were flat on her left side. She quickly twisted her hair with her fingers. Then she freshened up her makeup and left the room to register for the conference.

When she arrived, there were only a few women at the registration desk. She patiently stood in line waiting for her turn. The women behind the desk were wearing purple and white conference T-shirts. They smiled as she approached them. No one seemed stressed or rushed. They took their time explaining the contents of her packet before moving to the next person.

Misha looked at the women gathered for the conference. She was getting a good vibe from them. These women were pastors' wives, and they all came together to learn, grow and seek spiritual strength with ladies in the same position. This may turn out to be something she needed after all.

Walking from the convention center to the hotel she noticed a sign indicating a shopping mall to the left. She loved to shop, especially since she won the lawsuit against her employer which netted her a few million dollars. No one would ever know it by looking at her, but she was independently wealthy apart from Matthew.

Not only did her employer pay her, Courtney had a large trust fund that she would get when she turned twenty-one. God blessed her with a miracle baby and money to take care of her.

She decided to do some shopping for a little while before she had to get dressed for the evening service. She placed the straps of her conference bag over her shoulder and headed for the mall. It would kill time until God decided it was time to use her.

13

Deandrea stepped out of the dressing room wearing the black skirt she'd taken off the store rack. "How does this look?" she asked Shante.

Deandrea twisted in front of the mirror to get a better look at the fit of the skirt. Shante shook her head. The skirt was entirely too tight. Deandrea sighed and walked into the dressing room.

Shante thought the Lord was sending Deandrea to help her. Instead, she needed help too. She couldn't believe Deandrea had walked out on Jarrod. She seemed so quiet and meek when they first met. Once they got to know each other, Shante realized Deandrea was strong and confident. It was clear that everybody had a breaking point. Deandrea and Jarrod seemed so happy each time she saw them. No one would have ever guessed they were having problems.

They left the store and walked into the next one. There were a lot of nice preaching suits there. Deandrea pulled three suits off the rack and headed for the dressing room. Shante perused the racks of clothing, trying to find something that would look good on her friend.

"Oh my goodness, it's Shante Patrick," a lady screamed.

Not now, Lord. Shante painted on a smile and turned. The lady was staring her in the face. This was one of those moments when she wished no one knew her. She didn't have any privacy. People who followed her ministry thought they knew her. Today, she only wanted to hang out with her friend, and here, someone had recognized her. She never complained about it. She loved the people she ministered to. But sometimes, she just wanted to be left alone.

After speaking with the lady briefly, Shante turned to see Dee wearing the tightest red suit she had ever seen. "I know you are *not* thinking of buying that suit."

"It's cut too small."

"Is that what it is?"

They both laughed.

"Girl, take that suit off and let's go to another store."

Shante spotted a silver suit that she thought would fit Deandrea. She pulled one size larger than the one Deandrea said she wore and handed her the suit over the door. If it fit, she could wear it tonight.

"Excuse me. Are you Shante Patrick?" Shante heard another female voice ask.

Shante closed her eyes. *Not again,* she couldn't help but think. She opened her eyes. "Yes, I am."

"Hello. I'm Misha, Misha Taylor. I wanted to say thank you for a sermon you preached at The Rock of Life Church in Atlanta. It was like you were speaking directly to my situation, and it brought healing and I wanted to thank you for your obedience," Misha said.

"Misha, it was God, not me. You're from Atlanta?"

"I was born there. I live in D.C. now. Well, I don't want to take up more of your time. I look forward to hearing you preach. Enjoy the conference."

"Well, how do I look?" Deandrea bounced out of the dressing room turning as if she was a top model. The suit fit, but it was still the wrong suit. She stopped when she saw Shante and Misha standing side by side. "I'm sorry. I didn't mean to interrupt."

"No, that's okay. I was just leaving," Misha said.

Deandrea looked at Misha. "Do I know you?" she asked.

"You do look familiar." Misha placed her hand on her chest. "My name is Misha Taylor." She held out her hand to shake Deandrea's.

"Misha . . . Misha . . . " Deandrea repeated trying to remember how she knew Misha.

"Please forgive my friend," Shante said. "This is Copastor Dee Fuller."

"Fuller? Are you related to Pastor Jarrod Fuller, from South Carolina?" Misha asked.

"Yes, he's my husband."

"Now I know how I know you. It's me . . . Misha . . . from Atlanta."

Deandrea screamed and hugged Misha tightly. "I thought you looked familiar. How long has it been . . . two, three years?" Deandrea asked.

"Yes, it's been about three years. How have you been?" Misha inquired.

Shante cleared her throat. Deandrea looked at her. "I'm sorry, Tay. This is Misha, my shopping buddy from Atlanta. We haven't seen each other in a long time. See, God knew exactly what I needed. This girl should be a stylist."

It had been three years since Misha first met Deandrea at a prayer breakfast in Atlanta. After that meeting, each time Deandrea came to Atlanta, they would get together and go shopping. They lost contact after Misha met Matthew.

"Wait a minute . . ." Deandrea looked at Misha. "Your name wasn't Taylor, it was something else—"

"Holloway. I've gotten married since the last time we saw each other."

Deandrea screamed again and hugged Misha even tighter. "Oh my goodness. That's wonderful."

"And I have a little girl. Her name is Courtney."

"I have twins, a girl and boy."

"Looks like you two have a lot to talk about. But right, now you need to get out of that suit, Dee."

Dee looked at the suit she was wearing as if she had forgotten she was trying on clothes. "You're right," she said.

"I don't mean to be crass, but I hope you are not going to buy that suit. The fit's all wrong for your body. You have a beautiful figure. You should show it off," Misha said to Deandrea.

Deandrea looked at Shante. "See, Tay, this is why I went shopping with her. This girl knows how to buy clothes." She looked at Misha. "Do you have some time to go shopping with me? I have nothing to wear. I need something quick."

"Well, I guess I could. I'm here for the conference and had planned to go to service tonight."

"I think we can skip tonight," Shante said. "Dee *really* needs your help."

"Well, I guess it would be okay tonight."

"Perfect," Deandrea squealed and ran into the dressing room.

Misha looked through the racks of clothing with Shante following her. "I think this is the wrong store for Copastor," she said.

"You and Dee shop a lot?" Shante asked.

Misha smiled. "No, only a couple of times. Her husband was in town preaching at my home church. We lost track of each other. I'm glad we reconnected."

Shante watched Misha looking at the tailored suits. There was something about her that Shante could not put her finger on. Misha had a certain aura about her. She seemed very quiet and meek. She was certainly the opposite of Deandrea.

Deandrea finally joined the two, and they left the store. As they headed for another store, they passed the Christian book store. Deandrea spotted the display at the front that held Shante's latest book. There was a group of ladies gathered flipping through the pages. Deandrea ran into the store toward the ladies. After she spoke to them, all the ladies looked toward Shante, who was standing outside the door. Deandrea motioned for Shante to come into the store. Shante put on her smile and walked toward them with Misha in tow.

The manager of the store quickly found a table and chair for Shante. Deandrea talked loudly as she organized the women into a line and acted as Shante's assistant in her impromptu book signing. Shante signed books and took pictures until the display was almost empty. Gia would not like her doing this. Neither would Max.

"Let's find something to eat. I'm starving," Deandrea announced after the last lady left the store with her purchase.

Shante looked at her watch. It was not even six, and Deandrea was ready to eat again. It appeared she found her appetite in Philadelphia. She seemed more relaxed, smiling and humming. Taking a break was probably all she needed, Shante surmised about her friend. Shante knew how difficult it was working in a church and trying to maintain a happy home.

Shante and Dee had been in the mall for hours before Misha joined them. Shante had tried to get Deandrea to go into Lane Bryant or Ashley Stewart but Deandrea refused to admit she needed those stores. She had gained some weight since she had the twins. She wondered how Misha found it easy to get Deandrea to shop there.

Misha took Deandrea's arm and pulled her into one of the plus-sized stores. Shante felt offended. Why didn't Dee go in there when she suggested it? Deandrea protested, but Misha ignored her and went in anyway.

"You look like a sixteen. Here, try these on. Put this blouse with this skirt and this sweater with these jeans." Misha handed the clothes to Dee and pushed her toward the dressing room.

"I tried to get her to come in here, but she wouldn't go," Shante said to Misha once Deandrea was out of earshot.

"That's because you two are so close. Me, I'm, as she puts it, her 'stylist,'" Misha laughed and continued looking through a table filled with folded slacks.

"You know, there's something different about you," Shante said.

"That's what everybody says."

"It is. I can tell you love the Lord."

"I do. God has been so special in my life. My relationship with Him helped me through some tough times."

"Ta-da!" Dee shouted when she emerged from the dressing room wearing the jeans and sweater. Misha and Shante looked at each other and smiled.

"See, Pastor, these jeans fit so much better. The wide leg slims you and gives your figure more of an hour-glass appearance."

Deandrea twisted and turned in the full-length mirror on the wall. She rushed back into the dressing room to try on more clothing.

Finally, Dee had something to wear. She purchased four complete outfits from this store.

Shante felt the pangs of hunger. She decided to stop and get something to eat before she had another passing out spell. The trio headed for the food court. They ordered their food and took a seat away from the crowd.

Deandrea took over the conversation. She had some energy now. She told Misha how she got to Philadelphia. She was talking loud. She was around a lot of loud, country people in Snowhill and Shante felt Deandrea did not realize how much of their mannerisms had rubbed off on her. She laughed to think about how sophisticated and bourgeois Deandrea was. Now, she was beginning to blend right in with the country folk, and she didn't even notice it.

"Well, Misha, is your husband a pastor?" Shante asked trying to enter the conversation. They seemed to have forgotten she was there.

"Yes, we have a new ministry in D.C.," Misha replied. "It's only a couple of years old. We're growing though."

"Are you the copastor?" Shante asked.

"No, only the first lady. I don't sing or play the piano, teach or anything like that. From time to time, I will preach when Matthew's away ministering elsewhere."

"Well, girl, don't let him pull you into being a copastor. You might end up in a mess like me." Deandrea rolled her eyes. Then she took a bite out of her sandwich.

"Dee!" Shante could not believe what she just said. What was wrong with her? She didn't mind sharing the most intimate details of her life with this lady? They weren't real friends. They only went shopping a couple of times. They were going to have a long talk when they get back to the hotel room.

"I have to call my husband and check on my baby. I won't be long." Misha stood and walked away from the table.

"Dee, you should not have told that girl all your business," Shante was quick to say.

"She's okay. Look how God worked this thing out. She has a good eye for fashion. I found that out when we went shopping before. God knew I would need someone to help me pick out something to wear. Fooling with Jarrod, I look like an old country lady. I can't believe I allowed myself to go down like that."

Deandrea spewed bitterness and anger. Her pain was so deep. Shante was beginning to think Deandrea resented marrying Jarrod. She needed to be ministered to bad. It was a dangerous thing to have the combination of bitterness and anger. If one mixed that with loneliness, it was a deadly force that could lead to divorce, and Shante didn't want that happening to them.

Misha returned to the table, and after eating, the three ladies continued their shopping. Deandrea was getting into high gear with her shopping mode when Shante's cell phone rang. It was LaToya.

"Hi, LaToya . . ." Shante paused, listening to her assistant. She stopped her conversation and removed the phone from her ear. "Ladies, this is my assistant. This call is going to take awhile. Do you mind if I meet you back at the hotel? Dee, you have a key to the room. I'll be there when you get finished. It was nice meeting you, Misha."

Shante excused herself and completed her conversation before she reached the hotel lobby. She was tired and glad Deandrea had someone else to play with for a while.

Opening the door to her hotel room she felt lonely. She missed her sons and husband. She plopped down on the sofa and tapped Max's cell phone number into her phone. "Hey, Max. I thought I would check in and see how you guys were doing."

"We're eating dinner," he said flatly.

"At home?"

"No. We're eating out tonight. How's the conference?"

The conversation with Max sounded like a business conference. Since when did their conversations get so cold? He should have understood why she had to do this conference. She meant what she said that this one would be the last before she gave birth. She felt old, and this baby was already wearing her out. She wouldn't be able to keep up her usual pace much longer.

The conversation with Max quickly ended. It left Shante feeling sad and alone. Deandrea should be back soon. She would want to talk when she got in. Shante had to prepare herself to minister. She was still Deandrea's friend, and she loved her. Tonight, she would have to put aside her own problems to help her.

14

"Pastor Dee, try on these shoes. They will go great with your jeans." Misha handed Deandrea a pair of brown and tan boots with four-inch heels. They were now completing Deandrea's ensemble by shoe shopping.

Deandrea hadn't worn heels this high in years, not since she had the twins. She didn't know if she could still walk in them. They were nice, and Misha had been right so far. She reached for the shoes, slipped them on her feet and slowly stood.

Deandrea pranced around the shoe store pleased she could still walk in high heel shoes. There was only one drawback; they hurt her feet. She sat in the chair and pulled them off.

"Misha, I don't think I can wear these shoes. They hurt with just that little bit of walking."

"You just need to get half a size larger. It will give you a little more wiggle room in your feet." Misha handed her another pair of shoes. Deandrea put them on.

Deandrea couldn't believe that worked. The new pair fit perfectly and felt comfortable. She purchased four more pairs of shoes and left the store feeling revived. It had been a long time since she went shopping for something other than "first-lady" clothes. Before she met Jarrod shopping was her hobby. She wore all the latest styles. It was nothing for her to spend thousands of dollars on Jimmy Choo products, Dolce & Gabbana, Louie Vuitton, Vera Wang, Donna Karan, or Versace. She had to have all of them.

Wearing expensive clothing and driving luxury cars was the norm for her. She worked hard and felt she deserved all that God had blessed her with. She gave it all up to be with Jarrod.

She smiled as she carried multiple shopping bags. What would Jarrod think? She was having a great time running up his charge card. It felt like sweet revenge. It wasn't as if she didn't have any money; she had plenty. It was the fact that he was paying for her new wardrobe that felt so sweet to her.

Deandrea's phone beeped. She spotted her mother's name on the caller ID and answered the phone.

"Dee, what in the world is going on? I called Jarrod, and he said you were at a conference. He sounded worried. You didn't tell me about a conference. I could have watched the twins."

"It was a last-minute trip. Besides, Jarrod has the children."

"Jarrod said you were mad when you left. Were you two fighting?"

Deandrea placed her bags on a bench in the center of the mall. She sat next to the bags with the phone to her ear. The last thing she wanted was her mother interfering in her marriage.

"Pastor Dee, I'm going to run in this shop while you are on the phone," Misha said.

Deandrea nodded her head as Misha walked away. "Mom, I didn't do anything to Jarrod. He didn't do anything to me. I'm at this first ladies' conference in Philadelphia as a retreat. I'll be back on Saturday."

"He said he didn't know when you were coming back. He sounds pretty upset. You need to call him."

"I've only been gone one day. I'll talk to him tomorrow when I check on the kids."

"Well, I'll go over there and check on them, just to make sure they are eating. I'll take them a casserole."

"I'm sure Jarrod will appreciate that. I'll call him when I get back to my room, and I'll call you before I leave."

Deandrea finally got her mother off the phone. With any luck, she wouldn't try to dig too much into what was going on between the two of them. It was her problem to solve.

Her phone beeped again. It was Jarrod. She reluctantly answered the phone.

"Hi, honey. I just put the children to bed," he said. Now he was the hero for putting his own children to bed? Deandrea's shoulders tensed.

"What are you doing?"

"Shopping."

"Get anything you want. Use my card. Do you have it with you?"

Deandrea rolled her eyes. He just took all the fun out of spending his money. Then again, that was Jarrod. He never told her she couldn't wear designer clothing. No, it was the people in the church. They were always questioning where they got their money. Some people had an issue with everything—their cars, clothes and even how often she got her hair done. She toned it down so it would not interfere with the ministry. No more. She was getting her groove back. Being copastor was not who she was. She had to go back to being Dee.

"Jarrod, what do you want?"

"Are you alone?"

"I'm not alone. I'm in this mall, and there are hundreds of people around me."

"Oh. I'll call you later about ten thirty."

"Do what you want."

Deandrea pressed the power button to turn her phone off. She did not want to talk to her husband or mother. She wanted to have a good time, and she couldn't do it with the two of them constantly calling her.

She sat watching the people pass her in the crowded mall. Loneliness swept through her like a rushing wind. How could she be surrounded by so many people and shopping bags and still felt empty? Back in the day, shopping filled that void. Then Jarrod filled it. Now, neither did that for her anymore.

"Hey, why are you looking like that? You're not lonely now. You're here with friends. Come on, let's go," Misha said to her as she walked over, carrying the bags filled with the items she just purchased.

How did Misha know what Deandrea was thinking? Was she that obvious to everyone? She had to step up her game. She didn't want anyone feeling sorry for her. She didn't want her emotions to be so transparent anyone could tell what she was experiencing or thinking.

"Are you pregnant?" Deandrea asked her, noticing the bags from the maternity store.

"No. This isn't for me." Misha held up the bag.

"If you don't mind, let's call this a night. I think I have enough clothes for now."

They exited the mall entrance and encountered a mash of people leaving the convention center wearing conference T-shirts.

"Looks like we missed the first session," Misha said. She was disappointed. She wanted to attend the conference. Instead, she was shopping. There was always the next session. It was probably God's will for her not to attend the conference since Deandrea needed her tonight.

They stepped off the elevator, struggling with the many bags they held. Finally, they reached Deandrea's hotel room just as a bag dropped to the floor. Deandrea laughed and knocked on the door.

"Dee," Shante said when she opened the door. "Why didn't you use your key?"

"It was easier to knock." She reached down and picked up the bag.

Shante reached for the bags in her other hand. "What in the world . . . How much shopping can two people do in a matter of hours? Did you leave anything for anyone else?" She spotted Misha waiting patiently in the hall. "Misha, come on in."

Deandrea tossed her bags on the sofa. She opened one blue bag and showed Shante the tweed slacks and blouse she purchased. "Wait a minute. Let me show you how it looks on me. Misha has great taste." Deandrea scooped up the bags and ran to her room.

"Misha, thanks for shopping with Dee. I had to take that phone call."

"I enjoyed myself."

Shante walked to the small refrigerator at the minibar and opened the door. "Can I get you something to drink? The church has supplied me with orange and apple juice. I have water. I don't have any soda."

"No, thank you. I'm good."

A couple minutes later, Deandrea stepped out of the bedroom wearing a straight black skirt and ruffled blouse. The red belt she wore accentuated her waist. Her red pumps made the outfit pop.

"Now *that* looks good on you. You can wear that to the luncheon tomorrow," Shante said as she walked closer to get a better look.

Deandrea felt good. She twisted to get a better look at how the clothes fit on her.

"Luncheon? I didn't see a luncheon on the schedule for tomorrow," Misha said.

"It's something Shante has to attend with the other speakers and VIP guests. It's not part of the conference."

"Oh. That would be the perfect outfit for a luncheon," Misha repeated.

"Hey, you want to go?" Shante asked Misha. Misha shook her head. "I insist. It might be fun. Besides, where

are you going to eat lunch at tomorrow? You might as
well have a free meal with me and Dee."

"Since you put it that way, okay, I'll go," Misha accepted.

"Good. I better call Pastor Edmunds and let them know
you and Dee will be coming with me. I wonder if service
is over."

"It is. We saw a lot of people coming from it in the
lobby. I overheard a couple of women talking about it. It
sounded as if they had a good time," Misha responded.

Deandrea walked into the bedroom to change outfits.
Shante laughed at the way she twisted into the room. She
picked up the church card and tapped the numbers into
her phone.

Misha tried not to pay attention to the call but did she
just hear the tone of Shante's voice change? Talking to
her in the room her voice was high-pitched. But now as
she spoke with Pastor Edmunds, her voice was much
lower and more professional.

"Fuller. She's from South Carolina. Her husband is
Jarrod Fuller, pastor of . . . Yes, that's right. You know
him?" Shante asked.

Deandrea walked into the room and groaned when
she heard Jarrod's name. She should have known it
was possible this pastor had heard of Jarrod. He was on
television all the time.

"He talks about her all the time?" Shante continued.
"She'll be glad to hear that. Sing? Before I preach? Well,
I'll have to ask her. Wait a minute, she's right here. I'll let
you speak with her."

Deandrea stood in front of Shante waving her hand
no. She didn't want to speak with anyone who knew
her husband. She was there to get away from all things
Jarrod. Shante shoved the phone in her hand and walked
away. Deandrea took a deep breath and answered the

phone. "Pastor Edmunds, praise God. I hear you know my husband Jarrod," she said.

"Smooth and I have been friends since college. We pledged on the same line," Pastor Edmunds told her.

Chills went down Deandrea's spine when she heard her husband's college nickname. This guy was a close personal friend of his, a frat brother. She hadn't heard anyone call him Smooth in years. There goes her fun. From now on, she was going to have to be Copastor.

"Lord, Smooth talks about you all the time, you and your children."

"I hope he gives a good report," she gave a nervous laugh. Her nerves were all jumbled because she was teetering on hurt and anger. Jarrod talked about his family, but he didn't notice them when he was home.

"Oh, he is always talking about how good you can sing and play the piano. Do you think you can sing for us before Pastor Patrick speaks?"

"Well, I didn't come prepared to sing."

"I'm sure the Lord will put something in your heart. I'm going to have to call Smooth and tell him I spoke with you. I look forward to meeting you tomorrow. You can let me know something then."

Deandrea handed the phone to a laughing Shante. She was getting twisted joy from Deandrea's pain. She wanted to be invisible. She didn't want the people at the conference to know who she was. Now, she would have them looking at everything she did and said. They were even trying to force her to sing. She didn't come here to sing or do anything but talk to her friend. She couldn't do that with Jarrod's friends around.

"Misha, what's your husband's name?" Shante asked, still holding the phone to her ear.

"Bernard." Misha gave her husband's stage name because they would be familiar with him.

"Bernard Taylor?" Shante and Deandrea shouted at the same time.

Awareness leaped in Deandrea's mind. Now she remembered. Misha was the girl on the cover of every African American magazine in the country after she and Bernard married. She was Bernard's black wife. No one ever imagined he would marry a black girl.

"Misha, why didn't you tell us you were married to Bernard Taylor?" Shante asked after she ended her call. "I thought you said his name was something else." She tossed the phone into her purse.

"I call him by his first name, Matthew. Everybody else calls him by his middle name, Bernard. I try not to tell everybody."

"Why? Are you embarrassed to be married to him?" Deandrea asked out of curiosity.

"No, I'm not embarrassed. It's a long story." Misha sifted through the packages on the table and pulled out the Motherhood Maternity bag. "Pastor Patrick, here, I got you something," Shante stiffened at the sight of Misha holding the bag. "I hope it fits. You look like a size ten. I wasn't exactly sure how far along you are, but these should fit."

Shante couldn't move. She didn't remember telling them she was pregnant. There was no way she could have known. "How did—"

"Why are you giving that to her? She's not pregnant," Deandrea said, looking at the shocked expression on Shante's face. She walked to her. "Are you pregnant?"

"How did you know?" Shante asked Misha.

"Shante . . . You're pregnant?" Deandrea repeated.

"How did you know?" Shante was in utter shock.

"The Lord told me. Here, I think you'll like these." Misha smiled.

"Shante, you're pregnant!" Deandrea screamed in delight. She grabbed Shante and hugged her tightly. How could she be so selfish and not notice Shante was pregnant? She and Max must be so excited. Deandrea felt remorse bringing all her drama and she had not allowed her friend to share her good news.

Shante sat on the large mauve sofa and began to cry. Deandrea sat next to her and wrapped her arm around her. "I'm so happy for you. Why didn't you tell me?" she asked.

"You had your own problems. I didn't want to put mine on you," Shante sniffed.

"Girl, quit. You know Jarrod and I have been fussing since the day we met. Aren't you happy?"

Shante looked toward Misha who still held the bag waiting for Shante to take it. "There's something different about you. What is it?" she questioned Misha.

"Everybody says that. I'm no different than anybody else. Are you going to take these clothes from me? My arm is getting tired," Misha smiled.

"I'm sorry. Thank you. My first maternity clothes in twenty-four years," Shante reached for the bag and set it on the floor next to her. She reached for the box of tissue, pulled one out and wiped her nose. "I'm sorry, ladies. This pregnancy thing has me a little upset. Do you know how old I am? This is definitely a Sarah and Abraham thing. This is totally unexpected."

"Aren't you happy? How's Max taking this?" Deandrea asked.

"Max is enjoying every minute of it, except the fact that I'm here. He thinks I should . . ." She looked at Misha again.

"Looks like you two want to talk. I better leave," Misha said.

"No, Misha, stay," Shante pleaded.

Misha sat in the chair next to Shante and listened as Shante told them how she found out she was pregnant. Deandrea laughed hard.

"I can't believe you took nine pregnancy tests. The one at the hospital wasn't positive enough for you?" Deandrea laughed again.

"I don't know. I was in shock."

"Then why are you upset?" Misha asked.

Shante sniffed. "Do you know how old I am? I'm forty-six years old. How am I going to have the energy to keep up with a baby? I barely have enough energy to do what I have to do in ministry."

"Pastor Shante, God felt you could do it. That's why He sent this child to you and your husband. It has nothing to do with your age."

Deandrea was the psychologist, yet, she sat back and let Misha counsel Shante like a pro. If she didn't know better, Shante would have thought Misha was a licensed counselor. There was something about Misha that Deandrea couldn't put her finger on. It wasn't the fact that she was married to one of the biggest Gospel artists in the country or the fact that she was so young. There was something strange, mysterious even, about her.

"Pastor Shante, everything is going to work out. You'll see. Well, it's getting late. I better go." Misha excused herself and walked out the door.

Deandrea walked into her bedroom. All of a sudden her body felt tired and heavy. She was finally feeling the effects of her journey. She had been running on pure adrenaline, and now it had run out. She didn't even have the energy to speak with Jarrod. But she had to call him and see how the children were doing. She reluctantly punched in the numbers.

"Hi, Jarrod. How are the children?" Dee asked. Her voice was harsh and rough.

"Why do you sound like that?"

She didn't know. What was happening to her? She loved her husband. They needed to talk. They haven't talked in a long time. They had problems that they needed to resolve.

It took a lot for Jarrod to trust her in the beginning. It was hard for him to talk to anyone outside of ministry. There were times when they went out, and he would not say anything. Somehow they knew what each other was thinking. Then there were times when he revealed so much about himself to her she was shocked at what he said. He shared deep, personal thoughts and feelings, desires and longings. The conversations were so intimate.

He was interested in her every thought. If she didn't want to share, he had a way of pulling out the very things in Deandrea he allowed himself to release. Their bond grew close because they could communicate with each other. Now, she felt as if he didn't care. It had been a long time since he asked her how she was doing. Now, she felt, the world revolved around him and his purpose and nothing else mattered.

"What do you want me to do, Dee? I said I'm sorry," Jarrod pleaded. "What else do you want me to say?"

"If I have to tell you what to say, then it's not sincere. Jarrod, it's late."

"Please, Dee, don't hang up. We need to talk."

She was mad again. He had not asked her about her day or how she was feeling or even how the conference was going. He didn't care if she found something to wear in the mall. Did he think she was sitting in the hotel room waiting for his call?

"I love you. I can't wait until you get back home. When are you coming back?"

"Will you notice I'm there?"

"What do you mean by that? Of course, I will. I miss you already. Maybe I can get your mother to keep the children and I could join you there. We really need to talk—sooner than later."

Jarrod, come up here? No. That would ruin her trip. This was a first ladies' conference, not pastors and pastors' wives retreat. She was having too much fun for him to come and ruin it. She had to convince him that was a bad idea.

"You can't watch the kids a couple of days without pushing them off on my mother?"

"No, baby, that's not what I meant. I miss you. I want to spend some time with you. I don't like it when you're angry with me. I was wrong. I admit it. I promise you it won't happen again."

Was that violins she heard playing? It was the same old song. *I'm sorry. I promise.* Like the lyrics to a bad Country Western song, it kept repeating itself, never accomplishing anything. Deandrea lay on the bed listening to Jarrod give the same old excuses she had heard a thousand times before, not contributing anything to the conversation. She yawned loudly.

"Well, you must be tired. You're not saying anything. I'll call you tomorrow. Shag told me you're having lunch with him and his wife tomorrow."

Deandrea sat up on the bed. "Shag?"

"Pastor Edmunds. That's what we called him in college. He called me to tell me he talked to you. You're going to sing Friday?"

She should have known Pastor Edmunds was going to call Jarrod. But, she didn't expect him to use Jarrod to force her to sing. How could she minister to first ladies when she, herself, needed to be ministered to?

"What are you singing?" Jarrod asked.

"How are the kids?" She changed the subject.

"They're asleep. Have you decided what you are going to sing? You should sing my song."

His song? Be for real. She wouldn't sing anything that would remotely remind her of him.

"Well, I guess I better let you go. I'll call you tomorrow," Jarrod said.

"Don't you have to go to the church?"

"I took the day off."

"You took the day off? Why couldn't you have done that when I was there? You wait until I'm hundreds of miles away before you take the day off? I can see you really don't want to be with me anymore. Thanks, Jarrod."

"That's not true. I miss you. I can't focus with you gone."

"Do you realize that you haven't asked me about my drive up, how I'm doing or what I purchased today? You're not interested in anything I do. It's all about you. I can't even relax now since your friend is going to be watching my every move. I'm so sick of this. I don't know how much more of this I can take."

"What are you saying?"

"I don't want to talk with you anymore. Good night."

She pressed the end button so hard the tip of her finger hurt. She fell back on the pillows. Tears streamed down her face. She let them flow down the sides of her face and into her ears. She didn't want her children growing up in an unhappy, loveless home. She had to do something about this—just like Jarrod had said—sooner than later.

15

"Are you having a good time?" Matthew asked Misha as they talked on the phone.

She thought about her developing friendship with Deandrea and Shante. How could she tell him she was with people who had more issues than she could ever imagine? She had one who was angry with her husband and the other who was upset because she was pregnant. Then there was First Lady Moore who had another whole bucket of problems. Misha understood God sent her there to minister to someone, but major, prominent lady preachers? Did she even have enough time to minister to them? Although she was concerned about her own situation, Shante and Deandrea needed her.

Misha would have preferred to be with her husband and daughter than at the conference She had to remember she had a call for ministry on her life and she had to be obedient to God.

"I wish you were here with me," Matthew said to Misha in a soft, low tone.

"What would you do if I were there with you?" Misha asked him. His smooth, sexy voice pulled her right into him.

Misha and Matthew got married only a few months after meeting each other. Their lovemaking was often and passionate. Their conversations were few and most often before or after sex. Misha relished the time when they only talked. It gave them an opportunity to talk to each other about their hopes, dreams and passions. The sex was great, but the conversation was better. But now she feared every part of their relationship would be strained because of the lawsuit.

After her conversation ended, Misha fell off into a deep sleep. She was awakened by the sound of her room phone ringing. She looked at the clock and groaned. Slowly, she reached for the phone.

"Misha, we're ordering breakfast. You want to come up?" Deandrea's voice rang over the phone. It was early in the morning, and Misha needed to get dressed for Morning Glory service. However, she was compelled to go to their room and have breakfast with them. She accepted their invitation and headed for the shower. Hopefully, today, everyone would be in a better mood.

When she arrived at their room, she was surprised to see that neither Deandrea nor Shante were dressed. Deandrea was lounging on the sofa in pajamas watching television, and Shante was walking around, wrapped up in her bathrobe, talking on the phone. Her hair was wrapped in a silk scarf. Neither one seemed to be in a hurry. Misha looked at the table and didn't see any food.

"Pastor Dee, Morning Glory starts in twenty minutes. Aren't you getting dressed?" Misha asked them. She didn't want to be late for the service. Deandrea laughed as if she had said something funny.

"What's your hurry? Our breakfast will be here in a few minutes. Sit down and relax," Dee said. She then looked Misha up and down. "You look nice today."

Misha felt so overdressed standing in front of them with her gray pantsuit on. Matthew got her that suit. He even purchased the pink blouse and deep gray shoes she was wearing. He had good taste in clothing when he was shopping for someone else. However, when it came to himself, he usually went for the thrift-store look, which is why she took over dressing him.

"I'm sorry, ladies. LaToya is on the job early this morning. She wanted to make sure I had everything I need for today and tomorrow. She gave me my messages. I'll return my phone calls later. Is the food here yet?" Shante asked as she walked into the room, pushed Deandrea's feet off the sofa and plopped down beside her.

"What's wrong with you, Tay?" Deandrea asked.

"I'm going to gain a lot of weight. I'm hungry all the time. When is that food going to get here? Do we have anything to eat in here? What's in the minibar?" Shante shot off question after question.

"Probably a ten dollar candy bar," Misha answered. Shante laughed. Shante reminded Misha of her own pregnancy. She was hungry all the time. Matthew would laugh at her when she ate because she didn't hold back. She didn't care if he thought she was greedy. Courtney was hungry.

There was a knock on the door. Shante ran to answer it. After tipping the server, she sat down and ate as if she were starving. Deandrea laughed at Shante gulping down her food, her cheeks swollen with the large bite of muffin she had just taken.

"Tay, slow down. The food is not going to run from you," Deandrea said.

"Why did I have to get pregnant now? You know it's harder to lose the weight the older you are," Shante said as crumbs dropped from her mouth.

"You don't have morning sickness?" Misha asked. She wanted to be prepared in case Shante's meal wanted to make a surprise appearance.

"Not one day of morning sickness. I'm just tired and hungry all the time."

"I was hungry all the time when I was pregnant. In the beginning, I had a lot of morning sickness. How about you, Pastor Dee? Didn't you tell me you had twins?"

"Misha, let's get one thing straight before we go any further today." Deandrea set her fork down on her plate and eyed Misha. "You are going to have to stop calling me Pastor Dee. Just call me Dee."

"Call me Shante or Tay, whichever comes out first. You don't have to be so formal around us. We're plain folk," Shante chimed in.

"Well, okay," Misha smiled, pleased they had allowed her into their circle. Now the real ministry begins.

The trio continued eating as Deandrea overtook the conversation talking about her husband and children. Misha could tell she missed them. But Deandrea was stubborn. She wanted them to believe she was still mad at her husband. She was in a fight she did not want to lose.

Tell her about your trip to Daufuskie Island. Misha heard the familiar whisper in her ear. She had to be obedient to the voice of the Lord. He had never failed her. He was about to release something in the room, and Misha was curious to find out what it was.

"Pastor Dee . . ." Misha interrupted Deandrea's long rant. "I mean Dee. When we went shopping down in Atlanta, I don't know if you remember, I told you I was going on vacation to Daufuskie Island. You told me I would like it. Well, I had a ball. It was so relaxing."

Deandrea's face lit up. A smile spread across her face. It was the happiest Misha or Shante had seen her since she arrived.

"You liked it, huh? It is nice." Dee grinned from ear to ear.

"The beach was great. The spa and food were excellent."

Deandrea took a deep breath and sat back in her chair. Her eyes were distant, and the smile on her face caused Shante to stop eating.

"Dee, what's up? Look at you. You forgot we were in the room." Shante reached over and shook Dee on the shoulder.

"Oh. I'm sorry. For a minute there, I went back to the island," Deandrea said.

"You've been there?" Shante asked.

"That's were Jarrod and I got married."

Now Misha understood. The island held special memories for her and her husband. That was why she had that smile on her face. The mere sound of the island name took her back to the day she got married. Misha guessed God wanted to remind her of happier times and all it meant to them that day. God wanted her to know that everything was going to be all right. He was already moving in her situation.

"No, you didn't. You got married at your church. I was at the wedding, remember?" Shante said.

Deandrea looked at Shante and laughed. Misha was confused. She anxiously waited for the answer.

"That's right. You were at the wedding. But Jarrod and I had been married for almost a year before we had the wedding ceremony at the church," she said as she continued to laugh.

"What . . . No!" Shante screamed. She set her fork on her plate. Deandrea's revelation made her forget how hungry she was. "You're joking, right?" Deandrea shook her head. "How could you keep something like that a secret for so long?" Shante leaned back in her chair; then she quickly sat back up. "I told Max something was up with the two of you. I could look at you and tell. Why didn't you tell me?"

"We didn't tell anyone, not even his mother or my parents. My aunt and cousins lived with me, and even they didn't know."

Misha looked at the two of them. Deandrea seemed amused that her little secret was finally out. Shante could only stare at her in shock. Misha began to question God. Why did they keep their marriage a secret? Could this be the basis for the problems they were having now? Misha didn't want to interrupt their conversation, but she had questions.

"Dee, you eloped before you had your wedding. Why?" Misha asked.

Deandrea wiped her mouth with her napkin and placed it on the table beside her plate. She propped her elbows on the table and leaned her face into her hand. Shante and Misha leaned in closer to her as they anticipated the words that were about to come from her mouth. One could hear a caterpillar crawling across the carpet as they waited for her story.

"I loved my husband," Deandrea beamed. "He proposed to me in the Bahamas. It was so romantic. He had hidden the ring, and I found it. I wanted to make love to him so badly that day. He wanted the same. But we waited. We were trying to be good Christians."

Neither Shante nor Misha dared to interrupt her. This was beginning to sound like a true love story, one every woman craved and found hard to resist. Besides, Misha felt Deandrea had to release this, and she didn't want to interrupt anything God was doing in her life.

"We were in the process of building the new church. Jarrod insisted we should have the first wedding in the new church. With the construction schedule, it was going to take over a year to complete the building. I would have been satisfied having a small wedding in the old church, but he insisted. So, I agreed."

Deandrea leaned back in her chair. She noticed Shante's and Misha's keen looks. She leaned her head back and laughed loudly.

"Since my aunt, cousin and her kids were living with me, my house was always loud. I spent a lot of time at Jarrod's. He only lived right around the corner from us. We began traveling together. Sometimes he would go with me if I had a business conference to attend. They were our minivacations."

Deandrea's body sank into her chair as she shared her most intimate memories. She finally looked at peace. "Each time we traveled together, my aunt Jean would give me a handful of condoms. I think she thought we were having sex. We weren't, and I had a collection of various types of condoms for our honeymoon. Anyway, each time we had some intimate times together we would find ourselves getting more passionately involved. It was only a matter of time before we ended up in bed. So we decided to elope."

Something about that last statement made Shante sit up. Misha tried to focus on Deandrea's story, but now Shante seemed distracted, and it was bothering her. Shante fidgeted in her chair. She picked up her fork and picked at the hash browns on her plate. Misha could feel it. God was doing something in this room. She sensed a change . . . a shift.

"We took a day off and drove to Hilton Head to get a marriage license," Deandrea continued. "We didn't want to get it at home. It would have shown up in the papers. We devised the perfect plan. Luckily, there was a psych conference in Columbia the week we planned to get married. I told everyone I was going to the conference. He told everyone he was preaching a revival that was running Wednesday through Friday. I left on Tuesday to check on all the arrangements. He left Wednesday afternoon. He followed his regular routine of going over to my house to see what Aunt Jean cooked on Tuesday so she would not get suspicious. We got married Wednesday night on the beach. It was beautiful. The resort had placed candles along the shore. There was soft music playing, and the wind was slightly blowing. I wore a long white halter dress. It was sort of Grecian looking, and he had on a sand-colored linen suit with a white shirt and no tie. Neither one of us wore shoes. It was so romantic."

"How did you keep the secret so long?" Misha asked. She glanced at Shante who seemed antsy and had separated herself from the conversation.

Deandrea screamed and slammed her hands on the table. Shante jumped. "Let me tell you how his mother found out," Deandrea started. "Well, she was always talking about respecting her house and saying stuff like her house was sanctified anytime she caught us kissing or cuddling or something. Well, one day we thought she was at the plantation having a meeting with the senior missionaries. So we decided we had enough time to get in a quickie. Well, let me tell you . . . His mother came home early and caught us butt naked in one of the spare bedrooms. I thought we had killed her," Deandrea screamed and laughed so loudly Misha thought the windows would burst.

Deandrea jumped from her chair, waving her arms in the air demonstrating how her mother-in-law reacted when she caught them making love. "She started running around the house with her bottle of oil, rebuking the devil and telling us off at the same time."

Misha and Shante laughed so hard they were in tears. Deandrea ran around the room showing them how her mother-in-law anointed the house before she tried to kick them out of it. Misha leaned over in laughter as she held her aching stomach.

"Jarrod had to get on the Internet and go to the clerk of court Web page to show her we were married. She was still angry we had not told her."

Time went by quickly as Deandrea continued to tell funny stories about her and her husband. The room phone rang. Shante picked it up. She waved to Misha and Deandrea, who were still laughing, in order to silence them. A couple seconds later, Shante hung up the phone.

"Who was that?" Deandrea asked.

"The front desk. They said they got a complaint that someone was fighting in our room and they were checking on us."

Silence . . . Then all three screamed with laughter. Apparently they were having *too* much fun.

Shante looked at her watch. "Oh my goodness. Look at the time. I've got a book signing in thirty minutes. I better get dressed." She rushed into her room.

Misha left to go back to her room to freshen up. She felt good. God used her to break the angry spirit Deandrea had. He allowed her to remember the good times and the things she loved about her husband. Maybe next time when her husband called, she would talk with him. Misha felt it was only a matter of time and Deandrea's problem would be solved. But now, there was something about Shante that troubled her spirit.

16

Shante, Deandrea and Misha stepped off the elevator and were greeted by their escorts from the church. They walked through the hotel lobby into the convention center where a barrage of people ran to greet Shante. Her escorts surrounded them, making a path toward the vendor hall.

Deandrea's cell phone beeped. She smiled as she said hello to her husband, excusing herself. She dipped past the escorts and disappeared into the crowd. Deandrea seemed happier now.

Although she had just eaten, Shante was still hungry when they arrived at the hall. There were people lined up in front of the table waiting for her. Shante estimated there were about a hundred people waiting. She planted a smile on her face and walked toward the people. The sound of applause rang out in the room as Shante walked past the group. She stopped briefly to speak to a couple of people and shook hands with a few. She finally made it to her seat behind a long table. At the right of her, she spotted another table selling copies of her books, CDs and DVDs. *God, is this what my ministry has come to? I am a minister of the Gospel, not a celebrity.*

The first lady in line was directed by one of the escorts to approach the table where Shante sat. She had three books in her hands. This began a marathon of signing books, taking pictures, and speaking briefly to her fans. Shante's mind was jumbled as she listened to each one tell her how much they enjoyed her books. Did she write them for enjoyment or for their deliverance? Shante saw her books as a ministry. Yet, she realized, some people only read them for entertainment. Maybe Max was right. She should come off the road. It didn't seem as if she was accomplishing anything.

"Pastor, I brought you something to eat and some juice," Misha said as she set a plate filled with fruit and pastries on the table in front of Shante.

How did she know? Shante stared at Misha. She appreciated the help. If LaToya were here, she would probably do the same thing. But, Misha was different; it was almost as if she could read her mind.

Shante paused briefly to take a bite out of one of the pastries. She savored every morsel of the cream-filled flaky treat. One of the escorts approached her and whispered in her ear that there were a few more minutes before service started and they were cutting off the line for the book signing. There were so many people, she could not see the end of the line.

Deandrea walked up to the table with her lips curved in a sly smile. Apparently she and Jarrod were not arguing anymore. Shante welcomed the return of her old friend. Maybe now she could talk to her about her problems.

The large audience in the main convention hall erupted in applause and cheers as Shante walked onto the stage with Misha and Deandrea trailing behind. First Lady Edmunds, dressed so elegantly in her lavender designer suit and matching hat, stood to greet them and offered them a seat. Pastor Edmunds was on the stage addressing the audience.

"Aw yeah. I told you. She's in the house. Give it up for Shante Patrick!" he announced to the audience, who was now standing on their feet. Shante waved to the crowd of people clapping and screaming.

Shante felt that too much was put on her as an individual. Did they know she had issues? She wondered how they would react if they knew she was forty-six and pregnant. Or how would they react if they knew her perfect life was so imperfect.

"I'm going to introduce to you the ladies with her this morning." Pastor Edmunds looked at the paper he held in his hand. "We have Sister Misha Taylor. Y'all may not know her, but you do know her husband, a great Gospel singer and a powerful man of God, Bernard Taylor. Stand up, First Lady Taylor, so they can see you."

The audience gave Misha little applause as she stood and waved to the crowd. Pastor Edmunds continued addressing the audience. "The next lady—my God, seems like I have known her for years. She's the wife of my very best friend in college, my frat brother, my road dog, y'all know what I mean. Tomorrow night, she is going to minister to us in song. She's a powerful woman of God. Y'all give it up for Copastor Deandrea Fuller, wife of my friend Pastor Jarrod Fuller, all the way from South Carolina."

Deandrea stood and waved to the crowd like she was Miss America and sat back down.

"I didn't know she was coming to the conference. When I found out she was here, my spirit leaped, and I told my wife we had to get her to sing for us. She's a classically trained pianist and an anointed woman of God, and we are so blessed to have her here with us. Y'all, give these ladies a great big God Bless You. They have traveled near and far to be here with us today. Praise God."

The audience applauded.

"How long is this man going to talk?" Deandrea whispered in Shante's ear. Shante held back a laugh. She wanted the service to go forward too. She was delighted when he finally introduced the speaker.

Service proceeded quickly once Bishop began his sermon. Altar call was longer than his twenty-minute sermon. A throng of people jammed in front of the stage for prayer. Shante could feel the pain, sorrow and joy of the people at the altar. She felt connected with them. She wanted to run to the altar for prayer herself. Everyone expected her to be so anointed that she didn't need prayer.

What would people think if they knew she felt her perfect life was unraveling? Max, the man of her dreams, was so angry with her he couldn't talk to her. Her spirited sons had their own problems that were causing problems in her home, and what was she going to do with a baby? Shante shook away the thoughts and bowed her head in prayer.

"Pastor Patrick, I'm so delighted you could join us for lunch," Pastor Edmunds greeted Shante as she approached him in the small conference room set up to look like a dining room at the hotel. He hugged her tightly and poured out compliments back to back. It was so unnecessary. She was still going to preach tomorrow, if it was the Lord's will. Right now, the only thing she was interested in was the lunch menu.

Shante walked around the tables greeting the other ministers gathered there while Deandrea and Pastor Edmunds spoke to each other. She seemed to be enjoying the attention she was getting. Deandrea was in character, wearing her first-lady mask. She had that church talk down, and everyone around her seemed to be taking it all in.

"You know Jarrod talks about you all the time. It's good to finally meet you. I'm looking forward to hearing you sing tomorrow," Pastor Edmunds said.

"Thank you for inviting me to sing. I look forward to it. I'm glad I finally got to meet you too. Jarrod has told me a lot about you," Deandrea said.

Misha stepped beside Deandrea. Pastor Edmunds reached to shake her hand. The moment their hands met, Misha saw his life flash before her eyes. She saw tension in his marriage. She saw a troubled ministry. She heard his heart cry to God for help. She could not release his hand.

Deandrea noticed Misha's blank stare and the tight grip she held on Pastor Edmunds's hand. She tapped Misha's hand. "Misha . . . Misha?" Deandrea said trying to get her attention.

"Excuse me," Misha said coming out of her trance. "I'm sorry. You reminded me of something." She lowered her head in embarrassment and walked toward Shante who was observing the scene from the other side of the room. The wait staff announced the meal was being served. Everyone sat down to enjoy the lunch.

The three ladies returned to Shante's room. Shante kicked off her shoes and headed for the minibar. The meal of dried chicken covered in garlic sauce did not appease her appetite. She was still hungry, and she knew exactly where she wanted to go.

"Hey, y'all, let's go to Miss Tootsie's," she suggested to Deandrea and Misha. They had eaten very little of the dried up chicken and overcooked vegetables.

"Miss Tootsie's? What's that?" Misha asked.

"It's a soul food restaurant. I'm still hungry. I could barely eat that food with all that garlic. Do you want to go? We can take Dee's car."

"That's Jarrod's car. I took it. I let him drive the station wagon for a change," Deandrea said as she began undressing in her room. She slipped on her jeans.

Misha left the room to change her clothes. Shante walked into her room to do the same. She slipped on her jeans that were already tight at the waist. She held her breath and squeezed the jeans together, trying to get them to zip. It was not working. She gave up and dropped on her bed. Tears fell from her eyes.

"Hey, girl, what's wrong?" Deandrea walked into the room. "Are you that hungry?"

Shante shook her head. "My jeans don't fit."

Deandrea laughed. "What about the clothes Misha got you? What did she buy?"

"I don't know. I was so shocked, I didn't look in the bag."

Shante walked to the closet and pulled out the motherhood bag and looked inside. She pulled out a pair of maternity jeans and a casual soft pink maternity blouse. Shante looked in the bag again and pulled out a navy dress with a matching jacket.

She put on the jeans and blouse. It was a perfect fit. She was puzzled.

"Dee, these fit perfectly. How did she know what size I wore?"

"She's got the gift. You saw the clothes she picked out for me. They were a perfect fit too." Deandrea waved her hand. "Turn around. You look nice. She does have good taste." She placed her hands on her hips. "You should let her pick out some more maternity clothes for you."

Shante faced Deandrea. "What's wrong now?" Deandrea asked her.

"Don't you think there is something funny about Misha? I mean, she seems a little different."

"She is different. Didn't you see how she looked at Pastor Edmunds today? God showed her something. I've seen that look before. She had that same look Jarrod gets when he's about to prophesy to someone."

"You think she's a prophet?"

"I think she has the gift."

"But she didn't say anything."

"Maybe she wasn't supposed to. I've learned a lot of things about the gift by watching Jarrod. God reveals a lot to him about people. He doesn't always tell what's revealed until God tells him to." She thought for a minute. "Funny God didn't reveal to him how upset I had been."

"Maybe God wants the two of you to work this thing out on your own."

"I don't know. I don't know if it can be fixed," Deandrea sighed and walked across the room. She looked sad again. "Look at you and Max. You guys have the perfect marriage. That man loves you so much, and he hasn't taken away who you are. You have a successful ministry, and your writing career is great. You're still Shante. Me, I'm only the copastor and that title has no weight. It only means I'm in charge when Jarrod is not there. When he's there, I'm nobody."

Shante laughed. "You think Max and I have the perfect marriage? It's so far from it. He's mad at me for coming here to do this conference. I had to tell him I was in New York to help Camille with her wedding plans. That was the only way I was able to do the book signing and interviews. We don't have the perfect marriage. Nobody does. Everyone has disagreements."

"Well, at least you still have your career, ministry and marriage. I have nothing, no career, no ministry and—"

"Don't say it, Dee." Shante had to stop her. She couldn't allow her to speak death into her marriage. She couldn't let her friend go through this alone. She was in the danger zone; a point where she could no longer shed a tear for her marriage. She prayed God moved in her marriage quickly.

There was a knock at the door. Shante opened it to see Misha standing in front of her wearing jeans, a camisole, a jacket and some of the highest heels Shante had ever seen. She would love to be able to wear those shoes, but her feet would not allow it.

"Misha, come in for a minute. There's something I want to ask you," Deandrea said to her. "I saw how you looked at Pastor Edmunds today. You have the gift, don't you?"

"Gift? What gift?" Misha made a puzzling face.

"Don't act like you don't know what I'm talking about. Jarrod has the gift too. What did the Lord show you about him?"

"Now, Dee, if you really believe I have the gift, then you would know better than to ask me what God showed me, right?"

Shante laughed. Misha was smarter than she looked. She was so cool with her answer. "She got you there, Dee. Are we going to stand here and talk, or are we going to get something to eat?"

Shante left the room and picked up her jacket lying on the bed. She stumbled. She felt lightheaded again. She eased onto the bed. After a few moments, she felt better. The room was no longer spinning. She stood and joined them in the front room.

"Let's get out of here," Shante said. She had to remind herself to take the vitamins and iron the doctor gave her or else she had no idea how she was going to make it through the next several months.

17

"I thought you knew where you were going?" Misha asked Shante.

They were lost in a part of Philadelphia that would make you pray . . . hard. She didn't use her navigational system because Shante said she knew how to get there. Now, she was quickly punching in the address so they could get out of the gang graffiti-filled neighborhood they'd found themselves in.

Deandrea pressed her foot on the gas when the directions popped up on the screen. She darted in and out of traffic trying to avoid accidents. Shante and Misha held on for dear life as Deandrea drove through red traffic lights and dodged pedestrians.

Finally, Shante spotted the restaurant and was relieved when they pulled into a parking space. Misha leaped from the car as soon as it stopped.

"Dee, who taught you how to drive?" Misha demanded.

"I'm a good driver," Deandrea said. She stepped out of the car.

"Come on, ladies. Good food awaits," Shante urged as she led the trio down the sidewalk into the restaurant.

Shante had not lifted her head from her plate since they got there. She even ordered a carryout meal to take back to the hotel. It was hard for Misha and Deandrea to believe her pregnancy was making her eat like that. It was even harder for Deandrea to believe that Shante and Max were arguing about her traveling for her ministry. What was the problem with men? Did they know that women have a life too? Why can't men allow women to be who God wanted them to be instead of who they want women to be? Look how successful Shante had been in her ministry. Now, her husband wanted her to come off the road? She can preach pregnant. She could write pregnant.

Misha sat quietly across the table from Deandrea eating as slowly as possible. Deandrea could sense something was going on with her, but she wasn't going to ask. She was there to have fun. The last thing she wanted was to start a long drawn-out conversation about someone else's drama. Misha reminded Deandrea of herself. She was a little arrogant, probably because she was married to a superstar. Deandrea twisted her lips. She still couldn't believe Bernard Taylor married a black woman. What was he trying to prove? Wasn't it enough he was a white guy singing black Gospel music.

"That was good," Shante said when she finally lifted her head from the plate. She sat back in her chair with a look of utter satisfaction on her face. She wiped her mouth with her napkin. "I told you the food is good here. How did you like it, Misha?"

"It was good," she replied still holding on to her fork. Now she looked very distant.

Deandrea couldn't help herself. Ministry called. She had to know what was on Misha's mind. "What's wrong, Misha?" she asked.

"What makes you think something is wrong?" Misha answered. She briefly lifted her eyes and looked at Deandrea.

Her eyes said it all. Deandrea could see it. Why was Misha so sad? Deandrea looked around the restaurant. It was the middle of the day, and there were few people there. Restaurant employees were cleaning tables and changing the pans on the buffet table. She looked at Misha who now had her elbow on the table and leaned her head on her hand. She was no longer focused on them. Her eyes were distant.

"Misha, are you okay?" Shante asked.

"I was only thinking about my baby. This is the first time I've left her alone with Matthew."

"I don't think you have anything to worry about. That child looks so much like him he's probably showing her off to everybody. I'm sure he's taking very good care of her."

"Yeah, Misha," Deandrea jumped into the conversation. She understood separation anxiety. She was experiencing a little of it herself. She had to assure Misha that it was a normal feeling and everything was okay. "I'm sure your husband will take good care of his twin."

Misha's eyes stretched. Her glare sent a chill down Deandrea's spine. Misha threw her napkin on the table and stood. "Where's the ladies' room?" she asked a waitress. The waitress pointed, and Misha quickly walked in that direction.

"Who's going after her?" Shante asked.

"I'll go. I wonder what that is about. Did you see how she looked at me? Something's going on with her. I better go see about her."

Deandrea left the table and walked into the bathroom and saw Misha standing in front of the mirror fixing her hair with her fingers. She looked very frustrated. She was not crying. That was a good sign. She strolled over to Misha and wrapped her arm around her. Misha moved away.

"Can I help you with something?" Deandrea asked, trying to be as polite as she could. "Is there anything you want to talk about?"

Misha shook her head and exited the bathroom.

It was obvious to Dee something was wrong. Her trained psychological eye could tell. But if Misha didn't want to talk about it, Deandrea could not force her. Sooner or later, she was going to have to get help. If God had assigned her to help, then she was up for the challenge.

Misha and Shante were laughing when Deandrea returned to the table and sat. "What's so funny?" Apparently Misha had gotten over her little breakdown and all was well again.

"Excuse me. Aren't you Shante Patrick?" a woman interrupted them.

After the lady took a picture with Shante and left them, Misha asked, "People treat you like Matthew. Do you get tired of that sometimes?"

"No. I try to think about how I would feel if I were them. It's exciting. I know that. If you treat people nicely, good things will come back to you. Are you going to eat that cake?" Shante pointed at the piece of coconut cake in front of Misha.

Misha and Deandrea laughed at Shante reaching across the table for the small plate of cake. If she was not careful, she was going to be as big as a house. Shante slipped the fork filled with cake into her mouth. Her smile widened as she pulled the fork from her mouth.

"Shante, what are you wearing tomorrow?" Misha asked. "If your jeans won't fit, will the dress or suit you have to preach in fit?"

"You have made a good point. I don't know," Shante said.

"Well, we should go shopping and get you something to wear tomorrow."

"There's an outlet park here. We can go there," Shante suggested.

"Good. Then, I can get the children something too. I haven't gotten them any souvenirs yet," Deandrea agreed.

Misha googled the address for the outlet park on her phone and gave it to Deandrea, who put it in her car's navigational system, and soon, they pulled into traffic in the direction of the outlet park. Deandrea kept a tight grip on the steering wheel as she drove in the heavy traffic. She still could not believe she drove all the way there by herself. She must have been mad. Anger makes you do crazy things. Her cell phone beeped.

Shante reached for Deandrea's phone and looked at the caller ID. "It's your husband," she said to her.

"You can answer it. Tell him I'm driving and will call him when we get to the shopping center."

Shante did just that, then dropped the cell phone into the console in the center of the car and they continued to the outlet center.

Deandrea was supposed to help Shante pick out something, but she couldn't resist the temptation to shop for herself. The dress store they were in had some classy dresses. While Shante and Misha headed for the maternity section, Deandrea headed to the women's sizes.

She picked out an odd green-colored dress. She lifted it and got Misha's attention. Misha shook her head no. Deandrea looked at the dress. She liked it. She threw the dress over her arm. She was going to try it on anyway. Her phone beeped. She huffed when she saw Jarrod's name on the caller ID. He would only call back if she didn't answer. She tapped the answer button.

"I thought you were going to call me back," Jarrod said.

Did he have to call her all day long? He didn't do it when she was at home. Why was he doing it now?

"How is your day going? Shag told me you looked good this morning in service. He enjoyed talking with you at lunch."

An awkward silence loomed. "Jarrod, what is it?" Deandrea tried not to raise her voice.

"I want to know how your day is going."

"Well, we are at an outlet park, shopping. I'm getting ready to try on a dress. How are the children?"

Deandrea walked into the dressing room and set her purse on the stool in the tight room.

"They're at day care. I'll get them in a few minutes. We're having dinner at Mama's house today. I miss you."

Miss me? He is something else. She slipped her pants off and pulled the dress over her head, knocking the Bluetooth out of her ear. She adjusted the dress and looked in the mirror. Misha was right. This was not the dress for her. Disappointed, she pulled the dress off and noticed her Bluetooth on the floor. She picked it up and placed it in her ear. "Hello?" She couldn't believe he was still on the phone.

"What happened?"

"The Bluetooth fell out of my ear. I was trying on a dress."

"I hear Bishop is preaching tonight. I know you're looking forward to that. You know I met him at a conference in Texas, remember? Boy, did he preach."

Deandrea tuned him out. She didn't want to hear any of his preaching stories. If he really wanted to know how she was doing, he would ask her again. He hadn't realized that she did not answer his question. Yet, he continued to yap on and on about nothing.

"Dee?" she finally heard him say. In the time he was talking, Shante purchased a dress and they had left the store and were now in a lingerie store looking at maternity garments. "What are you doing?"

"I told you we were shopping," Deandrea answered.

"You never answered my question."

"What question was that?"

"I asked you how you were doing."

"I told you we were shopping. Didn't you hear me?"

"I didn't ask you *what* you were doing. I asked you *how* you were doing."

Deandrea rolled her eyes. Now, he was trying to turn the tables on her. He wasn't interested in what she was feeling. He was only trying to use one of the counseling techniques she taught them at the church. Didn't he think she could tell when he was using them? She was no amateur. She taught counseling classes at Tech. He can't psych her out. She knew all the tricks.

"What are you shopping for?" he asked. "What kind of store are you in?"

"Why?" She picked up some lacy pink boy shorts. *My fat behind will never fit in these things*. She hung it on the rack. She noticed Shante and Misha walking toward her. They were laughing. Shante was holding several items.

"Who are you talking to?" Shante asked.

"Jarrod," Deandrea whispered. Both had sly grins on their faces. Something sneaky was going on. "Jarrod, I'll call you later," Deandrea said and pressed the END button on her phone. "Okay now, what's up? You two look like you are up to something. What is it?"

"Misha had this idea I thought we would try," Shante said.

"What?"

"Well, I thought we could pick out sexy panties," Misha said, "take a picture of them and send them to our husbands."

"I'm not taking a picture in my underwear." Deandrea was appalled. With Shante's fame, why would she agree to do something like that? What if someone intercepted the picture and put it in the media—or worse, on the Internet. What was she thinking about?

"No, you don't get it. We are only taking a picture of the panties, not us in them. You know, to remind our husbands of what they are missing," Misha added.

"Young love. It must be nice. Wait until you're married a few years. Then you will be like Jarrod and me. He won't even know you are in the house. If I sent Jarrod a picture he wouldn't even recognize what it was."

"Come on, Dee. Don't be a party pooper. Let's do it and see what happens." Shante tried to persuade Deandrea to take the picture. If Jarrod was not turned on with Deandrea in a thong, a picture of ladies' panties will never do it.

Shante and Misha ran off to find sexy panties for their picture. Deandrea was jealous. She wanted a happy marriage like them. Maybe she should send Jarrod a picture of a church steeple or a pulpit. That would excite him. Or better yet, she could send him a picture of all the people gathered at the conference. That would really turn him on.

"Give me your phone," Misha demanded of Dee.

She hesitated at first, but then handed it to her.

Misha placed a lacy white thong on the front of a clothing rack and took a picture of it. "Now, let me see what I can say." She quickly typed the letters into the phone. Deandrea nervously twitched. She got anxious with every beep of the phone. She couldn't take it any longer. She reached for the phone. Shante dipped between them, and Misha ran to the other side of the store.

Misha returned after a couple of minutes and handed the phone to Deandrea. "Shante, are you ready?" Misha asked her. Shante and Misha pulled out their phones, took a picture of the thong and typed into their phones.

Deandrea placed her hands over her mouth as she watched Misha and Shante laugh at their messages to their husbands. These were supposed to be women of God, and they were sending risqué messages to their husbands. What if someone found out? What was going to happen to their ministries? What was going to happen to their husbands' ministries? She had to get this young girl away from Shante. She was going to hurt all that Shante had worked so hard for.

Shante and Misha continued looking at lingerie when Deandrea's phone beeped. Jarrod, yet again. Why did they do that? She had told them they hadn't had sex in ages. This was not going to turn him on. And what if it did? She was not there. He was not here. She shook her head and walked away from the laughing pair.

She hit the END button on the phone to stop the constant beep. Jarrod was probably mad. He could be self-righteous sometimes. Were Shante and Misha trying to cause more conflict in her marriage? She didn't need anymore problems.

Deandrea walked out of the store and sat on a bench in the breezeway. She felt like leaving Shante and Misha there to find their own way back to the hotel.

Shante scooted onto the seat beside her. "What did Jarrod say?" she asked.

Shante and Deandrea had been friends for many years, but this was the very first time she wanted to tell Shante off. How could she do something like this? Her marriage was already in trouble, and she and that little girl were sending provocative messages to her husband. Shante sat beside Deandrea grinning as if she had accomplished something great.

Deandrea's message signal chimed. Jarrod had sent her a text. Her mouth flew open when she saw the message. It was a picture of Jarrod's boxer shorts with the message, On or off?

"What?" Shante asked. She leaned closer to Deandrea to get a better look at her phone. Deandrea moved her phone away and deleted the message. She didn't want Shante seeing her husband's underwear.

Shante's phone rang. "Look, it's Max," she said and walked away from Deandrea. Misha's phone rang, and she retreated to another corner. Both of them were acting like silly schoolgirls trying to get the attention of the star football player. Deandrea was too grown for that.

Deandrea sat on the bench debating if she should call her husband. What was she going to say to him? Misha had sent him the picture with the same message he'd sent her. Her message chimed again. It was Jarrod. The message had a picture of the thong with the words, On then off, underneath it. He couldn't be for real. Deandrea knew the routine. She wasn't getting her hopes up.

Deandrea wanted to leave. Shante was standing to her left and Misha on the right, talking to their husbands like they were the happiest couples in the world. Deandrea was tired of both of them. Their husbands weren't married to the church. She and Jarrod used to be like them. Now, it took all she had inside of her to pretend everything's okay. Deandrea felt as if she had given all that she had. She had nothing more to give. She was emotionally drained. Why did she give up her career? She loved her psychology practice. Now, she needed to see a psychologist herself.

"Well, what did he say?" Shante asked Deandrea as she approached the bench.

Deandrea was not going to tell her what Jarrod said. Shante had a good husband. He cared enough about her to be concerned about her going on the road pregnant. It didn't matter to Jarrod that she left in the middle of the night to drive hundreds of miles alone. Now he thought everything was going to be patched up by him sending her a picture of his boxer shorts.

"Matthew is going to make me leave this conference. My husband is so sexy," Misha smiled as she walked toward Shante and Deandrea.

Deandrea sighed. Misha was so young. She would give it another year until the newness wore off and reality kicked in. Then she would see just how foolish she looked right now.

"Did your husbands like your message?" Misha asked them.

"Max sure did. It caught him off guard. He said I should not miss a single session if they are teaching us how to do things like that. He really liked it. That's something I never did before. It made him wish we were together. I had to remind him that's how we are about to be new parents at almost fifty years old. He thought that was funny. How 'bout you, Dee? What did Jarrod say?"

Deandrea walked away from them. It was none of their business what Jarrod thought. Besides, he wasn't sincere in his response. Why should she get all excited about nothing? When she got home, the only thing that will excite him was the fact that he would be able to go back to doing what he did. He would return to his mistress. She would return to her role as copastor that allowed his schedule to control her life.

She spotted a restroom and walked into it with Misha and Shante on her heels. Deandrea raced to one of the stalls, closed the door and allowed the tears to flow down her face. She allowed anger to direct her path.

18

Misha thought the message would be fun. A little flirting with each other would help their marriage get back on track. Sometimes, that was all it took. Guess she was wrong. She didn't want to cause any problems. She was only trying to help. How did she know it was going to turn out like this?

Misha wanted to apologize as Shante was trying to coax Deandrea out of the stall. "Dee, I apologize. I didn't mean to upset you. I thought your husband would like it. I thought a little flirting would put the spark back in your marriage."

Deandrea walked out of the stall. Her eyes were swollen from crying. Misha felt bad. She didn't mean to upset her this much. Shante moved to hug Deandrea, but she dipped out of the way and walked toward the mirror.

"I know you didn't mean anything by it," Deandrea finally spoke. "Jarrod actually liked it." She looked at Misha. "Next time, before you take someone's phone and send a message, ask first," Deandrea said roughly. She grabbed a paper towel, wet it and wiped her eyes.

"Dee, really, we didn't mean anything by it. We were just playing." Shante added.

Misha didn't understand. If he liked it, why was Deandrea crying? There was something deeper going on here. How could she get so upset about something that pleased her husband?

Deandrea straightened her blouse. She had her game face on now. She walked past Shante and Misha as if she didn't see them.

"Don't worry about it. She'll be fine. I'll talk to her later," Shante said as she hooked her arm in Misha's. They followed Deandrea out the door.

"I didn't mean to hurt anybody," Misha said.

"I know."

For the next hour Deandrea had enough energy to go on a wild shopping spree. She didn't ask for Shante's or Misha's opinion. She purchased clothing without trying them on. Misha and Shante followed her into a children's store, and Deandrea tried her best to buy everything she saw.

They bounced from store to store following Deandrea's antics. She seemed to find something in every store to purchase. Shante and Misha did not try to stop her. Eventually she would run out of steam. However, it was Shante who needed to rest, and the trio headed for the food court.

Misha sat at the table guarding all the purchases while Deandrea and Shante looked for something to eat. "God, what do you want me to do for these ladies? I've got to make sure I don't do something else stupid. I repent for the text. I thought it was a good idea. Dee's husband liked it. Why didn't she? I don't understand," Misha quietly prayed.

Deandrea and Shante returned to the table and sat down. Shante had a large sticky bun on a plate in front of her. Deandrea picked up one of her cheese fries and ate it. The atmosphere at the table was tense. Shante was trying hard to break the tension with light conversation. Deandrea was eating a burger and dancing to a tune only she could hear, trying to act as if nothing was happening with her. Misha felt uncomfortable. She looked up to these two women. Now, she was wondering why.

When she first went into the ministry, Misha would have killed to be where she was now. Being there was much different from what she imagined. She had often thought if she ever got the chance to sit down and talk with them, it would be so spiritually deep an angel would have to translate for her. She had imagined they would inspire her in a way that would change her focus and renew her spirit. She dreamt they would hit it off and be instant friends. She had imagined they would mentor her unlike anything she ever received in the ministry. Now that she was with them, she wished she wasn't. She enjoyed the fantasy more.

"Excuse me, miss," a lady tapped Misha on the shoulder. "I hate to interrupt you. I don't want to be a bother. May I ask you a question?" the woman's voice trembled.

"What kind of question?" Misha asked.

"Are you famous? You look like a lady I saw on the cover of a magazine I was looking at in the grocery store."

"That was her," Deandrea chimed in. "Her husband is Bernard Taylor."

"I'm sorry. I never heard of him. Does he play football or something?"

Misha loved it when people did not recognize her husband. It let her know there were still places they could go for privacy. She had to take note as to where this white lady with a strong midwestern accent lived. She had to keep it in mind for a retreat for her and Matthew.

"My husband is a pastor, and he sings Gospel music," Misha said.

"I love Gospel music. I like the Katinas, Point of Grace—"

"He sings *black* Gospel music," Deandrea arrogantly said.

Misha was appalled. She rolled her eyes. Deandrea needed to get over herself. In her house, they don't insult people, especially strangers.

"He's won a couple of Grammy's, and some Stellar awards and Dove awards. You never heard of him? He's anointed. He's cute too," Deandrea continued.

The more Deandrea spoke, the angrier Misha became. Her lips tightened in a forced smile. The lady asked an honest question. Instead, Deandrea was rattling off Matthew's résumé. Deandrea was only repeating what she read in magazines or heard on television. She didn't know Misha's husband. She had to rescue this innocent victim from Deandrea's insecurities.

"Miss, you recognize me from the cover? That was a few months ago. You have a good memory. I'm Misha Taylor. These are my friends, Shante Patrick and Deandrea Fuller," Misha pointed to Deandrea and Shante. "You like the Katinas? I love their music too. I saw them in concert a couple of years ago. Have you seen them?"

"Once. They came to my church. Well, I don't want to bother you any longer. You ladies have a good day," the woman said. She walked away, then returned to their table. "Excuse me. I hate to bother you again. Did you say your name is Shante Patrick?"

"That's me," Shante replied.

"The preacher?"

"Yes."

The lady jumped in the air and screamed. She grabbed Shante and hugged her tightly. Shante laughed. The lady waved over other ladies sitting at another table. The ladies joined her.

"We are here for the conference. Can we get a picture?" The lady handed Deandrea a camera. She snapped a picture of Shante and the group. "Thank you. I look forward to hearing you speak tomorrow. It has been a blessing meeting you . . . all of you. Enjoy the conference."

The group of women disappeared into the food court.

"How can you stand that?" Misha asked Shante. "People recognizing you wherever you go. Don't you get tired of it?"

"Never. These are the people God sent me to minister to. Sometimes ministry is not about how you preach from the pulpit. Sometimes, it's about how you treat people when they connect with you. In the pulpit or out, it's all ministry."

Now this was what Misha expected to get when she came in contact with them, not the whining or complaining. Maybe they could have a good conversation. "Did you see how that lady responded to me, and then to you? She recognized me from the magazine, but she screamed for you. That's how people act when I'm with Matthew. Sometimes they push me aside to be with him. It's like I don't exist. How does your husband handle it? Is he treated the same way?"

"Max? Well, he never said anything negative about it. He likes it when people recognize me. He says it sells books. He told me once he enjoyed having the virtuous wife. I think he likes the fact I have a career and ministry separate from his," Shante said in between licking her fingers of the cinnamon cream that dripped from the pastry she was eating.

"Misha, you need to embrace being Bernard Taylor's wife. You seem embarrassed by it." Once again, Deandrea put her unsolicited two cents in.

"You don't know anything about me. I've read the tabloids and the blogs on the Internet. They are always talking about him marrying 'that black girl'—like he's not black. I know he's light skinned, but they feel he's using me to prove his blackness."

"Well, is he?" Deandrea asked.

I can't believe that heifer asked me that. Excuse me, Lord.

Deandrea waited for an answer while Shante pretended to be unattached to the conversation.

"If you are suggesting that my husband only married me because I'm black, that's not true. I knew I was going to marry him long before we met. The Holy Spirit told me when I was a child, and He is faithful because I believed."

"Either way, that child looks just like him." Deandrea shoved another fry into her mouth. "What color are his eyes? On one picture they're brown. On another, they're blue. What's his natural color?" she asked.

Misha gripped her thigh in an attempt to control her tongue and anger. Deandrea was so insensitive, and she was pushing Misha's buttons.

"You don't have to tell me. Your baby has blue eyes. So his eyes must be blue too."

"Will you cut it out?" Misha yelled. "Courtney is not his baby, okay? Is that what you wanted to know? She's not his biological child."

Misha scooped up her two bags and stormed out of the food court. She had to find a phone book to call a taxi to take her back to the hotel. She looked at her watch. If she hurried, she could make it back in time for evening service.

These two women were not there to get anything out of the conference. They only wanted to hang out. Misha came to Philadelphia to worship and learn something that was going to make her a better first lady. She was beginning to think her assignment was to get revived instead of ministry.

Misha was sick of dealing with these two selfish women. Shante was here to teach. Yet, she had a lot of things to learn herself.

"Misha, wait!" Shante cried out.

Misha picked up her pace. She didn't want to be around them anymore. The respect she had for them was now gone. There was nothing either one of them could say to her to make her stay with them.

Misha felt a hand clamp down on her shoulder. "Please stop. She didn't mean anything by it. We didn't know. She didn't know," Shante said breathlessly.

"Misha, I'm sorry. I wasn't trying to get in your business," Deandrea said to Misha. She set her bags down and hugged Misha's stiff body. "I'm sorry. I didn't mean anything by it."

"I just want to leave this place," Misha said.

"It's about time we all went back to the hotel," Shante said.

The trio found the car in the parking lot and headed back to the hotel. The ride back was a quiet one. Misha stared out the window. She had to make it to service tonight. Her soul needed reviving. Her spirit was weak dealing with them. They had drained her energy.

How could she allow them to agitate her so much that she revealed a secret only close relatives knew? Now, it was going to be in all the tabloids. The pain she felt now in her belly was for her husband and his ministry. If this became a problem, it was all her fault. She didn't know how to rectify it.

Misha rushed to her room without speaking to Shante or Deandrea. She tossed her bags on the bed and called Matthew. She had to let him know her mistake before he heard about it.

"Hey, Babe," Matthew said. Before he could say anything else, Misha spilled everything that happened.

"Honey, don't worry about it. Besides, what would they gain by telling people?" he asked her.

Misha's leg shook nervously. She didn't need any more stress right now. She had enough at home.

"Call me back on the videophone. Courtney wants to see you."

Misha hung up the phone. She reached into her purse and pulled out her tablet, then called Matthew. She laughed at the sight of Courtney answering the phone wearing a baseball cap turned backward and dark sunglasses. Her hands reached for the cap until she spotted Misha. The baby's fat arms reached for the tablet. She babbled.

"See, I told you we are okay. We are just chilling, watching the Binky Frogs and sipping milk," Matthew said as he adjusted the tablet to show him and Courtney. He laughed loudly.

Matthew always had a way of cheering Misha up. She smiled at the sight of her happy family. She missed them dearly. Forget the conference. She wanted to go home to take care of her husband and child. She wasn't needed here with these selfish women. Shante and Deandrea were ungrateful for what they had, and they needed to lie before God and repent.

A knock on her door caused Misha to end her conversation. She looked through the peephole and spotted Deandrea and Shante standing at her door. If she remained silent, maybe they would go away. She walked into the bedroom and sat on the bed. Deandrea and Shante continued knocking. Finally, Misha ran to the door and yanked it open.

"We come in peace," Deandrea said, her lips spread in a wide smile. "May we come in?"

"I thought the two of you would be at the evening session."

"No. It looks like you are not going either. May we come in?" Deandrea replied.

Misha stepped to the side, and they walked into the room. She closed the door and stood with her arms folded, waiting for them to tell her why they were here.

"You have a nice room. You didn't tell us you had a suite," Deandrea said acting as if nothing happened. "Misha, I'm sorry. I didn't mean to get up in your business. I didn't know."

Misha did not move away from the door. She was well aware that Deandrea could not have known about Courtney. None of it was in the tabloids and blogosphere. Much of the stuff printed about them was untrue. But, people like Deandrea continued to question his identity and his sincerity in his ministry and marriage.

Misha tried to ignore it, but it was hard. She and Matthew never talked about it. He was still sensitive about the abuse he experienced as a child. She only talked about it when he brought it up. He didn't realize that he had habits that were developed because of his abuse, and he was not aware of the things he was doing. He thought he had defeated his past. However, it continued to show up. It made him overly sensitive to other people's opinions. Misha had to be his protector just as he had been hers. Now that she had told their secret, she felt ashamed, as if she had abused him all over again. How was she going to fix this?

19

Shante had never seen Deandrea act like this before. She was rude and insulting. She was taking out her anger at Jarrod on everyone else. She had pushed poor Misha to the limit. Misha wouldn't move from the door, as if she was waiting for the opportunity to kick them out.

"Misha, please forgive us. We didn't know. Dee was only trying to make conversation."

Misha frowned and moved to the large window. She had nothing to say to them. She was hurt. Not only from Deandrea's comments, but from everything that was going on in her life.

Shante stood in the center of the room looking at Misha gazing out the window, as if they were not there, and Deandrea leaned back in a chair. It was time to bring healing in this room.

"Ladies, I feel we need to pray," Shante said.

"That's a good idea," Deandrea said as she bounced from the chair and walked to Shante. They joined hands. Misha did not move from the window. "Misha, come and pray with us."

Misha huffed. She didn't want to do anything else with them. Prayer was different. It wouldn't hurt anything. She sluggishly approached the two who held out their hands to her.

As Deandrea prayed for forgiveness, Shante couldn't help but feel sorry for Misha. They were having fun until Deandrea messed things up. She should not have invited her. She wanted to talk to Deandrea about her problems but she had more issues. Shante could never leave her husband and children, especially her children, no matter how mad she was at Max. Deandrea's nonstop opinionated talking had gotten on Shante's nerves too. Frankly, she was tired of it.

Deandrea's cell phone rang as she concluded her prayer. She glanced at it, saw that it was Jarrod, and sent it to voice mail.

"You should talk to your husband and stop treating him like that," Misha said, looking at Deandrea.

Deandrea's eyes widened, and she took a step toward Misha.

"Misha, we should stay out of it," Shante said as she leaped between the two of them.

"You should stay out of my business," Deandrea fired back at Misha. Her body stiffened.

"You're in *my* room. Therefore, it *is* my business," Misha said just as quickly as Deandrea shot at her. "Your husband is a man of God. You should honor the anointing on his life."

"You don't know anything about me," Deandrea inched closer to Misha. "You need to take care of your own house. You're the one who's embarrassed of your husband."

"I'm not embarrassed of my husband. You don't know what it is like to be me—Mrs. Bernard Taylor. You're not with me when people push me to the side to be with him. You're not the one people all over the world are talking about, and most of it is a lie. You're not the one where women threaten to take your husband every single day of your marriage."

"Now, I can say I have that problem," Shante interjected. "Women approach Max all the time. Bold, daring women, and ones who don't care if he's married or a minister of the Gospel."

"You can say that again." Deandrea waved her hand in the air. "As long as you are married, you're going to have women approach your husband. That's why you have to pray for him every day. Some women come in the church only to make a pass at my husband. They quickly find out we don't play that in our church."

They finally had a connecting factor, something they all had to deal with. Deandrea walked away from the two women and flopped on the sofa. Shante walked to the small dining table and sat in one of the chairs. Misha joined Shante at the table.

"When Jarrod and I first got married, I was so dumb. I thought no woman would be attracted to him because I wasn't, at first. Then I saw a woman make a direct pass at him, and I almost lost it. I asked God to show me the women before they approach him."

"Well, did He?" Misha asked with much interest.

"Yes. Usually I can spot them when they walk in. When he travels, I have to trust God to give him a spirit of discernment so he can see the traps of the enemy. Temptation is everywhere. You have to pray as a wife of a minister."

Misha listened to Deandrea. She had to learn to deal with the burden of being married to Bernard Taylor. He was famous, and women were attracted to the money and fame. It didn't help that he was good-looking.

"I almost got in a fight with a woman at the church. She was all up in Matthew's face. I wanted to let her know she wasn't dealing with a little girl fresh off the farm," Misha laughed. "I guess it was the wrong thing to do. But, it felt good at the time."

"Misha, you can't go around fighting women over your husband. You have to pray," Shante said, hoping to give her some clear direction and godly advice.

"I know. I'm learning. But, it did feel good," she said, continuing to laugh.

"Was she scared?" Deandrea asked.

"I think I was more frightened than she was. I'm glad Matthew has security. You can talk a whole lot of junk with two big bodybuilders standing with you."

The three of them screamed with laughter. Misha was tiny and fragile looking. It was hard imagining her trying to fight anyone.

Shante sat at the table with her hands folded in front of her, relieved the tension had left the room. "Hey, is anybody hungry?"

"Tay, if you don't stop eating like that, you're going to be as big as a house before that baby is born," Deandrea remarked.

"I don't care. I'm hungry. I have to order room service. Y'all want anything?" she asked them.

"Maybe some fruit," Misha answered.

"Nothing for me," Deandrea said.

Shante reached for the phone, placing her room service order and charging it to her room, then sat the phone on its cradle.

"Shante, you're famous. Have you ever been approached by an admirer . . . of the opposite sex?" Misha asked.

Shante returned to her seat. "All the time. Men in the church are just as bad as the women. But, they approach you differently." Shante stood, lifted her shoulders and leaned into Misha. "Uh, Pastor Patrick, are you happy at home?" she said in a deep voice, mimicking the men that approached her. She sniffed. "You smell mighty fine. Is that husband of yours treating you right? Apparently not; he's not here. If you were my woman, I'll never let you out of my sight."

Deandrea and Misha laughed at Shante's crude imitation.

"Then there are the ones that use or misuse scripture to make a pass at you. Always talking about greeting you with a holy kiss. There is nothing holy about the kiss they want to give you."

"How does your husband deal with it?" Misha asked.

"When I tell him, it doesn't bother him. He usually takes it as a compliment that his wife is so fine, men still approach me. I haven't seen him get mad or jealous yet. Hopefully, he won't. He knows I love him and am committed only to him."

Deandrea and Misha nodded their heads in agreement. A knock at the door startled them. Shante beat Misha to the door. It was room service with their order. Shante reached for her food as soon as it was placed on the table. She lifted the cover off the plate and picked up her cheesesteak. Misha tipped the waiter and closed the door.

"Shante, you better stop eating like that," Deandrea said as Shante munched on her sandwich.

"I'm eating for two now. That's my excuse, and I'm going to stick with it and suck the life out of it for as long as I can."

That was her plan. Although Shante was a minister, people expect her to be perfect. Sometimes, she didn't feel as if people were seeing her as a preacher but a movie star. They wanted her to have the same characteristics as the latest theatrical princess. Her agent told her to watch her weight and get Botox injections to smooth out the lines around her eyes. Then there were the scars on her face she wanted Shante to see if she could have removed. But her scars were her ministry. Shante ministered to women who had been in abusive relationships like she had and the scars were the outward signs of her deliverance. She would never have them removed.

Misha ate the fruit salad she had in front of her. Deandrea reached for a fry off Shante's plate and put it in her mouth.

"I love my husband. I really do," Deandrea said as she sat back on the sofa. "Sometimes it's hard. I gave up everything for him." Her eyes shifted downward.

Shante felt bad for her. Deandrea always acted as if everything was perfect with her. Now, she realized Deandrea could turn it on and off at will.

Misha joined Deandrea on the sofa. They were back in the friend zone.

"I love my husband too. I know it can be hard," Misha added.

"You don't understand. Sometimes I feel like a single parent. He's never at home. We never spend time alone. The children barely know him." Tears filled Deandrea's eyes. She adjusted herself and continued. "I try to schedule time alone, but he always has something better to do—a meeting, a revival, a conference. It's never ceasing. I'm concerned about his health. I don't know how long he will be able to keep this up."

"It sounds like you are lonely," Shante said, trying to understand her situation.

"It's more than that. It's like he's forgotten he has a family until he needs us. We are the ones that stand when he introduces his family before he preaches. It's almost like he's saying 'These are my trophies, look at them.' When it is over, he puts us back on the shelves until he needs us again."

"It couldn't be that bad," Misha stated.

"You don't know the half of it. He used to tell me how beautiful and intelligent I am. We used to make time for each other. We could talk for hours about anything or nothing at all."

Misha walked back to the window. She folded her arms around her body and leaned against the wall. Her eyes seemed distant. It was the same look she had when she shook Pastor Edmunds's hand.

Deandrea continued her rant of the trials of Deandrea Fuller. Shante knew it was hard for her. Could Max feel the same way? Shante tried to give him lots of attention when she returned home. She prepared meals for them and left cooking instructions for Max before she left to preach. She wrote Max and the boys special notes, letting them know how much she loved them. She called them regularly when she was away. As soon as she stepped in the house from one of her trips, Max was there, waiting for her.

"You know, one day I got really frustrated and talked with an attorney," Deandrea confessed.

Shante snapped back to the conversation. "No, Dee, you didn't." She stopped eating and joined her on the sofa.

Deandrea continued, "I'm not going to do anything. That day, I only wanted to know my options. Jarrod and I have a lot of property, and I needed to find out where I stand if we ever came to that. I don't want to divorce him. I only wanted to know."

"Who has your ear?" Misha said out of the blue.

"What?" Deandrea questioned her.

"Who has your ear?" Misha walked boldly toward them. "Who have you been listening to? I'm not talking about the attorney. Somebody else has your ear. Who is it?" she asked fearlessly.

"You keep trying to push my buttons. You don't know what you're talking about." Deandrea rolled her eyes.

"That's how you know I'm telling the truth. Now, I ask you again, who has your ear?"

Misha stood her ground and didn't back down.

Deandrea twitched in her seat. She stood and paced the floor. "One day I was at the church. Jarrod was gone . . . again. One of his friends dropped by the church to see him. He invited me to lunch since Jarrod wasn't in. At first, I turned him down. But he was insistent. So I went."

"You're having an affair?" Shante gasped.

"No, girl. We only went to lunch. I had fun though. I have to admit it. It was like when Jarrod and I started dating. I missed that. He drove me back to the church, and I never saw him again."

"Is that it?" Misha asked. "Is that all you did?"

"Misha, if I didn't respect the anointing on your life, I probably would have cussed you out by now. But I know it's God." Deandrea walked back to the sofa and sat down. "He calls the house for Jarrod. When he's not there, we have a good conversation. I enjoy talking to him."

"That's dangerous territory. Remember, lust . . . then sin," Shante said.

"It's nothing like that. We only talk," Deandrea said, her mouth curved to a wide smile.

"Do you know how dangerous 'just talking' is? Talk allows you to become intimate in other ways before you step into a physical relationship," Misha added.

"Yes, Dee. That's how adultery starts, with conversation. You should cut it off, especially since it's Jarrod's friend."

"I did. I realized it was the wrong thing to do. Now, if Jarrod is not there and he calls, I don't even pick up the phone. I want to. I know if I did, I will hear compliments and will feel special when I get off the phone. Jarrod does not make me feel special. He doesn't compliment me anymore. He's gone all the time. We haven't had sex in months. He takes care of other people's families more than his own."

If Deandrea was expecting Shante and Misha to say it's okay for her to do a little creeping, she was dead wrong. Neither could condone such actions. This man was no friend of Jarrod's if he was so willing to come in his house and entertain his wife when he was gone.

Shante had so many questions she wanted to ask but was afraid to. Deandrea's situation was making her look at her relationship with Max in a different way. She never thought about Max cheating on her. Max had integrity. Listening to her friend, she began to wonder if this was God showing her how Max really felt.

She tried to focus on Deandrea's continuous whining. Frankly, Shante wished she would shut up. She could relate to Jarrod's ministry. They both were on the road a lot. She knew how draining it could be. Deandrea didn't understand.

Misha moved back to the sofa and wrapped her arm around Deandrea. Shante wasn't buying the pity party Deandrea was having. She was playing hard on Misha's sympathy.

"I wish he would realize that I need him too. He doesn't care," Deandrea cried.

"You don't care," Shante said.

"Yes, I do. If I didn't care, I probably would have divorced him a long time ago. I gave up everything to be with him. I had my own business, property, money and ministry when I met him. Now, it's all about him."

"No. It's all about you," Shante fired back.

"What's your problem?"

"I'm sitting here listening to you whine and complain about your life. Have you ever thought about how Jarrod feels when he comes off the road? Do you ever think about how tired he may be? What do you do to welcome him home?"

Misha sat quietly on the sofa not intervening in their conversation.

"Everybody can't be perfect like you and Max."

"Perfect? Perfect? How can you say something like that? You don't know what goes on in my house. You think we're perfect?"

"Look at the two of you. You have the perfect marriage, family and church. You don't have all the drama Jarrod and I have. He respects you. You guys knew each other for years before you got married. You still get along. He hasn't taken you . . . from you. So to me you are perfect."

Shante shook her head and walked away. Deandrea didn't know half of the story. She was on the outside looking into what she felt was the perfect world. She didn't realize even in their house, everything seemed out of control. But, Shante was not going to tell her that.

"Stop acting like a jealous little girl," Shante said to Deandrea.

"I'm not jealous of you. I want to be me, not Copastor—me."

"Shut up! Please shut the heck up," Shante shouted so loud the neighboring guests would probably complain.

Misha's hand flew to her mouth.

"Yeah, I said it, and I'm not taking it back. All you have done since you've been here is complain about Jarrod. You don't know what it feels like coming home after a tiring trip ministering the Gospel. It is draining being on the road with everyone pulling at you and making demands on your time and energy. When you get home, all you want to do is sleep for three days. But you can't because being home has its own issues. Jarrod is probably drained and tired, and he has to come home to your whining and complaining. If I had to listen to it, I'd talk over you too."

"What are y'all doing? Both of you are ganging up on me," Deandrea cried.

"You don't understand. Max and I are far from perfect. We have our problems like everyone else. Foot, we even had sex before we got married."

A loud gasp filled the room.

Shante rewound the words in her head. *Oh no, I didn't say what I just said . . . did I?*.

"Well, well, well, the famous Shante Patrick and her husband were busy with the hanky-panky before they were married," Deandrea said with a satisfied smile on her face. At last, misery had company.

20

"Shante, it's okay," Misha consoled her as she sat with her hands covering her mouth, a stunned look was on her face.

It pleased Deandrea that she was not the only one hiding something. God pushed that one right out of Shante's mouth. At least she and Jarrod waited until they got married to have sex. They wanted to engage in premarital sex, but they wanted to live what they preached even more. They didn't want to preach against fornication, leave the church, and shack up.

Shante wiped her face with her hands. It was out there. She might as well finish it. "Max asked me to go with him to D.C. to take the children to visit their grandparents for the summer," Shante said. She was overwhelmed and relieved at the same time that her secret was out. Misha escorted Shante back to the chair.

"It was a long drive back from D.C. We both were tired. He dropped me off at my house. After I took a nap, he called and invited me to dinner. We decided to eat takeout at his house."

"Why his house?" Misha asked.

"I lived out in the country. He was closer to restaurants. By the time I got there, he already had the food. Well, we ate dinner and watched a movie. It wasn't really romantic. We both were still tired. We had spent a couple of days with Dr. Yakenowa and his wife Suki."

"Dr. Tom Yakenowa, the neurosurgeon?" Misha asked.

"You know him?"

"He's my father-in-law's partner. Matthew's dad is a neurosurgeon in D.C."

"Oh my God, really? I think I may have met your father-in law while I was there. Is he a tall white guy?"

Deandrea hated to interrupt this family reunion, but she wanted to hear the rest of Shante's story. "So, Shante, how did it happen? I mean . . . You don't have to tell us if you don't want to." *But I hope you do.*

"Well, it was late. We were lounging on the sofa holding each other. I was about to leave, and Max said he wanted to give me something before I left. He reached into his pocket and pulled out the ring. That evening he proposed to me."

Misha had that look on her face again as Shante continued her story. Deandrea leaned on the sofa and crossed her legs. It was about to get good. God was getting ready to reveal something about Shante, just like He did for her. This could get interesting.

"So the two of you celebrated your engagement by . . . well . . . you know?" Deandrea urged Shante on.

"No. It wasn't like that." Shante walked to the table and sat down. "Well, I was about to leave. It was already late when he proposed. After that, I stayed another hour or so. Anyway, it was real late, and he didn't want me driving home that late at night. He asked me to stay.

"I had spent the night at his house numerous times. I didn't think about anything. He gave me one of his pajama shirts, and I went to Jonathan's room for the night. I don't know what happened. I couldn't sleep. I got up and was walking down the hallway to go to the den to watch TV. Apparently he couldn't sleep either. He heard me walking down the hall and came out of his room. He was wearing the pants to the shirt I was wearing. He didn't have on a shirt. Although the lights were dim, I could see every muscle in his well built body."

Misha didn't move. She still had that look on her face. She had completely zoned out. This concerned Deandrea. Misha had called her out. What was she getting ready to do to Shante? She could barely focus on Shante's confession for trying to figure out what Misha was going to do next.

"Well, he picked me up and carried me to his bed. I guess the rest is history. We spent a lot of time at each other's house that summer."

"Did you repent?" Misha said, finally coming out of her trance and staring intently at Shante.

"What?" Shante asked.

"Did you repent? You said you and your husband committed fornication. Did you repent?"

"Misha, we were planning our wedding and got married shortly after the boys came back home."

"Did you repent?" Misha did not back down on her question. Apparently Shante did not want to answer her. Misha stood directly in front of Shante. "If you and your husband don't repent, you will find your sin being manifested in your own house."

Shante's face went blank. Misha was not one to be played with. God spoke to her. She was anointed. Deandrea sat back waiting for the move of God.

"How can you say something like that? You can't curse me," Shante said.

"I'm not trying to curse you. The Lord says, if you and your husband don't repent for your sin, you will find it manifested in your own home."

Shante placed her hands on her hips and moved toward Misha. Deandrea jumped between them. She had to stop this before someone called the front desk.

"Ladies, let's calm down," she said.

"She doesn't know anything about me," Shante snapped. "I love my husband, and I know he loves me. He would never do anything like that to hurt me."

"I didn't say anything about your husband," Misha fired back.

"Shante, don't get too excited. Remember the baby," Deandrea said.

Shante released the breath she held and sat down. Deandrea faced her and said, "I don't think she meant it like you took it."

There was a brief silence.

"Y'all want anything to drink? I'm going to get some ice." Misha picked up the ice bucket and left the room without waiting for their reply. The air was tense in the room.

Deandrea sat in front of Shante. "You okay, girl?"

Shante looked at Deandrea. "Who is that girl?"

"I think she's a prophet. Do you see how she looks before she says anything? Jarrod gets that same blank look."

Shante took a slow, deep breath. "This is taking a lot out of me. She seems to know all about us. It's weird. Do you think God sent her here to correct us? I've got to speak to all those women tomorrow. Instead of studying and praying, I'm here with you guys, and I can't seem to leave. This is so weird. I've never seen anything like this before." She looked around the room. "I'm hungry. Do we have any of that food left?"

Shante walked to the tray on the cart near the door and began picking at the food left behind earlier. Misha entered the room carrying a couple of sodas and the ice bucket filled with ice. She walked past Shante and set her items on the coffee table.

"Anyone want ice? I got us some sodas out of the machine. Shante, I got you a caffeine-free drink." She handed the drink to Shante.

"Thank you," she said, reaching for the soda Misha handed her.

"You and your husband need to repent," Misha said again. She was not going to let this go.

Shante's eyes stretched. She set the soda on the cart and finished chewing the bread she had in her mouth. "Max and I got married. We love each other. You want me to repent for marrying him? I don't regret marrying him."

"Shante . . ." Deandrea raced between them again. She was trying to figure out what was the big deal. Misha was only telling her they needed to repent for the sin of fornication. Shante should know that.

"You need to tell your husband he needs to repent too," Misha said to her.

"Who are you to tell me what to say to my husband? You don't even know him," Shante said as loud and as firm as she could. The veins popped out of the side of her neck. "How can you judge me? You are the one who was pregnant before you got married, and it wasn't even your husband's baby. You said it yourself. So how can you judge me?"

"Shante!" Deandrea screamed.

The soda can perched on the tip of Misha's lip gave her a mannequin-like appearance. A lone tear rolled down her face. She lowered the can and placed it on the coffee table.

"You are not the person I thought you were," Misha said to Shante. "I looked up to you. I wanted to be as bold and confident as you. Not anymore. After I tell you this I want you, both of you, to leave my room." Misha could barely talk. Shante's words hurt her deeply.

"The school district I worked at in Atlanta hired a consultant to study ways to improve our school," Misha started. "He was a white guy and had the most gorgeous blue eyes. He kept asking me out." She tried hard to fight the tears from falling. Deandrea put her arm around her shoulders. Misha shrugged it off and walked to the other side of the room. "I kept feeling like there was something weird about him. To make a long story short, he raped me. He put a gun to my head and pulled the trigger three times, and thanks be to God who is my protector, it didn't go off."

"Oh no . . ." Deandrea shouted.

"Misha, I'm sorry. I didn't—" Shante began.

"Don't . . ." Misha waved her hand for them to be silent. "I guess this is what you want to hear. When I found out that I was pregnant, I almost had an abortion, but Courtney was a part of me and I couldn't do it. I'm so blessed to have found Matthew. He didn't look down on me or judge me like others did. A pregnant single minister, it was the talk of the town. God ordained him to be Courtney's father. So much so, they look and act alike. You even noticed it. Now, if the two of you don't mind, please leave my room. Close the door behind you."

Misha walked into the bedroom and closed the door, leaving Shante and Dee standing alone in the front room.

"Let me go talk to her." Deandrea walked to the bedroom door and knocked. "Misha, let me in. Let's talk." There was no response.

Shante cried uncontrollably. Deandrea's mind was jumbled. She couldn't leave Misha here alone, knowing she was dealing with reliving the rape. But she had to minister to Shante who was weighted down with guilt for what she said to Misha. Deandrea hugged Shante.

"I didn't mean anything by it. She was raped? I didn't know," Shante's speech was broken by her sobs. "Dee, what are we doing here? It's not by chance the three of us are here. What's going on?"

"I don't know, Tay. I don't know." They hugged each other again. "Come on, let's give her some time alone. I'll talk with her later."

The women exited the room, hoping God would answer their query soon. Why were they there? What exactly was God trying to tell them?

21

"Honey, do you want me to come and get you or will you try to catch a flight?"

Matthew's voice usually soothed Misha. It was not working now. Forget the conference. She wanted to go home now. How could she listen to Shante tomorrow? She didn't have any respect for either of them. They were old bitter women, and she was not going to let them contaminate her mind against her husband or their marriage.

"No, I think I will stay until Saturday morning. I ran into First Lady Moore. I wanted to talk to her before I leave. I can stay until the conference ends."

"Okay. Well, if you need me, just call," Matthew said.

"I will. I love you. Good night, Babe."

Misha hung up the phone. The fight in her welled up in her belly. She was not going to let these two run her away from the conference. She came here on a mission, and she wasn't leaving until she had ministered to First Lady Moore.

Misha never imagined Shante and Deandrea would act the way they do. They seemed so together. Yet, they had more issues than she did. She thought their lives would ooze with an anointing so great, no sin could overtake them. She was wrong. "If these are the women that are leading the church," she said, "then, God, we have a problem."

It baffled Misha how she could tell them about the rape. It wasn't anything she willingly told anyone. She thought she had gotten over what happened to her. Matthew helped her deal with the nightmares and flashbacks that would attack her day and night. Often she cried, wishing the tears would wash the feel of her rapist's touch from her body. How could she have allowed them to force her to relive that painful event over again? They kept pushing her and pushing her. She hoped they felt as bad as she did right now. She wanted them to feel the pain.

Misha was tired of crying about the same thing over and over. The hurt, pain and memories of that horrible day repeatedly flood her mind. She had to do something to change her focus. Television did not help. She tried to read her Bible, but her concentration was lost. How could she allow Shante and Deandrea to take control of her emotions and make her lose her joy?

She should have attended the conference instead of hanging out with them. At least she would have some Word in her to focus on. She didn't even have a CD of one single service.

Tomorrow was a new day. She would overload her mind with the Word, and all this pain will go away.

There were so many images running through her mind, Misha could not sleep. She looked at the clock. It was late, too late to call Matthew. The sound of the phone ringing would wake Courtney. Then he would be up all night, trying to get her back to sleep. Misha rolled off the bed and knelt. She had to pray for peace.

After attempting to pray, Misha's body trembled with nervousness. She was afraid to go to sleep, afraid of the nightmares that may come. Why did they have to bring up that horrible time in her life? She slipped on jeans and a sweatshirt and headed downstairs toward the hotel convenience store. She didn't really want anything but peace of mind. Hoping a change of scenery would help, she left her room. Misha turned the corner toward the store and ran into Deandrea.

"Misha. I didn't expect to see you here," Deandrea said.

That was the last person Misha wanted to see. "I wanted to get some air. Excuse me." Misha quickly moved past her.

"Misha, wait," Deandrea said.

Misha no longer wanted anything to do with Deandrea. Her father-in-law was wrong. The conference was not good for her. It had been an emotional roller coaster, and she wanted to get off. Three days was too long to be on this ride. She had to get down to business. Tomorrow, she was going to find First Lady Moore and do thus saith the Lord and be on her way.

"Misha, wait," Deandrea cried out again. She pulled Misha's arm. Misha flipped around with such rage in her eyes, Deandrea released her arm and stepped back, fearing Misha would hit her. "Hey, I'm sorry." She lifted her hands.

"About what?"

"About what happened in the room. Shante and I didn't know. Shante . . . Well, she didn't mean anything by what she said. She was on the defense. Do you understand? She was trying to protect herself. I understood what you were saying to her. She never answered your question. I guess we both know what that means. She needs us. We need each other."

"Really?" Misha said sarcastically. She felt the only one she herself needed was God. She did not need the two of them. Misha turned and walked away.

"Why are you here?" Deandrea asked. "Why did God send you here? How can you minister angry?"

Misha stopped. Deandrea was right. She could not be effective in ministry angry. Angry ministers beget angry parishioners. Misha learned that from experience. She had to get this negative emotion out of her.

Deandrea walked up to her and whispered, "How can you minister hurt?"

Immediately, the tears started to flow down Misha's face. She felt weak and felt her legs betray her. Her body fell to the floor. She felt as if all the air had been sucked out of her body.

Deandrea reached under Misha's arms and lifted her, dragging her to a nearby chair. Misha's limp body lay laggardly in the chair. Deandrea pulled out her cell phone.

"Shante, come to the lobby quick. Misha has passed out." Deandrea hung up the phone and stood over Misha and wiped her forehead until Shante arrived by her side.

"What happened?" Shante asked.

"Help me get her to her room," Deandrea answered.

Misha felt the two of them lift her body. She was afraid to open her eyes, afraid it wouldn't be Shante, Deandrea, or Matthew. The thought of that man dragging her body and trying to kill her took over her mind again.

They entered the elevator. Deandrea pressed the button to take them to their floor. They heard the beep, but Misha heard the click of the trigger. As the elevator moved, she heard it over and over. Misha flung her arms wildly, trying to fight the man off her body. If she was going to die, it wouldn't be without a fight.

"Misha, open your eyes. It's us!" Shante screamed.

Deandrea grabbed Misha's hands, trying to control them before she or they got hurt. "In the name of Jesus, Satan, release her," Deandrea prayed.

Misha's eyes felt glued by her tears. He had her arms, holding her down. She threw her legs in the air. She had to get away from him. She felt him on her body, touching her in places reserved for her husband. She felt the barrel of the gun on the side of her face. She saw his face full of hatred and lust. She had to fight. She yanked her body from side to side, trying to get away from him.

"Misha, open your eyes. It's me . . . Shante and Dee. You're safe. You're with us . . ."

Misha slowly opened her eyes. She looked at Shante and Deandrea. She looked around her. She was in an elevator. Deandrea was holding her hands and praying. Her body went limp.

Shante and Deandrea lifted Misha's body and helped her to her room. They placed her on the simple green quilt covering the bed. Deandrea ran to the bathroom and returned with a wet towel. She placed it on Misha's forehead. "Misha, wake up. You're safe," Deandrea said.

Misha opened her eyes. She felt as if she had been running a marathon. Her chest hurt. She was tired and weak, but she garnered enough strength to sit up against the headboard.

"Shante, give her some water," Deandrea said.

Misha looked around the room. She was in her suite. "What happened?"

"You fainted," Shante answered. She handed her the cup of water. "How are you feeling now? Should we take you to the emergency room?"

"No. No. I'm fine, I think." Misha removed the towel from her forehead. "Thanks for getting me to my room. You can leave now."

"You want to talk about it?" Deandrea asked.

Misha shook her head. "I'm fine now," She couldn't talk to them. She thought she had built up enough walls to protect her from the memory. Somehow, they seem to slip in when she least expected it.

"We can't leave you alone. At least let us pray for you," Shante requested.

"Okay," Misha agreed. She placed her face in her hands.

"Release it. Release it right now in the name of Jesus," Shante prayed.

Misha could feel the tingle of Shante's words all over her body. She felt herself getting weaker and stronger at the same time. Her mouth was moving, but nothing was coming out. Deandrea and Shante prayed, but their faces were blocked by Misha's tears.

"They tried to kill me. They wanted me dead. They wanted me dead," Misha blurted out as her body slid off the bed and sank to the floor.

Deandrea and Misha sat next to her with their backs against the bed. Shante continued praying.

"Who tried to kill you?" Deandrea asked.

"Everybody; my family, my doctor, my church, that man, everybody," Misha said. Strangely she felt calm. She took the tissue Shante handed her and blew her nose. She accepted another tissue and wiped her eyes. "They all thought they could kill me. They didn't know that I serve a true and living God."

Misha couldn't hold anything back. She sniffed and the words flowed. She was unable to stop their release. "My mom had me when she was over forty. You would think she would love me since I was her first child. But I never felt loved. She was mean and evil. Her beatings went far beyond a simple spanking." She gave a slight laugh. "A year after I was born, she had the son she always wanted. She loved my younger brother Justin. Many times he was my savior. We are real close. I spent my childhood hearing her tell me I would never be anything. All I wanted to do was get away from her—from Atlanta."

"Misha, I'm so sorry," Deandrea said.

"It wasn't your fault. Our relationship is better now, thanks to my husband. But as if that wasn't enough, I went in the ministry under a pastor I thought was great. He kicked me out of the church and called me a witch because of my gift. Then he and my ex tried to destroy my reputation and attempted to make me lose my job."

Misha blew her nose again, sniffed and continued. "Then I was diagnosed with cancer and was told I couldn't have children." She smiled. "God had a different plan. I still don't understand why He chose the way He did. But, He had the perfect plan."

"What happened?" Shante asked.

"Well, I told you about the school consultant. He was attacking one of my students when I walked in on them. I fought him, and my student ran off to get help. He pulled a gun on me. He beat me up pretty bad. He tried to shoot me, but the gun didn't work. Praise God. I had to go through the healing process by myself. No one in the church came by to see me, even when I had cancer. I couldn't understand that. I was a worker in the church. I helped so many people. But when I needed help, no one was there for me.

"When I found out I was pregnant, I thought it couldn't get any worse. I was determined to go on and be all that God wanted me to be, with or without help from family or the church. Then things began to change. I met Matthew when I was six months pregnant. He accepted me for who I was. He accepted Courtney. He was there at her birth. He cut the umbilical cord." Misha smiled and scooted up.

"Let me tell you how God blessed me. I filed a suit against the school, the consulting firm and the agency that did the background check on that man. I won all three. Courtney has a multimillion dollar trust fund, and I won a couple million myself." She laughed. "God had a plan after all. Now I don't have to work for anyone but Him. It gives me the ability to go where God sends me."

"You are a prophet," Deandrea said.

Misha shook her head. "I don't know about that. I do know a lot about people that I should not know.

Sometimes I don't understand the words that come out of my mouth. I have to be obedient. But I can't escape those memories."

"Misha, look at me," Shante said. "You see these scars on my face?" Shante pointed to the long scar that extended from her left brow to her cheek and the smaller one on the side of her lip. "My ex-husband tried to kill me. He used to beat me unconscious. I used to have nightmares too. I was paranoid. I thought he was stalking me. For a time, he did. God delivered me. He's in jail now. Not for what he did to me—for stealing money and credit cards. I'm a witness it will get better, but you can't hold all that in. That's how it controls you."

"I'm sorry, Shante. I didn't know how you got those scars. See, God doesn't tell me everything," Misha smiled. Then she hung her head. "The parents of the guy who raped me want to take my child now."

"What?" Shante and Deandrea said in unison.

"How could they do that? Do you want me to ask Max about it?" Shante asked.

"No. Our attorney is handling it. He said they can't do that. They are trying to block Matthew from adopting Courtney. My in-laws think it's all about money. I'll give them whatever they want just to leave us alone."

"Don't give them anything. If you do, you will never get rid of them. They will spend it and come back for more. You've got to fight it," Deandrea said.

"I know. We are going to fight. They are not taking our child. Matthew was ordained to be Courtney's father."

The trio sat silently taking in all that had happened.

"Misha, as you heal, be careful that you deal with the residue of abuse," Shante said.

"I don't understand," Misha said.

"Well, God began to minister to me about the residue of abuse. Behaviors, habits and attitudes I had because of the abuse. One of those was living in secret."

"Secret?" Misha didn't understand.

Shante stopped her story and sighed. "Yes, secrets. Sneaking around in relationships. Not wanting anyone to know anything about me. Being overly private. I almost lost my husband because of it." She sighed again. "Secrets," she said in a low faint voice. "I thought I had been delivered. I pulled Max into my secret world, leading both of us to sin. God, forgive me. We need to repent."

"God will forgive you," Deandrea added. "If He can forgive me for all I have done to Jarrod, He can certainly forgive you."

"What did you do?" Misha asked wondering how many more secrets Deandrea could possibly have.

"You already know. I treated Jarrod pretty bad when we met. I had that strong-black-woman-and-I-don't-need-a-man-to-give-me-anything attitude. When I get stressed, it comes back out. I'm here because of it. I realize that now. I thought I had been delivered. Yet, sister-girl keeps showing up."

Deliverance was in this place tonight. Misha could feel it. All three of them had issues that had been keeping them in bondage. Tonight, they were able to release them. They had been delivered from secrets, hurt and pain.

A cool breeze swept throughout the room as the three of them sat side by side on the floor, leaning against the bed. No one wanted to move. They simply wanted to allow God to move.

"Misha, how does your husband feel about the rape?" Deandrea asked. "You don't have to tell us if you don't want to."

"We never really talk about it," Misha said. "When we met, I showed him the newspaper articles and told him how I wanted to move on with my life and raise Courtney the best way I can."

"You guys have to talk about it." Shante adjusted her body to face Misha.

"Sometimes, I think Matthew is uncomfortable talking about it. Everybody thinks he is talkative and outgoing. In reality, he's very quiet. With everything that's going on now, we need to talk. When we start, we usually end up making love instead of talking. I guess it's our way of avoiding the subject."

"You and your husband are going to have to learn how to sit down and talk with each other," Deandrea said. "Every problem cannot be solved by having sex."

"And you and your husband?" Misha added.

"I know. I know. I need to take my own advice. I will when I get home."

Tell her to call him now. He's up praying, Misha heard in her spirit. "Dee, you should call him now."

"Misha, it's . . ." She looked at the clock on the night-stand. "It's 3:12 in the morning. I can't call him now."

"Call him. He's up praying. He'll be glad to hear from you."

Deandrea gave Misha a quizzical look. She pulled her cell phone out of her pocket and punched in the number. She walked out of the room while the phone was still ring-ing. A few seconds later Dee peeked her head in the door. "You were right. He said he was up praying. I'm going to the room now and talk to my husband. Are you going to be okay?" she asked Misha.

"I'm fine. Thank you for everything." Misha got up and hugged Deandrea.

Shante didn't move from the floor. "You're a prophet-ess," she said to Misha.

"I am who God says I am."

"You're a prophet. How did you know her husband was up praying?"

"The Holy Spirit."

"That's why you've had so many problems in your ministry. That's how you knew your bishop's secret. It made him uncomfortable—like it made me. He had to do something to destroy you and make your word ineffective. It wasn't you. It was the anointing on your life that intimidated him."

Misha laughed. If she only knew what he's up to now, she may think another way. She held her hand out to Shante, who grabbed it and stood. Misha smiled.

"What's so funny?" Shante asked.

"Bishop has been trying to get me to come back to the church. He's only doing it because I'm married to Bernard Taylor. He doesn't want me. He wants Bernard Taylor."

"How do you know that's true? He may want to apologize to you. You said he was uncovered in a public way. Maybe he's trying to apologize to you in front of the very people who witnessed you being thrown out of the church."

"That's the same thing Matthew said."

"Well, think about it. No, pray about it. Don't just brush him off. If God is working on you, Dee and me, he could be working on that bishop too. The ball is in your court. You have to decide what you are going to do." Shante threw her arms in the air and stretched. "It's late. I better go," They walked to the door. "When I learned to forgive, I found out I could face the enemy and feel sorry for him. I no longer had to hide from him. I could face him head-on and not fear what might happen or how he tries to use me. Forgiveness has a way of bringing healing into every area of your life."

Shante left the room. Misha leaned against the door. Forgive Bishop? She thought she had already forgiven him. She still remembered the things he did to her and said about her. How could she walk into his church, knowing all the things that she knew about him? She tried to warn him, and he brushed her aside and belittled her and called her out of her name.

Suddenly, she heard herself. She was still angry. There were things within her that she needed to forgive. She vowed before she went to bed she would pray for God to help her forgive anyone and anything that allowed her to walk in unforgiveness. She smiled. Her father-in-law was right. This conference was good for her after all.

22

Shante lay on the bed with her legs propped up by one of the pillows. Her phone was perched between her ear and shoulder as she listened to Max talk. She only had about six hours of sleep. Under normal circumstances, this would have been more than enough. Now, she could use another six hours. It could be the baby or the fact that she was getting older. Whichever it was, she had to get up, pray and study for her sermon this evening.

"The polls show I'm in the lead. This has been a difficult race," Max said.

Shante tried hard to focus on the conversation, but she was exhausted. The conversation last night was intense. However, she, Misha and Deandrea had a breakthrough. They had issues that took each other to sort through.

Misha was right; she and Max had to repent. She would talk to him when she got home. She couldn't bring up something so deep with him now. He was excited about being in the lead in the race for councilman. She couldn't burst his bubble by talking about sins of the past. It was not that serious. They did get married.

Last night was the first time she realized that she had drawn Max into her abuse. She tried to keep their relationship secret for a long time. She learned how to keep secrets when her ex-husband was abusing her. She didn't want anyone to find out what was happening in their house. She became an expert at excuses for fear it may ruin the way people thought about them. She tried to uphold their elite middle-class lifestyle and gave the appearance that everything was fine. She learned to cover up the evidence of abuse by makeup and hiding. No one ever knew until she left him.

Shante thought she had been delivered from her secret lifestyle. She still hung onto a few secrets, though. The summer of passion she spent with Max was only a residue of the abuse she still clung to. They knew it was wrong, even when it felt right. They convinced themselves they were getting married anyway and it was okay. They even had a secret ceremony with only the two of them where they recited the wedding vows to make themselves feel better about what they were doing.

Shante didn't realize it then, but that summer, she and Max were out of the will of God. They had spent the entire summer sneaking around with each other—living their secret life. It amazed her that two pastors could easily walk in sin and not feel guilty. For years, she had ministered to others regarding fornication, and she ended up doing it herself. How could she condemn them when she did the same thing?

"How are you and the baby?" Max asked, drawing her back into the conversation.

"We are doing fine. We wish we were home."

Shante ended her call with Max and quickly fell asleep. The following morning she woke up early and ordered food from room service for herself and Deandrea.

Shante sat down to eat when Deandrea walked sluggishly from her room with her hair sticking straight up in the air as if she was Buckwheat's twin sister. "What are you eating?" she asked Shante, who was hunched over her plate.

"I ordered enough for both of us."

Deandrea reached for the coffee pot and poured the dark brew into a cup. She pulled out a chair and sat. Her eyes were weak with big puffy circles under them. Shante was afraid to ask her what happened with Jarrod.

"What time did you go to bed?" Shante asked.

"About five," Deandrea said with a wide smile. "Jarrod and I talked a long time. I think we are beginning to understand each other."

"That's good. Looks as if everything is going to work out."

"Girl, if he had been here last night, I would just be getting some sleep now. We haven't talked like that in a long time. We laughed. He was doing his impersonations again. We talked about everything but the church. He even apologized to me, and I think it's real this time. I can't wait to get home. He said he was taking all of next week off so we can spend some time together." Deandrea reached for a piece of toast.

"God is working in all of our lives. Last night was something, wasn't it?"

"We all needed it. We had to release all those things we have been keeping inside for years. I feel great. I know God is in this. He uncovered things that had been covered for years. God won't allow us to hold this stuff in anymore. He's making us whole."

"Amen, sister. I think we all needed it." Shante took a swallow of her orange juice. "Hey, Max called. He said the polls have him in the lead in this election."

For the first time in this trip, Deandrea seemed more interested in someone other than herself. "That's fantastic. I have to call and congratulate him." Deandrea raced to her phone that sat in its charging cradle.

Shante smiled. This was the friend she knew. She always had a way of encouraging people and making them believe they could do anything. Shante sat listening to the brief conversation on the speakerphone. When Deandrea hung up, her phone rang. It was her husband. She held the phone to her ear and picked up a muffin with her other hand; then she turned and walked into her room, kicking the door closed behind her.

There was a knock at the door. Shante walked to open it, hoping it was not Misha wanting to go to the morning session. She looked through the peephole and saw her daughter.

"Oh my goodness," she said as she pulled open the door. "Camille, what are you doing here?"

"Hi, Mom! Surprise!" Camille walked into the room wearing her pink city coat and gray slacks.

"Camille? I wasn't expecting you here. Why didn't you tell me you were coming?"

"I thought I would surprise you." They embraced each other. Camille walked to the center of the room and pulled off her coat, flinging it onto the coffee table. "Mom, look at you. Why aren't you dressed? It's almost lunchtime. I thought we could get some lunch. I know you want to have the rest of the afternoon to prepare for your sermon."

Deandrea walked out of her room and screamed when she saw Camille. She ran to embrace Shante's younger twin. "Camille, Shante didn't tell me you were coming."

"I didn't tell her," Camille replied, smiling.

Deandrea spotted the large pear-shaped ring on Camille's finger, and she screamed again as she lifted her hand. "Look at this rock! That Aaron has good taste. I know you can't wait to get married."

"Actually, we decided to postpone the wedding."

Shante stopped chewing the muffin in her mouth. She quickly swallowed and said, "What do you mean postponed."

"We talked about it, and I wanted to have my little sister or brother at the wedding. So we are going to get married in the summer or fall. We haven't decided on a date yet. But it will be after you have the baby."

Shante was relieved. That sounded reasonable to her . . . until it hit her—*Camille doesn't want her pregnant mother in her wedding. She's embarrassed.* She had thought Camille was more mature than that.

"As much as I wanted a brother or sister, I'm not going to miss having him at my wedding. Aaron didn't want to change it. I think he's mad right now. He'll get over it." Camille flung her hand in the air and walked to the table and picked up a strawberry and put it in her mouth.

Shante shook her head. Camille was spoiled. Now she was acting selfish. She had to learn that marriage was a compromise. She'd obviously made up her mind, and it sounded as if she didn't discuss it further with Aaron. Shante suddenly realized how Aaron must feel having someone making an important decision about his life without discussing it with him. She had to speak with Camille privately.

Noticing the stunned look on Shante's face, Deandrea walked into her room to get dressed.

"Camille, I will talk to you later about this. Are you sure this is what you want?"

Camille sat in the chair next to Shante. "I'm sure, Mom. I'm so excited."

Shante gazed at her child. Camille was not saying something. She was going to have to pray before she spoke with her.

"Sorry I can't stay. I've got sound check. I'll be back in an hour or so," Deandrea said when she entered the room a short time later. She slid her arm in her jacket and headed for the door.

"I've got to study for my message tonight. Before you go, will you show Camille how to get to the mall?"

"You trying to get rid of me?" Camille asked.

"No. I haven't had time to study yet. I need to go before the Lord. Why don't you guys call Misha to go with you? She can help you pick out something for me to wear tonight."

"That's a good idea." Deandrea made the call, and within a few minutes, Misha was at the door. Shante introduced her to Camille; then the group left the room.

Relieved she was now alone, Shante had to go before the Lord. She didn't know what she was going to preach. She thought she had the perfect sermon, but things had changed. What she really wanted to do was take a nap. She looked at the clock. If she took an hour's nap, she still had enough time to study. It sounded like a plan to her. She headed for her bed.

23

Deandrea, Misha and Camille walked through the lobby of the hotel. They were greeted by the many passing ladies with conference bags hanging from their shoulders.

"I'm so excited about Mom being pregnant. I always wanted a brother or sister," Camille said.

Deandrea wished Shante would be as excited about the baby as Camille. If it were her, she would be dancing on the rooftop. She wanted another baby—just one this time. Now that she and Jarrod had made up and were back on good terms, they could give it a try. They would have that talk when she got home.

Deandrea couldn't wait to get home. If she hadn't told Pastor Edmunds she would sing, she would probably be on the road right now. This time away from Jarrod had been good for both of them. They needed a break from each other. She needed time for herself, and he needed time to be a father.

When she gets back home, they will be in the mood to be each other's spouse . . . with all the benefits. Deandrea wondered if she had the time to go buy something sexy for Jarrod. He already said he wanted to see her in something sexy, but then he wanted it off. That could also be arranged.

Deandrea waved good-bye to Misha and Camille and headed toward the main conference hall. She stepped through the door and spotted the thousands of chairs in the empty hall. She couldn't believe tonight she would be performing there. This was the largest space she ever performed in.

She walked to the stage and spotted a man giving directions to the band.

"Excuse me. I'm Dee Fuller. I'm here for sound check."

"Good to meet you, Pastor Fuller. Pastor Edmunds told me you would be here. I'm Craig the music director. What are you singing? We can play anything."

"I think I'll sing that new CeCe Winans song."

"Okay," Craig nodded his head in approval. "We know that one. A girl in our church sings it too." He handed her a microphone, and Deandrea walked to the center of the stage. She nodded to him to begin.

Deandrea stopped singing. The music was not right. It was as if they were in two different keys.

"It's an A minor," Craig said.

The music sounded a little weird to her. She didn't need all these musicians around her. What she wanted was a piano and for them to let her do her thing.

"Can you bring me a piano?" she asked Craig.

He and two other men rolled a baby grand piano onto the stage. Deandrea sat on the cushioned bench in front of it. She placed her cell phone beside her and pressed the record button, then she bent her head and prayed, "God what should I sing? That first song isn't working. I want you and only you to be glorified here tonight." She placed her hands on the black and white keys in front of her and massaged them until a song began to form.

It had been a long time since she had played anything other than Gospel music. She moved her fingers back and forth while the classical song began to soothe her spirit. The sound resonated through the large room. The echo wrapped around the room and into her ear, sending her into the presence of the Lord. Deandrea had been in many conferences, both preaching and singing, but nothing like this. The thought of it made her stomach quiver. But the music relaxed her shaking nerves.

Deandrea felt alone with her music now. She could feel it. The beats, although scattered and erratic, sent peace throughout her soul. Suddenly she heard a Gospel tune melting its way into her Chopin. Like a spiritual mix that could only be construed by a divine deejay, the rhythms collide and come together in a way she had never heard before. She opened her mouth and allowed the Holy Spirit to use her.

"Whoa, that's deep. Show me how you did that," Craig asked Deandrea when she concluded her song.

"It's a classical-Gospel mix." It was all she could say. She wished she could show it to him. She had been taken away by the Holy Spirit. Thank goodness she recorded it. She could listen to it in the room so she could get the music in her head before she performed tonight.

"Pastor, that's all the time we have for your sound check. Everything should be fine tonight. Do you have any questions?" Craig asked.

"No, thank you, Craig." Deandrea shook his hand and walked out of the room toward the mall. She was going to pick up something for Jarrod and hopefully run into Camille and Misha. She figured Shante didn't need her in the room while she studied.

Deandrea plowed her way through the crowded mall. Her hands shook at the sight of the large number of women carrying conference bags. When Shante invited her, she thought it was a small local conference, not an international one. The sight of the people minding their own business was making her nervous. Many of these people were the same people whose eyes would be focused on her, and only her, tonight. They would have great expectations of her. She held her belly to keep it from trembling. What a great assignment.

Deandrea finally reached the lingerie store and entered to find something special for her homecoming. She wanted to believe Jarrod was sincere this time. He sounded repentant on the phone. This time, she believed, he would pay more attention to her and the children. On the phone last night, he listened to her like he used to do when they were dating. The conversation was fun and enlightening. Jarrod had found out things about the children he never knew. Now he understood why she said R. J. was just like him. His son had the very same humorous personality and his daughter sang all the time. Simple things he should have known. He now knew what he was missing.

Deandrea's phone sounded. It was Misha. She tapped the phone to answer it.

"Have you finished your sound check?" Misha asked.

"I have, and I'm in the lingerie store. I'll wait here for you."

Deandrea had let time slip by as she tried to find the perfect lingerie for her return home. She didn't want anything too stank. She needed something so sexy, Jarrod would want to rip it off her right away. She wanted to give him what he asked for. She took her time looking at the racks of clothing until Misha and Camille joined her.

It was nearing dinnertime when they decided to find a restaurant. They went to the mall food court and sat at the small round table.

"I better call Shante and see if she wants something to eat," Deandrea said. "Too many people would recognize her if she came down before she preaches tonight."

"Mom doesn't usually eat before she preaches. She'll probably eat after service," Camille volunteered.

Deandrea had forgotten Shante had a nervous stomach before she preached and didn't eat until after service. She placed her phone in her purse again.

"Ladies, it's late. Why don't we just get something to go, and that way, we can get some rest before service."

Camille and Misha agreed. Deandrea was relieved. She didn't know why she was so nervous. Her legs were shaking. Was it the shear size of the event or the fact that she came here for one reason and God changed it? She had to remember she was singing for the glory of the Lord, not for the approval of people. It was her desire to usher the attendees into the presence of the Lord by God using her ministry. They purchased their food and headed for their rooms.

Deandrea and Camille stepped into the room in time to see Shante stuffing a large barbecue rib into her mouth. Camille blinked. Deandrea's mouth flew open.

"It's about time y'all got back. They'll be here in about forty-five minutes to get us," she said, barbecue sauce dripping from the corners of her mouth. "What?"

"Mom, you're eating before you preach." Camille was shocked.

"Strange, isn't it? I was starving so I ordered room service. Y'all want some?" Shante held out a rib to them.

"No," Camille shook her head and held up her hand. "I better go take a shower." She walked into Shante's room with her hands loaded with the items she purchased at the mall.

"I need a camera," Deandrea laughed at the sight of Shante with her head in her plate. Her hair was still wrapped in a black silk scarf, and she was dressed in her robe. "Have you finished your sermon?"

"All finished. You sure you don't want any of these ribs. They brought me too much."

"No. You enjoy it. I'm going to get dressed."

Deandrea walked into her room and began undressing. She was so nervous she was about to pee in her clothes. She peeped into the other room at Shante who seemed relaxed. How did she do it? Deandrea held her hands out in front of her. They trembled. Would she be able to play the piano tonight? She placed her hands on her hips. She was being ridiculous. She had performed many times. Tonight should not be any different. Thinking a shower would help her to relax, she walked into her bathroom.

The warm water of the shower trailed down her body, taking paths only directed by its own impulses in a relentless effort to calm Deandrea's nerves. Her cell rang. She stepped out of the shower and wrapped the large towel around her body. She smiled when she saw Jarrod's name on her phone. "Hello."

"Hey, baby. I just wanted to see how you were doing before you sing tonight. Don't be nervous and do what you do. The Lord's got you," he said.

"Thank you. I was kind of nervous."

Just hearing Jarrod's voice this time calmed her nerves. She placed her phone on speaker and moved the towel around her body, removing the remaining droplets of water. Jarrod always knew how to minister to her. Listening to him pray for her while she dressed was exactly what she needed.

This time away from Jarrod and the kids showed Deandrea how the enemy could step in and influence the decisions in her life. She had to repent for allowing herself to be entertained by the messages the enemy was sending her. Yet, in all her rebelliousness and disobedience, God showed up in her situation and brought healing in her marriage. Now, her feelings for her husband had returned. She was excited about seeing him again. The anticipation masked the anxiety she had about performing. Now, all she had to do was sing this one song, and she could get up early in the morning and go home to her husband and children.

***

The escorts from the church arrived on time and walked with Shante, Deandrea, Misha and Camille to the green room to await the start of the service. Deandrea placed the earphones in her ears and pressed the audio replay. Her fingers moved to match the song she was listening to.

Deandrea hoped no one in the room could tell how nervous she was. Was she ready for this? For years now she had been praying for her own ministry, her own identity. Now the spotlight was on her. Never mind the audience was there to hear Shante. She would be in the spotlight before Shante. Very few, if any, of those people knew her husband. After tonight, they would know her. There was only one thing she needed to do—stop worrying and glorify God.

There was a knock on the door, and a young man escorted Deandrea, Camille and Misha to the side of the stage. She stood behind the thick black curtain waiting to be introduced. She removed the earplugs from her ears and handed them and her cell phone to Camille. Then she moved closer to the edge of the curtain as she listened to Pastor Edmunds introduce her.

"Give a big God Bless You to Copastor Deandrea Fuller."

Deandrea walked out on the stage and greeted Pastor Edmunds with a hug. He passed the microphone to her. She walked to the center of the stage and said the well-worn introductory statement, "Praise the Lord, everybody. Somebody praise the Lord in this place."

The audience stood and applauded her. Deandrea smiled, delighted that the audience acted as if they knew her. A rush of adrenaline flowed through her body as she sat down on the bench in front of the piano and place the microphone on the stand at her side.

Deandrea allowed the Holy Spirit to take over her once again as she began to drum her fingers across the keys. She didn't know what happened after that. It was as if she had an out-of-body experience. She remembered singing and playing the piano, nothing else. She looked around the stage. She was sitting next to Camille, who was fanning her. The musicians were still playing and people were praising God all around the building.

Next to her sat First Lady Edmunds who was in tears. Pastor Edmunds sat next to her, but he seemed distant and unconcerned. He stood and walked to the center of the stage, motioning to the musicians. The music slowed.

Stray voices shouted, "Hallelujah," "Praise Him" and "Thank you, Lord." There were faint sounds of women crying. Deandrea could not remember the words she sang. Yet, she felt calm and peaceful, as if a weight had been lifted off her. Camille handed her a glass of water. She took a sip as she listened to Pastor Edmunds give Shante a glorious introduction.

Shante walked onto the stage with a big smile on her face and waved to the crowd who were on their feet. Only Shante could make maternity clothing look fashionable. There was a loud roar from the audience as she took the microphone from Pastor Edmunds and hugged him. She whispered in his ear. He laughed and walked off the stage.

"That's my girl, Copastor Fuller, a mighty woman of God. I invited her here. If I had known she was going to show out like she has tonight, I would have left her at home." The audience laughed at her joke. "You know you don't take your friends to job interviews and you don't take them when . . . you . . . have . . . to preach," she said slowly as she opened her Bible that sat on the large podium in front of her. The audience laughed with her at everything she said. She knew how to work her audience.

"I want to thank Pastor and First Lady Edmunds for inviting me here. It has been a life-changing conference for me and my friends. If this conference has blessed you, stand to your feet and give the visionaries of this blessed event a great big thank you for putting together such a wonderful event."

After the audience sat down, Shante continued. "I want to introduce you to some special people with me. You have already met Copastor Fuller. Didn't she bless our soul?" Shante waited for the audience to finish their applause. "My other friend was introduced earlier, but I wanted to do it again because she has blessed me at this conference. Her husband is the dynamic Bernard Taylor. She is a woman of God with an awesome ministry. Everybody, say hello to my friend, Misha Taylor."

Misha stood and waved to the audience.

"Now I want to introduce you to the best part of me, my twin, my daughter, Camille."

Camille stood and quickly sat down.

Shante flipped open her notebook and turned some pages. She opened her Bible and turned to Isaiah 43:18–19. "When I first got the invitation to preach here, I thought God had given me a message to preach to you about the twenty-first-century virtuous woman. I had it all planned out. I was going to talk to you about being a well-rounded first lady . . ." She stopped and shook her head. "Y'all, it was going to be good." The audience responded with laughter.

"But God had another plan. As you sit and listen to me today, God has uprooted my life in a way that I never would have thought and never asked for. You see, I'm forty-six years old, and I just found out that I'm pregnant."

A loud gasp filled the air as the audience responded to her statement.

"That's the same thing I said before they had to pick me up off the floor," Shante laughed.

Deandrea sat in her chair listening to Shante begin her sermon with a scripture. Isaiah 43 was one of her favorite chapters in the Bible. She opened her Bible and read.

Remember ye not the former things, neither consider the things of old. Behold, I will do a new thing; now it shall spring forth; shall ye not know it? I will even make a way in the wilderness, and rivers in the desert.

It felt as if God was giving her instructions without hearing Shante's sermon. When she returned home, she had to forget all the things that went on before she left. God was indeed doing something new in her and her marriage. She had to have faith that God was going to do something new in her life, period. The thought of it made Deandrea's pulse race. Only a few more hours and she could see God's mighty work. She couldn't wait to get home.

24

The four women sat in Shante's room after service eating food they ordered from room service.

"Dee, I like how you sang Bernard Taylor's song. You messed up everybody. I even had to get my praise on," Camille said, lifting her hands in the air.

Deandrea had heard Bernard Taylor's new song many times on the radio as she drove to Philadelphia. It had taken its place in her psyche and worked its way into her classical song. It was such an original twist, many of the musicians stopped playing because they could not figure out what she was doing.

"I'll have to tell my husband about it. It was a wonderful mix of his new song," Misha added. She stood and stretched. She was tired, but she did not want to leave.

After Deandrea messed everyone up with her song, Shante wiped the place out with her sermon. Her impassioned message on forgiveness struck Misha in her heart. She realized that she had to forgive Bishop for all the things he did to her, and she had to forgive the man who violated her. From their abuse, God had turned it around and given her very special wonderful gifts in her husband and her daughter. She vowed that each time one of the negative memories came up, she would replace those thoughts with something good. She would even stop talking about it unless it served as a ministry help.

Misha thought she had forgiven them. Each time she and Bishop crossed paths, she would treat him with honor as if nothing had happened between the two of them. Tonight, she realized she constantly brought the incidents up, not necessarily mentioning Bishop's name, but to tell the world how badly she'd been treated. This allowed her to hang on to unforgiveness. But not anymore.

Matthew and Courtney were the new things that God had placed in her life to bring healing and wholeness. They were constant reminders of God's unfailing, unconditional love. Shante had encouraged them to embrace the consequences and use it to glorify God.

Misha loved Courtney. Courtney was the result of abuse like she had never experienced before. There were days when she would look at her sleeping baby and see that man and didn't want to touch her. Then there were those days when Misha did not want to let her baby go. Either day, Courtney loved Misha unconditionally. She was the perfect example of how God could take a horrible situation and make it a blessing.

"Mom, Pastor Edmunds gave me these CDs to give to you of your sermon while you changed clothes," Camille said as she handed the box of CDs to Shante, who was stuffing a piece of watermelon in her mouth. "When are you going to stop eating?" she asked.

Camille said what everyone else wanted to say. They laughed. Shante reminded Misha of herself when she was pregnant. She ate a lot too. It was one of the things that attracted Matthew to her. She wasn't shy about food around him, like other women he had dated. He said he would rather see her eat a large hoagie than play with a salad. In Misha's case, she ate both the hoagie and the salad. He loved that about her. She gained so much weight that after Courtney was born, she immediately switched to a healthier diet and was back in great physical shape.

"Tay, you messed me up tonight," Deandrea said.

"That wasn't me. What about you? I thought those people were never going to stop praising. After you sang, I could have gone home," Shante replied. She looked at Camille who was tapping numbers into her phone. "Who are you calling?"

"Aaron," Camille replied.

"You can't leave that man alone one minute," Deandrea said. "I bet March can't get here soon enough for the two of you."

"We're not getting married in March now—possibly in the fall, remember?" Camille said.

"What? Why not?" Deandrea said, forgetting the particulars of the previous conversation.

"I've always wanted a brother or sister. I want my sibling to be at my wedding. If we wait until Mom has the baby, then I will be happy." Camille pressed the end button on her phone.

"What did your fiancé say about that? Is he happy about the baby?" Misha asked her.

"Well, he doesn't think we need to change the date. But I told him that we were going to change it. I want my sibling to be at my wedding. That's it. He doesn't like it. He'll get over it." Camille flung her hand in the air.

Deandrea sat beside Camille. "Do you know why I'm here?" Camille shook her head. "I'm here because I was angry with Jarrod."

Camille turned away and looked downward. It was a telltale sign of why she was probably there too. She and her fiancé had an argument about their wedding. It was obvious there was no compromising with Camille, so nine times out of ten, she'd react the same way Deandrea had—hit the road to Philly.

"You have to talk to him. Don't just make decisions all willy-nilly," Deandrea said. "Marriage is compromise. Both of you have to give a little and get a little. It's not all about what you want. He has a life full of dreams, wants and needs, and so do you. Sometimes those things clash and interfere with what the other wants. That is when talking to each other is most important.

"My husband is very career- and ministry-oriented. He lives and breathes ministry. Not that he does not love his family, he does. It is through his ministry that he provides for his family. He will do whatever it takes to take care of both his family and ministry. Many times this has clashed with what I wanted to do. I gave up my practice because he needed help. I didn't know that I would feel totally neglected in the process.

"My problem is, I never talked to him about how I felt. We had an argument, and now I am here. In the past couple of days, I actually talked to him. He stopped everything to hear me. We're getting along much better now. You have to do the same. You are going to have to stop and listen to him."

"I agree with Camille," Shante butted in.

Deandrea's eyes stretched. "Why?" she asked.

"Well, I am going to be as big as a house when they get married. I know it's selfish, but, I should have some say-so."

"Thanks, Mom, for agreeing with me," Camille said sarcastically.

"You don't have any say-so. This is between Camille and Aaron. They are the ones who will determine when, and if, they will get married. Yes, I am sure they will take your feelings into account, but the final decision is theirs." Deandrea stood with her hands on her hips.

"You're right, Dee. But . . . I *am* the mother of the bride." Shante wiped her mouth with a napkin and set it on the table. "However, I do agree with you in one aspect." Shante addressed her daughter. "Camille, you have to talk with Aaron. Unspoken words often mean unspoken anger, fear and other deeply held emotions that can build a wall between the two of you. You should talk to him. Go call him now and listen to him." She stood. "In the meantime, I'm going to the bathroom."

"I'm going to call my husband too," Deandrea said as she walked into her room.

Misha stood to leave. These women ministered to her without them knowing it. She needed to talk to her husband. Many times when they had a problem, they would always say the cliché that God will make a way or it will be all right. Yet, the feelings were still there, unspoken and pushed aside. It was time they voice those emotions. It was time for her to call her husband.

The following morning as Misha picked up her purse to go to the final session, there was a knock on her door. She was surprised to see Shante, Deandrea and Camille standing in front of her when she opened the door. She stepped to the side and invited them in.

"I'm surprised you are here. I thought you were going to leave this morning," Misha said.

"Well, we thought we would attend the final session this morning. What time are you leaving?" Shante asked.

"I'm heading to the airport shortly after the morning session. My flight leaves at one," Misha answered.

"Good. I already called Edmunds's people and let them know to meet us here," Shante told her.

"Dee, don't you have a long drive home? When were you planning on leaving?" Misha asked.

"Right after service," she replied. "I'm going to drive until I get tired. Then get a room and start early Sunday morning. I can't wait to see Jarrod and the kids." Deandrea's face glowed with her unending smile.

Suddenly, someone knocked on the door. Their escorts had arrived, and they paraded out of the room toward the auditorium. Once the women arrived in the auditorium, they noticed the audience was much smaller than the last few days. It had been filled to capacity, but now, there was plenty of seating left.

Misha looked around the audience trying to see if she could spot First Lady Moore. She sighed when she did not find her. Apparently, it was not her duty to minister to First Lady because God never gave her the opportunity. She looked to her side and saw Shante and Deandrea clapping their hands and enjoying the service. This was her assignment. Not only was she there for them, they were there for her.

Misha smiled and stood to enjoy the service along with the others. Her peripheral vision caught sight of First Lady Edmunds. Her smile looked forced as she watched the service progress.

She is very depressed. She has even thought about suicide. Go to her, Misha heard in her spirit.

Misha moved next to her, took her hand and whispered in her ear, "I need to speak with you alone."

First Lady Edmunds looked at Misha, tears welled in her eyes. She nodded and followed Misha off the stage and into a dressing room behind the stage.

"The Spirit of the Lord told me you're depressed and suicidal. I want you to know you're not alone. God loves you," Misha said to her. "God loves you."

First Lady Edmunds sank into the director's chair in front of a large mirror. She cupped her face in her hands and wept. Misha handed her a tissue from the box that sat on the dressing table.

"I'm not going to kill myself. Yes, the thought has come up." She shook her head and blew her nose. "But I'm not going to do anything. That's just the devil. I'm just tired."

"Would you like to talk about it? I don't think anyone will mind if we talk a few minutes."

First Lady Edmunds paused, then said, "I think you know how hard it is being a first lady. My husband is never home. Before, I filled my life with my son and all his activities. I wanted him to have a normal life. Now, he is away at college. There is nothing to do except church stuff. Everyone is pulling on me, and the gossipers were spreading more lies than usual. I just feel alone at times."

The door of the room opened up. Deandrea stepped into the room. She stopped at the sight of the two women. "I'm sorry. I was wondering if anything was wrong. Can I help?"

God knew who to send. "You have perfect timing. First Lady is having some of the same issues that you just experienced. You two need to talk." Misha patted First Lady on the shoulder. "I'm going to leave you with Pastor Dee. She is very capable of helping you. You two have a lot in common."

"Thank you," First Lady Edmunds said.

Misha left the two of them alone in the room and returned to the stage. She sat next to Shante.

"Is everything all right?" Shante asked.

"Dee's taking care of it."

The service was as exciting and spirited as the others they had attended. Deandrea and First Lady Edmunds walked to their seats on the stage right before Pastor Edmunds introduced the speaker. Deandrea's phone chimed. She'd forgotten to turn it off. She rushed to reach into her purse to quiet her phone. After she peeped at the ID, she stood and left the stage.

A few minutes later an usher slipped beside Shante and whispered in her ear. Shante leaped to her feet and left the stage. Misha and Camille followed her. They walked into the dressing room and found Deandrea with her phone in her lap crying.

"Dee, honey, what's wrong?" Shante ran to her.

"Miss Essie. It's Miss Essie. She's had a stroke. They don't think she's going to make it."

"Oh my God," Shante shouted. "How do you know?"

"Step, Jarrod's sister, just called me. She said Jarrod didn't want me to know until I got home. But she felt I should know, and she called. Oh my God. How am I going to make that drive?"

"Why don't you fly with me? I've got the plane. Someone can pick you up in Columbia."

"Dee, I can take your car to Washington, and Matthew and I will drive it to your home. It will be okay. Take the plane. Don't worry about your car. We'll get it to you," Misha suggested.

Shante called her crew to make different flight arrangements and to tell them that Deandrea would be joining them on this flight.

For them the conference was over. They hurried back to their rooms where they packed and loaded their luggage into Deandrea's car. Deandrea had much hope that her return home would be a joyous one. Instead, it was a disaster.

Misha drove Camille to the Thirtieth Street train station so she could catch a train back to New York. Then she took Shante and Deandrea to a private airport outside the city. Misha hugged Shante, she then hugged Deandrea, praying for her mother-in-law before letting her go. They stepped into the small jet. Misha programmed the GPS to lead her to the highway and headed for home.

Misha walked through the foyer of her home, down the hall past her formal dining room toward the kitchen. She could hear Matthew humming. She stopped when she saw him pouring formula into a bottle. His back was turned away from her. She gazed at Courtney peacefully gnawing on her rattle in the playpen. She was back at home. It was peaceful. Perfect.

She stepped toward Courtney when the baby spotted her and released a loud scream. Misha rushed to pick her up. Courtney pulled the sides of the crib trying to get to Misha who lifted her from the pen. Tears poured from Courtney's eyes as she held her head against Misha's chest and whimpered.

Matthew turned and stopped at the sight of Misha holding Courtney. She turned and smiled. Her eyes were radiant as she gazed at her husband. They quickly stepped toward each other. Misha held onto Courtney as her husband wrapped her in peace and serenity as their lips met. This was the love she sought all her life, a bond that could never be broken.

"Honey, I didn't expect you here until later. I was just getting ready to go to the airport. You take an earlier flight? You should have called me. I would have picked you up," Matthew whispered in her ear. Neither moved from their meeting place.

Courtney whimpered. Misha kissed the top of her head. "I am so happy to be home." She leaned in and kissed Matthew again. Then she sat on the sofa and held Courtney in her lap.

"Pastor Dee had a family emergency, and I drove her car home. I told her we would drive it to South Carolina for her. I hope you don't mind."

"No, that was the right thing to do. You should have called me." Matthew sat next to her.

"I know. Everything happened so fast. The drive was not too long." She laughed. "I think I broke every speeding law getting here. I hope God forgives me. I wanted to get home."

"I'm sure He will forgive you for that. We missed you."

"I missed you too." Misha looked at Courtney leaning against her breast, content, her hair unkempt as if Matthew had not touched it since she left.

"Tell me about the conference."

Misha wanted to but how could she explain all that she experienced to him? There wasn't enough time to explain the deliverance, healing, salvation, correction and instruction she received.

As Courtney tried to force her eyes to stay open, Matthew gently kissed Misha's lips. He stood and lifted Courtney from Misha's lap. She whimpered, but her head fell in a sound sleep. Misha followed him upstairs and watched as he laid her in the crib. He had established his place in her life as her father. As long as Misha had a say, nothing or no one would change that.

25

A month had gone by since the conference. The ladies spent a couple hours every Thursday evening on Skype talking and encouraging one another. It was their time. In the meantime, Shante had completely cleared her schedule, and Max won the council race. The press eased up on the constant search for dirt in his and Shante's lives. Now, they were looking at the eager new county councilman who had already shown he had a heart for his constituents.

"Honey, don't forget I have a council meeting tonight. I'll be home late," Max said. He gave Shante a quick peck on the lips and kissed her abdomen and rushed out the door.

The holidays were upon them, and Shante waited for Camille to return from taking the boys to school. With her there a few days before Thanksgiving, it gave them a chance to talk and make plans for her summer wedding. The conference was good for Camille. She and Aaron got together and talked about their wedding and agreed to get married in August.

Today, they planned to spend the day shopping for Christmas gifts and food for Thanksgiving. Their house would be filled with friends and family who were spending time with them for the holiday. Shante wanted everything to be perfect.

"Mom, are you ready to go?" Camille asked as she returned from taking the boys to school. She bounced into the room full of energy and ready to go shopping.

Shante was four months pregnant and tired. She no longer had her obsession with food, and, in fact, now the smell of certain foods turned her stomach. Camille still expected her mother to be able to go and go. She seemed to have forgotten Shante was nearly fifty years old and did not have the energy she had before. But there was a lot to do, and Shante didn't want to waste time thinking about what she couldn't do. She picked up her purse and headed for the garage.

Their first stop was at the most expensive bridal boutique in Columbia. Why Camille had to order a new dress was beyond Shante. She could have used the one she already purchased. Instead, she wanted a dress for a summer wedding.

The bridal shop was filled with women looking at aisles of white wedding dresses, colorful bridesmaids' outfits and shelves of accessories. Mothers were advising their daughters about the fit of the dresses. Friends of brides-to-be were giving their opinions about everything, and Shante sat back in the corner, wishing Camille would hurry up and find something she liked or admit defeat and leave for another store or lunch. After an hour in the store, Camille settled for a simple tiara. She headed for checkout with a thankful Shante behind her.

"Mom, I think I left my wallet in my other bag," she said, looking in her large handbag. She pulled items out and set them on the countertop, looking for her wallet. The people in the line behind them huffed at the sight. Shante reached into her purse and pulled out money and handed it to the cashier. They left the store and returned home to get Camille's wallet.

Camille pulled the car into the driveway of Shante's house. "I'll only take a minute. I know exactly where my wallet is," Camille said as she opened the door to the car and ran into the house.

Shante exited the car to use the downstairs powder room. As she entered the house she heard a strange noise coming from upstairs. Someone, other than Camille, was in her house. Against her better judgment, she followed the sounds of people talking up the stairs. She knew she shouldn't go exploring. The wise thing to do was call the police, but she could not resist. There was something familiar about the voices.

She took the last few steps toward Jonathan's room. Two people were talking. One of them sounded like her son who was supposed to be in school.

Shante pushed open the door and rushed into the room. She gasped. "Oh my goodness." She blinked. She could not believe what she was seeing. Her oldest son and that fast little girl Marshay stood in her house, barely clothed, looking as if they were ready to do something neither one of them were ready for.

"Jon!"

Jonathan and Marshay jumped and pulled apart from each other. Jonathan reached for his shirt as Marshay pulled her blouse over her head.

"Mama Tay! It's not . . . we were just—"

"Don't say anything, Jon. You're in enough trouble as it is. Why aren't you in school? Didn't Camille take you to school this morning?" The veins in Shante's neck pulsed. Her head hurt at the sight of the two of them trying to dress as fast as they could.

How could he do this to them? He was raised in the church. He knew the Word of God. He knew fornication was a sin. Yet, Shante found him in their home about to get his freak on with this little girl. Marshay stood behind him with a look of terror on her face.

"Mom, what's wrong?" Camille rushed into the room. She spotted the two teenagers. "Whoa . . ."

"Camille, make sure the two of them are dressed and downstairs in the family room in five minutes," Shante said before she turned on her heels and exited the room. She'd seen enough.

Shante headed downstairs. How in the world was she going to handle this? Max was going to kill him. Cutting class, having sex, Jonathan was in more trouble than she could have ever imagined. How many times had he done this? She took deep breaths as she paced the family-room floor trying to come up with a plan. First, she needed to call Marshay's parents and let them know she was out of school. Then she will deal with her son.

Jonathan and Marshay walked into the family room as if they were walking to the gas chamber. Fear filled their eyes as they watched every move Shante made. She continued pacing the floor with her arms wrapped around her waist.

"Mama Tay—" Jonathan started.

Shante lifted her hand for him to stop. "Jon. Be quiet. Don't say anything right now. Marshay, go call your parents and tell them to pick you up here. Camille, you go with her. Tell them I will talk with them when they arrive. I have to deal with Jon."

Camille and Marshay left the room to call her parents.

"Well, Jon, what do you think I should do?" Shante asked.

"Give me another chance."

"To do what?" Shante stopped pacing.

"We didn't do anything!"

"And what if I hadn't come home? What would have happened then? What were you thinking?"

He hung his head down. Shante knew exactly what would have happened. Thank God Camille forgot her wallet.

"We taught you better than this. I expected so much more from you."

"Like father, like son," Jonathan smarted off.

What did he just say to me? Shante balled her hands on her hips. Jonathan was pushing every button he could, and he didn't have the right to do so. "What do you mean by that?"

"We know about you and dad," he said in a harsh, accusatory manner.

"Know what?" What could he have on them? He didn't know anything about the summer they got engaged. He was out of town.

"My friends told me you lived with dad when we were visiting Obaasan and Jiji."

Shante's hand flew to her mouth. Who told him they lived together? They never lived together although she was at his house a lot.

"They said you were there all the time. We found some of your clothes in the laundry when we got back. Dad made up some excuse. I could tell you had been there."

Shante looked away. Guilt ran through her, giving her chills of condemnation. "Jon, go to your room until I can get myself together enough to talk to you."

Camille and Marshay returned to the room.

"Marshay's mom will be here in about twenty minutes," Camille said.

Shante was so filled with guilt she could not look either one of them in the face. She stared into the mirror above the fireplace as Misha's words filled her mind, *"If you don't repent, you will find your sins manifested in your own house."* Today, she had seen the fulfillment of that word. This was not about Jonathan and Marshay. It was about her and Max and their secret sin.

She had forgotten what Misha said to her at the conference. She failed to discuss it with Max, and now, she was paying for it. How could she rectify the situation? Should she call Misha and ask for advice? She was too young. She wouldn't know how to handle this.

"Jon, go to your room," Shante said again. "Camille, can you and Marshay give me a minute."

Everyone left the room.

Shante paced the floor and prayed for God's direction. Their home was finally calm . . . and now this. She didn't want another fight between Jonathan and Max. She had to tell Max what happened or he was going to hear it from Marshay's parents.

She stopped pacing. "God forgive me. I should have repented the night Misha warned me. Please forgive me and show me what to do."

Jonathan sat on his bed staring blankly at the television, not focusing on it, when Shante walked into his room. He did not acknowledge her presence. She sat beside him. He did not move. "What do you think I should tell your father?"

"Tell him what you want." He seemed peeved.

"I'm trying to be civil. You need to talk to me before he gets here. Marshay's mother just left. I talked to her. She's mad. I don't think Marshay will be able to see you anytime soon."

"Whatever," he said as if it didn't bother him.

"I know you're upset, Jon, but we need to talk," Shante picked up the remote and turned the television off. "Camille is downstairs. It's just the two of us. So let's talk. I'm going to begin. I don't know who told you your father and I lived together, but it's not true. We never lived together. I was at your house a lot while you were away. We were planning the wedding. It was no more than usual. So whoever told you we lived together, lied. It is absolutely false." She stood and faced him. "Jon, did you two ever . . . I mean . . . before we got here did you—"

"Have sex?" he blurted out.

"Well, yeah. You know there are a lot of things out there worse than having a baby. There are diseases that can kill you."

"I got protection."

What! My child has condoms? Shante could not believe this was the same child that sang in the youth choir and recited Easter speeches every year. Was this the same child who was such a good example for the youth when they moved to Columbia? What happened to the child who was on fire for God? "Where did you get condoms?"

"From Dad. They were in his nightstand when we moved. I kept them."

Shante turned away embarrassed and afraid that her expression would show that she was the one who drove to another state to buy condoms for their tryst. At the same time, she was relieved to know that he hadn't opened the package. If he had, he would have found out they were too old to use. It had been years since she purchased them. They would have crumbled in his hands. Nevertheless, now was the time for Max to have a talk with him, not an argument. Their son was growing up.

"Why don't you really tell me what's wrong?" She sat beside him again. She brushed his slick black hair away from his face so she could see his perfectly formed Asian eyes. He had changed so much, she hardly recognized him. He was no longer the little boy. He was maturing into a young man. "Talk to me, Jon."

"You don't care. Don't you have a conference or a book to write or something?"

"Now you know I'm not traveling anymore. No, I don't have another book to write, but I do have an ear to hear. Is this what all this is about?"

Jonathan stood and leaned on the bookcase in the corner of his room.

"You and Dad don't care. Dad is always working at the church, in the community and now the county council. You're always traveling. The only reason why you're not doing it now is because of the baby; otherwise, you wouldn't be here. When was the last time you went to my football games? Did you even notice I made the honor roll or that I made varsity basketball this year?"

"You made varsity?"

He looked at her, shook his head in disgust and walked across the room. "Marshay is there for me all the time. She is the only one in the crowd that shouts my name and congratulates me when I'm doing well. You and Dad used to do it—until you got married and started doing your own thing. Now with the baby, you really won't have time for us—none of us."

Shante had an overwhelming feeling of guilt. She knew she should be mad with him and lay down the law. But, she could feel his hurt and anger. Did her other sons feel the same way? She and Max had been very busy. They hadn't done a lot of things with the boys lately. She had spent more time with them when they were dating than they did now. Shante held back tears. She couldn't believe she didn't even know he made the varsity basketball team. Did Max know?

"Sometimes I wonder what our lives would be like if Mom had lived."

Now that was a low blow, a straight punch in the gut. He didn't have to go there. After all these years, he still missed his mother. He was so young when she died. How could he have any memories of her? Something in Shante was saying he only said that to punish her, and something else told her he longed for a loving motherly relationship, one Shante thought she was giving him. She had nothing more to say. She left the room.

Camille met Shante in the hallway. "How's he doing?" she asked.

"I can't talk to him right now."

Shante breezed past her and into her room. Closing the door, she allowed the tears to flow. She couldn't allow Jonathan to see her cry. He would think he had the best of her. She couldn't let him have the advantage in the house. He was still the child and she the parent. She would let Max punish him when he got home. She was drained. She lay across her bed and prayed.

Shante was awakened by the sound of Max's voice in the room. "Hey, baby. Camille wants you to know dinner's ready." Apparently, neither Camille nor Jonathan said anything. Max was smiling.

"Camille cooked?" Shante sat up in the bed and leaned on the headboard.

"The only thing she knows how," Max said with a smile.

"Spaghetti," they said together with a laugh.

Shante fluffed a pillow and placed it behind her back. "What are you doing home? I thought you had a council meeting."

"I do. I don't have to be there until seven. I've got a little over an hour. Besides, Camille told me what happened today."

"What happened?"

"She said you two caught Jon and Marshay skipping school." *Why did Camille do that?* Shante wanted to talk to Max first. Now all hell was about to break loose in their house. Shante couldn't stand another fight or an unhappy holiday. The season was supposed to be a joyous one. She couldn't allow their guests to come into a house full of pain.

"I can't believe they had the nerve to be at the mall when he knew the two of you were going to be shopping today. I think he wanted to get caught. Well, how did you punish him? We've got to stick together."

"I thought we would talk about it first."

"Well, the first thing is that little girl and no phone—"

"Max did you know Jon made the varsity basketball team?" she interrupted him. He stopped talking. "Did you know he made the honor roll?"

"He made varsity?" He leaned back and laughed. "That's my son, in the ninth grade and on varsity. Like father, like son."

A soft groan escaped Shante's mouth. That's the second time she had heard that today, and she still didn't like the sound of it. She can't let this go on any longer.

"Max, did you know the boys think we lived together before we got married?"

"What? Where did they get that idea?"

"One of your neighbors told them." Shante adjusted herself on the bed and took Max's hand. "Jon was not at the mall. He knew Camille and I would be out shopping all day. He was here with Marshay. I caught them undressing . . ."

"Did they . . ."

"No. I'm pretty sure they didn't. But I feel he may be heading in that direction. He really likes Marshay."

"You think so?"

"I can't really say. But you need to talk to him. He did cut school today."

Max gave a pained look, as if he feared having "the talk" with his son. "You're right. I'll talk to him."

"Max, before you do, there's something else."

"What is it?"

"Well, when I was in Philadelphia at the first ladies' conference, Misha told me something I had forgotten until today."

"What was that?"

She took his hands. "She said if we didn't repent of our sin, we would find it manifested in our own home."

"What was she talking about? Sin? What sin?" Max asked. "You know you can't listen to everyone who wants to prophesy to you. I know she's your friend, but what does she know about us?"

"She knows about the summer we spent together. Everybody knows. We thought we were doing something in secret. But everybody knew. We need to repent before the sin of fornication shows up in our house. Max, we need to repent."

"We were getting married. We had the ceremony." He stood and paced the floor in deep thought. Max was only silent when he was trying hard to focus on something, searching for an answer to whatever situation was at hand. Like Shante, he never thought about it before. They had the same mentality, that they were getting married and their secret ceremony made it right. But it wasn't. Sin was sin, and there was nothing they could do to change that. He looked nervous.

"Max, we need to repent, and we need to do it now."

Max fell onto the bed and hugged Shante tightly. "I loved you then, and even more now. I wouldn't do anything to hurt you," he said, "to hurt this family."

Shante and Max repented of their sin and prayed to God for forgiveness of their sin and to purify their bodies and household of any unrighteousness.

26

Deandrea stood over the stove stirring oatmeal for Drea's breakfast. R. J.'s pancakes and Jarrod's omelet were cooking on the griddle. The children were running around the house screaming at the top of their lungs. Jarrod bounced down the steps and kissed her on the cheek.

"Honey, the home health nurse called and said she is running late. She'll be here about eleven," he said.

With all the commotion, Deandrea could still hear the tap of Miss Essie's walker slowly moving toward the kitchen. Deandrea checked to see if the water was boiling for Miss Essie's grits. "Hey, hey, hey, stop pulling on your grandma's walker. She can make it to the table by herself," Jarrod yelled at Drea who was pulling on the walker and R. J. who was trying to climb it. "Come to the table and eat your breakfast."

Miss Essie struggled to speak to them with the slurred speech of a recovering stroke patient, her mouth slightly twisted to the right. "Morning," she said barely audible. Jarrod stood and helped her sit in her chair.

It had been six weeks since Miss Essie's stroke. Although Deandrea was happy she pulled through and was finally out of the rehabilitation center, there were days when she wished Miss Essie did not live with them. At the time she thought it would be a good idea. Snowhill didn't have a rehab center and the other medical treatment she needed. Greenville was a better option. But, the agreement was that Jarrod and his siblings would all share a role in taking care of her. Since Jarrod was the only one of his siblings that did not live in Snowhill, they got stuck with twenty-four hour, seven-day care.

Deandrea loved her mother-in-law like her own mother, but the reality was she was the one who was responsible for Miss Essie's daily care. It pained her to see Miss Essie go through all her troubles. Yet, it was another task that had been passed to her that she didn't ask for; more work for her while Jarrod was away. Now, not only did she have to take care of the children, she had to take care of his mother.

Deandrea was under incredible stress right now. She did not feel like eating. Her weight was down at least two dress sizes since she returned from the conference, and no one noticed. She had thought when she came home from the conference things would be better since she was looking at life a different way. Never would she have thought tragedy would meet her at home. She was thankful Shante had a plane to get her back faster than driving. She was also thankful for Misha who called her once, sometimes twice, a week to check on her and see how she was doing.

She still felt alone, more than before, however. She and Jarrod barely spoke to each other outside of talking about the children and his mother's treatment. There had been days when she felt as if he booked preaching engagements and various meetings just to get out of this house. Deandrea didn't have an outlet. The pattern continued. When he was away, she was at his church doing the work he should be doing. When he was at home, she was taking care of his mother, and on top of all this, she had to take care of the children and house.

Charlene and Miss Nellie tried hard to encourage her, but, as usual, Deandrea put on her fake smile and did what she had to do to get through the day. She had to keep the faith to believe God would work everything out. She didn't want to walk away from her husband, even though the thought flashed in her mind during moments of great frustration. It was those times when Jarrod tried to make things better by taking the children to day care. At times, he would even try to spend some time alone with them by taking them out for pizza or to the park. Deandrea wasn't sure if that was his way of getting out of the house, away from her and the pressure cooker atmosphere there. It was her hope it was his way of keeping his promise of helping her out.

Deandrea did have one day to look forward to: Thursday nights. Those were the nights when she, Misha and Shante video chatted. They prayed and talked about whatever came out of their mouths. It was Deandrea's only refuge. Jarrod understood she needed it. On Thursday night he took care of the children and his mother and allowed her the time to spend with her friends. She looked forward to hearing about the exciting things that were happening in her friends' lives. She lived through them and wondered if her life with Jarrod would ever return to the way it was when they first got married.

"Honey, can you preach on Sunday? I don't have anything in me," Jarrod asked as he gulped down his eggs.

Deandrea placed the bowl of grits in front of Miss Essie and placed a pat of butter on top.

"Can one of the associates preach?" she asked.

It was the holiday season, and Jarrod was working overtime. He spent much of Thanksgiving serving dinners and handing out boxes of groceries to the poor. He had preached at events in multiple churches. Tomorrow night, he had to preach at Star of David's annual Christmas gala. The exhaustion showed on his face.

"I guess they could. But I would like you to do it. I know it's short notice. You only have to preach one service. If you like, I can ask someone else to do the second service at least."

"I'll preach both services. Mom will have the children. I'll have time to study."

"Thanks."

Deandrea left her family eating at the kitchen table and walked to her room. It was still early in the morning, and she was already exhausted. She had thought she would have some time to enjoy the weekend. She had already packed the children's bags to spend the weekend with her mother. Miss Essie's bags were packed too. She was going to Snowhill with Jarrod today. Jarrod's niece was staying with Miss Essie during the weekend so she and Jarrod could attend the church gala. However, instead of relaxing, she had to prepare to preach.

Deandrea walked into the walk-in closet in her master bedroom searching for something to wear. She used to enjoy going to the gala. It was Jarrod's and her first official date. It always brought a smile to her face when she remembered the antique ball gown she wore and the tuxedo Jarrod wore that night. It was on her birthday back then. She spotted her jewelry box that sat atop the chest of drawers in the large room. She pulled out the beautiful black opal necklace Jarrod had given her for her birthday. It was a perfect match for her dress. Everything that night was so perfect. That was the night he taught her to dance.

"Babe, are you in here?" The sound of Jarrod's voice snapped her out of her memories. She returned the necklace to the box and walked out of the closet.

Jarrod sat on the bed putting his socks on, a languid expression on his face. Deandrea walked past him to the bathroom. She looked over her shoulder to see if he still sat on the bed. She opened the medicine cabinet and pulled out a small bottle. She counted the pills inside. Jarrod had not been taking his blood pressure medicine. This was one of those times when she felt like his mother instead of his wife. She shouldn't have to do this. He was a grown man. He knew he should be taking his medication. She returned to the closet and pulled the blood pressure machine off the shelf; then she placed it next to him on the bed.

"Hold out your arm. Let me take your blood pressure."

Jarrod rolled up his sleeve and held out his arm. Deandrea wrapped his arm in the cuff and pressed the on button to take his pressure. His pressure was up. Deandrea rolled her eyes. Resisting the urge to scold him like a child, she removed the cuff. She feared for Jarrod's health. He worked too hard, and it seemed as if she was the only one that cared. The intercom buzzed. Deandrea hesitated, then turned. Miss Essie needed her. She had to leave her husband to minister to his mother. She made a vow, for better or worse, twice. She hoped it did not get worse than this.

Saturday night arrived quickly. Miss Essie was at her home in Snowhill, and the children were with her mother. Deandrea and Jarrod had barely spoken to each other all day. She awoke early to prepare her sermon while Jarrod slept. When she took a nap, Jarrod worked on his sermon. Then they drove to Snowhill and checked into the hotel. They attended the gala, barely speaking to each other in the process. Deandrea and Jarrod presented themselves as the happy couple and danced the night away.

After the event, they returned to the hotel in silence. Deandrea had worn the formal dress she purchased weeks ago for the gala. It no longer fit. It was too big in some places, and she had to use safety pins to tighten it up. She didn't have time to take it to her mother's dress shop for alterations.

"Honey, you look beautiful tonight." Jarrod wrapped his arms around her waist and pulled her close to him. "Have you lost weight?" he asked.

Deandrea was surprised and delighted he noticed. At least it told her he was paying attention to her.

Jarrod twirled her around. He wrapped his arms around her tightly and swayed as if they were dancing.

"Remember the first time we danced?" Deandrea whispered.

"Uh-huh," he replied as they continued to hold each other and move slowly around the room.

"What happened to us?" she asked.

He stopped dancing and pulled away from her, his eyes not leaving hers. Deandrea was tired of living like this. Tonight, she was going to get an answer.

"We've got a lot going on now with the church, the kids, Mama. You know, a whole lot."

"We had a lot before, and we found the time for each other. What happened?"

He sat on the chaise. She sat beside him, resisting the urge to embrace him. "Are you sick?" she asked.

"No. Tired. It's late. We better get some sleep. We've got early services tomorrow."

He stood and removed his tie. Only moments ago Deandrea could feel his security and peace. He was in a safe place, and she messed it up with her questions. There was something deeper going on here. *Is he having an affair?* She rebuked the thought. Her husband was a workaholic and can be a pain in the butt sometimes, but he had integrity. He was not an adulterer.

Jarrod walked into the bathroom and closed the door. Not knowing what to do, Deandrea fell to her knees and prayed.

"Copastor, you preached this morning," a member of their church told Deandrea after the second service. "Were you at my house last night?"

Deandrea was emotionally spent. She purposely did not preach anything that had an inkling of resemblance to anything that was going on in her life. A powerful message on holiness and salvation every now and then does a church good. It was well received.

Deandrea sat in her office dreading the ride to Miss Essie's house to pick her up and taking that long ride home. Why were they still living in Greenville? It took too long to drive back and forth to work. That was one of the problems they had. They spend four hours a day on the road. They eat in the car, work in the car and return phone calls in the car. They practically lived in their cars.

It didn't matter when they were dating. Living in another city, away from their ministry, allowed them to date openly and freely without the constant watchful eyes of their devoted congregational members. They enjoyed the long rides back home. It would give them time to talk and connect with each other in ways Deandrea never imagined. They joked, laughed, cried, prayed and danced on those long rides home. Many times when they arrived home, they would sit in the car for hours and talk. They hated the moments they had to leave each other's sight. Right after they got married, there were times when they would not leave the car before ripping each other's clothes off and making love.

Today, they were a two-car family. Their schedules were so different, they needed to travel separately. Even today, they were in separate cars. They couldn't even ride in the same car for their once-a-year date night. Jarrod had to have a separate car. He never knew what he had to do after service on Sunday.

"Honey, we're going to eat at Mama's." Jarrod poked his head through the door. "The children are riding with me. I'll meet you there," he said and left.

Deandrea did not feel like being cheerful around Jarrod's family today. She gathered her coat and purse and walked to her car. She tossed her stuff onto the passenger seat and headed for the strip mall. She entered the department store and walked straight to the sporting goods section, where she got all the items she intended to purchase, and then made her way to the checkout counter.

"That will be one hundred sixty dollars and fifteen cents," the clerk behind the register said.

Deandrea paid for her items. She walked back to her car and returned to the church. Once inside the church, she changed into her newly purchased athletic wear and running shoes. It was cold outside, but she had to do something to get this stress off her. She felt like running. She wouldn't be able to run the entire five miles into town and back like she used to do. But today, if only for today, she was going to run as far and as fast as she could until she got tired.

Deandrea ran down the sidewalk as people honked their car horns as they passed her. She waved and kept her slow jog. She dodged traffic with a hat covering her head and gloves on her hands. Her jacket filled with air as the wind whipped her face, making tears fall from her eyes. She wanted to run longer and faster, but her tired body wouldn't allow it. About two miles into her run she stopped, turned around and walked back to the church.

Deandrea leaned on the hood of her car that sat in the empty church parking lot and wept. No one was there but her and God. She asked God for answers, but He didn't answer her. She wiped the frozen tears from her face and went and sat inside her car. She couldn't be around Jarrod's family today. For a few moments today, she just wanted to be alone. She started her car and turned onto the road for her long ride home.

27

"Hey, Mama, we're here," Misha shouted as she walked into the kitchen of the small brick ranch house she grew up in. The smell of homemade biscuits cooking filled the air. She felt good about being in Atlanta for the holidays and to celebrate Courtney's first birthday.

Her mother rushed down the hallway headed straight for Courtney who was crouched in Matthew's arms.

"Wait," Misha said. She threw out her hands to stop her mother's approach. Matthew stood Courtney on the floor.

Courtney gripped Matthew's leg as if she was holding on for dear life. She looked from side to side, trying to assess her environment or find what she can get into. Then she relaxed and released one arm from his leg.

"Call her," Misha instructed her mom.

"Courtney, baby, come to Nana." Her mother held out her hands toward the baby who was trying to steady herself.

Courtney released her other hand and fell to the floor. She looked to see if anyone was going to pick her up. When the adults did not run to her aid, she rolled over and crawled to a chair. She grabbed the seat of the chair and stood. After gaining her balance, she took a few unsteady steps toward her grandmother who was patiently waiting for her.

"She's walking. Oh my goodness. Look how big my baby has gotten," Misha's mom said as she reached for the baby in front of her.

Matthew walked to his mother-in-law, hugged her and kissed her cheek. Courtney gripped his arms trying to pull him to her.

"I can see who's spoiling her. Here take her. I've got to check on my food in the oven," She handed Courtney to Matthew. "Y'all come on in and make yourself at home."

Misha, Matthew and Courtney sat at the small kitchen table. Nothing much had changed in the room. The old clock was still hanging from the hook near the door. The curtains were new, but still the familiar green color.

Misha wanted to purchase her parents a new home when she got her settlement, but they refused. They were comfortable in their community with their friends, neighbors and church. They did not want to leave all that they had worked hard for.

There weren't many good times for Misha in this house, except the time Justin found out she knew Matthew. Misha smiled. She was pregnant. That was the first time her mother did not send her on the multiple holiday shopping trips to pick up one or two forgotten items. She sent her brother instead. That's when he spotted Misha and Matthew's picture in a magazine near the checkout lane. The rest was history.

"I want y'all to know I'm anointed to cast out devils. Anybody got a devil in them?" Misha's father entered the room with his usual wit and charm.

Matthew laughed loudly and stood to embrace him. Misha smiled and did the same. Somehow her daddy seemed shorter and wider than she remembered. He definitely had less hair.

"Hey, pumpkin. How are you?" Misha's father said, kissing her on the forehead. "Look at my beautiful granddaughter. Come to Papa." He took Courtney from Misha's arms and walked into the adjoining family room with her.

"Misha, can you do me a favor?" her mother asked. Misha already knew what it was. "Can you run to the store for me?"

Misha laughed. She was back at home now. Some things never change.

"I'll go with you," Matthew said.

"No. You stay here. You draw too much attention. I want to get in and out in a hurry." Misha lifted her purse and took the grocery list her mother was extending from her hand.

About fifteen minutes later, Misha pulled into the parking lot of the Piggly Wiggly and rushed in to purchase her mother's first list that was comprised of chicken broth—Campbell's only—Lipton tea bags—family size—and five pounds of sugar.

"Mimi? Is that you?"

Misha rolled her eyes. She knew that voice. Why did she have to run into him? She plastered a smile on her face and prepared to give her perfect life speech to her old boyfriend, Roger. Watching him approach her, she couldn't understand what she ever saw in him. She searched his face and body to find a reason and failed to find one.

"It's funny running into you here. Are you here for the holidays? Look at you. Married life looks good on you. Now you know if he doesn't act right, I'm still here." Roger laughed. He was the only one laughing.

He's got to be kidding. Never in this lifetime or another would he and Misha get together for any reason. He left her at a point in time when she needed someone. He chose his career over their life together. Then he tried to destroy her. God had the last laugh though. She survived and came out on top, despite all the foolishness he put her through.

"I called you at the church. Did you get my messages? I wanted you to come and preach on Women's Day at my church."

She did the women's day thing with him once and got burned. She was not going to jump into that oven again. "No, I didn't get the message," she lied and immediately repented. He should have gotten the hint when she didn't return his phone calls.

"Look, you don't have to wait until Women's Day. I'll call you, and we can make arrangements for you to preach. Where's Bernard? He can come with you and sing if he wants to. We can have a couple's night, and you can minister to the couples."

Be for real. Couples night? Who was he fooling? He was trying to get Bernard to sing at his church. He didn't realize Matthew was a better preacher than he was a singer. He would rather preach. Misha was not about to tell him that. She had to get away from this man. Although he aggravated her, she felt sorry for him. They had dated for several years. She could easily pick up on his moods. He was having a hard time. She was not the one to rescue him.

"Roger, it's good seeing you. I have to get back with this stuff for my mom. You know how she is with her never-ending shopping lists." Misha held up the paper in her hand.

"She's still doing that? Well, okay. Call me after the holidays and we can schedule something."

Misha waved and walked away from him. She could almost hear her grandmother's voice saying, "He ain't no count." She never did like him. She was right about him.

Misha sat with her family watching television and waiting for her brother Justin and his family to arrive.

"Misha, don't forget church starts at ten Sunday. Pastor will be happy to see you and Bernard," her mother reminded her.

"Matthew and Courtney are going to church with you. I've got something to do."

"What's more important than going to church?"

"I've got something to do, that's all." Misha walked into the kitchen and poured a glass of tea. "Guess who I ran into at the store. Roger," she answered before anyone had time to reply. "He looks like he's doing well."

"What is he doing, stalking you? He called here a few times looking for your number. I didn't give it to him," her mother said. The topic of Roger seemed to distract her for a moment as she filled Misha in on the latest gossip surrounding Roger and his church. Misha tuned her out. Tomorrow was an important day for her. She was going back to Bishop's church. She thought she was never going to step foot in that church again. But it was time for her to move on. In order to move forward, she had to come to terms with her past. This was the same past that had come back to force her to deal with it.

She learned a lot from the conference, not from the conference itself, but from the people God placed her with. They had built a strong bond. The last time they spoke, she hated to get off the phone. Her life was much better now that she had friends who understood what it was to be her and didn't judge her when she did something silly. Misha especially loved the way they corrected her when she needed it. They were not afraid of the gift. Shante and Deandrea said they were more afraid of her going to hell than about her being able to prophesy. God had blessed her with two friends who were real.

Misha always enjoyed being with her family at Christmas. The lights and sounds of the holidays helped her to forget her troubles. However, she couldn't keep what she had to do off her mind. Misha had an uncomfortable sleep. She tossed and turned all night until she finally got up and walked to the den, not wanting to disturb Matthew from his sleep. The night was long and daylight finally shown through the window. Misha reluctantly began her routine and began the day that could change her life.

Misha walked up the stairs to the traditional red brick church. She was greeted by a young lady who looked as if she was stunned to see her. "Misha?" She looked as if she had seen a ghost.

Misha acknowledged the usher at her old church and walked into the sanctuary. Her legs seemed to fail her. She could feel them shaking as she took a seat in the back of the church. She didn't know if she could do this. People filed past her as if they did not see her, as not one of them greeted her. How could they miss her in the bright red suit she wore? She selected this suit because it screamed power, authority, confidence and boldness, all the characteristics she needed to get this over with.

Bishop Moore and the associate ministers paraded into the sanctuary and took their place in the pulpit. Bishop scanned the congregation as if he was looking for someone. His and Misha's eyes connected. He leaned to one of the associates and whispered something in his ear. He then looked up with a staunch look on his face.

Misha could not tell if he was happy or not. His facial expression was tight. She did not come there to distract the service, but she was prepared to leave if asked.

The service progressed much like it did when she attended there. The first day she walked in here everything was so different than the Pentecostal church she was used to. Bishop taught, and it moved her in ways she could never explain. There was nobody that could preach like Bishop. He was definitely old school with a new twist.

Misha looked at the many familiar faces and a few new ones. There seemed to be fewer people in attendance this morning. The sanctuary felt smaller than she remembered. On the front pew, First Lady Moore sat proudly in her place, wearing a deep purple suit with matching hat. She always knew how to dress. Some things don't change.

Bishop stood at the "sacred desk," as he called it, and began his remarks.

"I see one of my daughters has returned to visit with us this morning. Misha Holloway, or should I say, Misha Taylor, please come join us here in the pulpit. You know we always have a seat for you in our pulpit."

Misha's legs shook. She hesitated. She didn't know if he was trying to set her up to embarrass her. Was he about to make good on his threats? She came here to set things straight and sitting in the pulpit would help her do what she needed to do. God had already showed her what to do and say.

"Misha, I know you might be reluctant to join me here. Please, I invite you to join us in the pulpit of your church."

My church? Where did that come from? Misha gripped the pew in front of her and pulled her body upward. She walked as fast as possible toward the pulpit. She climbed the four steps leading into the pulpit and shook the hands of the associates as she approached the center where Bishop stood.

"Y'all welcome Misha Holloway Taylor back home. The prodigal daughter has returned," Bishop told the congregation as they stood to their feet clapping their hands. These were the same people who yelled, "crucify her, crucify her," when Bishop called her a witch. Now she was the "prodigal daughter." He had some nerve.

"Misha, come up here and give us a few words."

Misha tried to control her temper. She had a few choice words for him. The church may not be the appropriate venue for them, however. Bishop wrapped his arms around her and hugged her tightly. He stretched out his hand toward the sacred desk and offered her the microphone.

Misha took a deep breath. She tried to get focused as she watched the congregation return to their seats. Suddenly, the door opened and in stepped Matthew, Courtney, her parents, in-laws and a few other extended family members.

Immediately her anger left her. Why was she angry anyway? She knew exactly how Bishop was before she walked into the church this morning. Nothing he said or did should have surprised her. She smiled as Matthew waved to her.

Bishop Moore joined Misha and took the microphone.

"I see Pastor Bernard Taylor just walked into the church. Please, Pastor Taylor, come join us in the pulpit." A loud rumble went through the church. Matthew handed Courtney to his mother. The congregation clapped as he walked toward the pulpit. Bishop continued. "Ushers, we have some seats here on the front. Please escort Pastor Taylor's family up here."

Bernard entered the pulpit and shook everyone's hand before greeting Misha with a kiss on the lips. He stood beside her as she approached the podium.

"Well, I didn't expect my husband and family to be here this morning." She took a quick breath trying to organize her thoughts. "It has been said this morning I'm the prodigal daughter. I don't agree with that comment. You see, *prodigal* means wasteful. Nothing has been wasteful about my life since I left this church. I have a beautiful family and a successful ministry. I have trusting and loving friends I can depend on and an extended family that supports me. However, sometimes, in order for some of us to move forward, we must first reconcile with our past. That's why I'm here today."

Misha turned toward Bishop. "Bishop, I want to say I love you. You taught me a lot while I was here, and even after I left. I have grown tremendously. I thank God for you. If I said or did anything to offend or bring harm to you or your ministry, please forgive me." Next, Misha directed her attention to the first lady. "First Lady Moore, I love you, and I hope when I'm your age, I can still look as good as you."

Next, Misha addressed the congregation. "Although it's exciting to be back, my stay is brief. You see, I must move on. God has placed me in ministry with my husband in Washington, D.C. We have a great work there. We must be committed to working in the vineyard we have been assigned to. I just stopped by to tell you thank you for everything, and I love you with all my heart. May the peace of God be with you all," Misha concluded her comments. She looked out at the congregation, her past and future reconciling in the same place and time, as if God was saying now she could move on. When she left there today, she could truly leave her past behind and walk out into her future.

28

"Okay, Mrs. Patrick, her head is out," Dr. Consuelo Neves said to Shante. "You can stop pushing until I tell you."

Shante leaned her head back on the pillow. Sweat covered her brow. Max stood in front of her staring down between her legs. That's how they got here in the first place. Shante gave a weak smile. There was a soft sucking noise, and then the loud wail of her newborn baby girl.

Jessica Renee Patrick was making her grand appearance. They had decided early on they would call her Jessie. Dr. Neves held up the screaming baby so she could get a quick look at her, then passed her into the hands of the waiting nurse. Max wiped the tears from his eyes and joined Shante at the head of the bed. This was their fifth child, the fourth Max had witnessed the birth of.

Shante could not believe she just had a baby when she was old enough to be a grandmother. This should have been Camille, but God chose her to have a child for such a time as this.

The nurse handed Shante the tightly wrapped baby who whimpered until she heard her mother's voice talking softly to her. Shante examined every feature of the baby's face.

"She's beautiful. She looks like you," Max said as he leaned over and kissed Shante. "I better go tell the boys."

The past few months had been trying ones. Little Jessie wanted to make sure her mother didn't gain a lot of weight during the pregnancy. She returned to sender much of the food that was sent down to her. The last month on bed rest didn't help either. But with all the problems, she was here, healthy and strong. Shante held the peaceful child in her arms. She looked so comfortable, and Shante was tired. She didn't remember being this tired when she had Camille. But that was a long time ago.

The boys quietly entered the room. They stood against the wall, afraid to approach Shante and the sleeping baby in her arms.

"Come on, guys. You won't hurt her. Come meet your little sister," Shante said.

Jonathan was the first to make a dash to the bed. "Can I hold her, Mama Tay?" he asked.

"Sure. Sit down in the rocker. Max will give her to you."

All three of the boys ran to the rocker in the corner of the room. Jonathan sat on the seat while Joshua and Jacob stood on either side. Max placed the baby in his lap.

"Hold her head," Max said as he shifted Jonathan's hand behind Jessica's head. Jonathan looked at his dad. A wide smile spread across his face.

Max walked to the bedside table and picked up the digital camera. He took pictures as the boys posed for the camera with their little sister.

These past few months had been hard for Jonathan. Marshay broke up with him after they got caught skipping school. She didn't understand why his parents would not let him date until he was sixteen. At first, he was extremely sad. His grades fell. He almost got kicked off the basketball team. Then he learned Marshay was not the girl he thought she was, so he swore off girls until he was thirty. That was . . . until Elise came along.

The boys took turns holding their little sister and posed for the camera. The phone was ringing nonstop with Max's family calling from Alabama, church people, council members and the media calling. There was a joyous atmosphere, but Shante couldn't help notice someone was missing. "Max, have you heard from Camille?" she asked.

"She's still trying to get a flight here. She's on standby. She said she would call when she gets a flight."

"Where are Sara and Abraham?" Deandrea screamed as she entered the room holding a wrapped gift in her hand. She was country-loud. She hugged Max. "Hi, guys," she greeted the boys. "How do you like your little sister?" She bent down to get a closer look at the baby who cracked open her eyes. "Oh, she's adorable. What did you name her?"

"Jessica Renee," Max said.

"Thank goodness you named her something I can pronounce. Jessica. I can remember that." Deandrea reached for the baby. She cradled the child in her arms.

"Hey, guys, are you hungry? Let's go downstairs to the cafeteria and get something to eat. Tay, can I get you anything?" Max asked Shante.

"No, I'm okay. Dee, you want anything?" Shante asked Deandrea.

Deandrea shook her head. Max and the boys exited the room.

"Dee, look at you. How much weight have you lost?" Shante asked.

"Forget about me. How are you?" Deandrea sat in the rocker. Jessie whimpered.

"She's probably hungry. She has a bottle on the table beside the bassinet," Shante said, pointing.

Deandrea reached for the bottle. She balanced the baby in her arms. She removed the protective cap from the bottle and placed the nipple in Jessica's mouth.

Shante leaned back. Her friend was back. She looked happy, although Shante couldn't tell if it was the fake façade Deandrea could flip on and off at will. In their weekly calls, Deandrea said she wanted to take time out for herself, and it looked as if she had. She had dropped a considerable amount of weight. Even though things were no different between her and Jarrod, her personality was so different than when they went to the conference.

"Hey, I didn't come to stay a long time. I wanted to see the baby. If you guys need anything, give me a call. I've got to get back to Snowhill to pick up my mother-in-law from the adult day center. Love you, guys." Deandrea held the baby to her chest and lightly patted her back until she released a burp. She placed the baby in the bassinet, hugged Shante and left the room.

Shante had dozed off to sleep when she was awakened by the sound of a crying baby. She turned to see Camille sitting in the rocker holding Jessica.

"Mom, she is so cute." Camille stuck the bottle in the baby's mouth silencing her cry. She seemed so natural with it. She did have a lot of practice helping with Joshua after his mother died. He was a baby then. "Can I take her back to New York with me?"

"Only if you want Max and the boys to move in with you." Shante adjusted the head of the bed and sat up, trying to find a comfortable spot to help her trembling body adjust to being single again. "How long have you been here?"

"About twenty minutes. She started crying. I thought she was hungry." She held up the bottle. "Looks like she was."

Camille rocked back and forth in the chair with the satisfied baby. "When are you going home?" Camille asked.

"Tomorrow, if everything is okay."

"Good. I'll be here until Friday. Aunt Gwen and Aunt Patrice will be here this weekend. They can help you then. I'll have plenty of time to go shopping for my little sister."

Shante leaned back in bed. She had finally found balance in her life. This time not working had allowed her to see what was really important in her life. Her family, friends and home church are the most important things secondary only to God. Her relationship with her sons had improved. She and Max had reworked their schedules and learned to delegate work to other ministers in the church. Max still had his council duties, but he found the time to attend games, recitals and other family events.

As for Shante, right now, she was satisfied with being a stay-at-home, work-at-home mom. It would be at least a year before she got back on the road. She was taking this time to take care of her own household. She could see the manifestation of the sermon she preached at the first ladies' conference. God had done a new thing in her life, and she was going to embrace and enjoy every moment of it.

29

Deandrea sat in her office stringing the laces on her running shoes, preparing for her daily run. Just then, Jarrod walked into her office. "How's Shante?" he asked. Deandrea peeped up at him and noticed he was dressed very casual in a jogging suit.

"She's fine. The baby is so beautiful. You should have seen her. She looks like Max. They named her Jessica."

"We should go visit her."

Jarrod had been away for several weeks. Spring revival season had kicked into high gear. He had only been home a couple of days a week in the last month. His schedule was always full this time of year. This was the first day Deandrea had seen him since Sunday. The children would be happy to see him. Tomorrow he would have his regular Saturday meetings, and she wouldn't see him until late in the afternoon. Until that time, she vowed to keep her strict schedule and continue to take time for herself. It helped to keep order in the home.

"Mind if I run with you today?" he asked.

"I've been running a few months now. It's been awhile since you ran. I don't think you can keep up with me." Boy, had things changed! When she had first arrived in Snowhill years ago in all her arrogant glory, the tables were turned. Jarrod was running ten miles a day. Deandrea was very out of shape. She had been determined to make the ten-mile trek despite his criticisms and doubt that she could finish the course.

Now, she was running six miles a day. Jarrod wouldn't be able to keep up with her. She ran to get rid of stress. The weight loss was an unexpected benefit and pleasant reward that came from sheer determination in a fight not to lose her mind. It was also a time when she could pray and connect with God without the distraction of children or ministry. People saw her running around town, smiling and waving at them, not knowing she was praying and worshiping God the entire time.

For the past two weeks she had been fasting and praying for her marriage. Deep intercession for Jarrod and her marriage was urgently needed. Jarrod was working too hard. He was off taking care of everybody else's house and not his own again. It was like he couldn't say no to an invitation. When he arrived home, he was exhausted and burdened by the things he saw at other churches. Deandrea loved her husband and didn't want the church to kill him.

They left the church running the same path they ran many years ago. Deandrea slowed her pace so Jarrod could keep up with her.

"Wait. I need to catch my breath." Jarrod stopped, bent over a brick retaining wall and took deep breaths.

Deandrea rushed to his side. "Are you okay?"

"It has been awhile since I ran. I didn't think I was that out of shape. Give me a minute," he said breathlessly. He leaned down, gripping his thighs, trying to slow his breathing.

Deandrea stood next to him and heard a voice in her spirit. She reached out to rub his back, but her hand paused midair. It was as if she was receiving instructions on what to do. It had to be the voice of the Lord. She vowed to be obedient to what she was hearing. She caressed his back until he stood. "Are you ready?" she asked him. He nodded. "We'll walk the rest of the way." He smiled.

They strolled back to the church, talking along the way. Jarrod was totally beat by the time they reached the building.

"Jarrod, can you pick your mother up from the center? I have an errand to run. I'll get the kids."

"Go ahead with your errand. I'll pick up Mom and the children. I'll pick up something for dinner too, if that's okay with you."

"Sure. Stop by Miss Nellie's. She will pack a cooler for you. She knows what I usually get. It will be fine when you get home. I will meet you there."

He nodded and limped into the building.

Deandrea took a quick shower and put on a change of clothes. Then she jumped in her car and headed into town.

"We can see you tomorrow. You need to have this information completed when you come in," the receptionist in the office said as she handed Deandrea some forms to complete.

So far, Deandrea's plan was working out. The appointment was scheduled. Now, she only had to get Jarrod to come along. That was the hard part.

The following day, Deandrea sat in her office wondering where Jarrod could be. She had searched all over the church looking for him. He had to be there. His car was in the parking lot. She picked up her phone to call his office one more time when he walked into her office.

"Kira said you were looking for me. What's up? I have a meeting in a few minutes," Jarrod said.

"Close the door, honey. There's something I need to ask you privately."

He closed the door and met Deandrea in the center of the room. She wrapped her arms around him, and her lips met his, softly, then passionately as her tongue danced with his.

"What was that for?" he asked when their lips separated.

"It's a secret," she said playfully, her lips curving to a sly smile. Her hands caressed the back of his head. "I'm the copastor of this church, right?"

"What kind of a question is that? Sure you are," he said softly.

"That means I have some authority around here, right?"

He leaned back giving her a curious look. "Right."

"Well, I have taken executive authority and cancelled all your meetings for the rest of the day."

Jarrod released her and stepped back, saying, "What did you do that for?"

"I wanted to spend some time alone with you. Your mother is at the center. The kids are in day care. I thought we could take an early lunch and see where that leads. We used to do it all the time."

"The budget meeting at eleven is important. I can't—"

"Rescheduled for tomorrow at the same time."

"I have to meet the contractor about repairs to the old church at one thirty—"

"Rescheduled for Monday."

Today, Jarrod was going to do what she wanted him to do. She had taken away all his excuses. He was going with her, even if she had to drag him, kicking and screaming.

"I can't. Not today. I have a lot of work to do."

"Your first ministry is to your family. Isn't there some place in the Bible that says, 'How can a man take care of the affairs of the church if he can't take care of his own family?' or something like that?" *Thank you, Lord, for that one.* "I need to spend some time with you. I love you. Yesterday, I loved walking and talking with you. We used to do that all the time, remember?" A smile spread across his face. "We haven't really seen each other the past few weeks. I just want to be with you. I want to have a few minutes alone with my husband. Please have lunch with me, Jarrod."

"Sure. We can have lunch," he surrendered.

"Good. I'll drive. I have something special planned."

Deandrea's plan was now in full gear. It was time for phase two. She and Jarrod left the church and drove the short distance to the office where Deandrea had scheduled their date.

"Honey, I've got to run in here and pick up something. Come on in with me. It will only take a minute," she said softly.

Jarrod agreed. They got out of the car and held hands as they walked into the office.

"Hi, we have an eleven o'clock appointment with Dr. Chandler," Deandrea told the receptionist sitting behind the enclosed area guarded by a sliding glass window.

"Patient's name?" the receptionist asked.

"Jarrod Fuller."

"Me? I don't have an appointment with Dr. Chandler," Jarrod jumped in.

"Yes, you do, honey. I made it for you yesterday. We need to see about your blood pressure."

Jarrod's face went blank. He realized he had been tricked. He sat quietly, waiting for his name to be called. It was exactly how Deandrea knew he would respond. He was not the type of person who would cause a scene. She knew he would go through the motions and later voice his opinion. That was the risk she had to take. She knew that when she scheduled the appointment.

After sitting silently in the stale waiting room for a few minutes, Jarrod was called to the examination area. Deandrea went with him.

Jarrod barely said a word when Deandrea presented Dr. Chandler with the paper she had used to keep track of his blood pressure when he was home. Jarrod answered direct questions with short answers.

"Did that medication I gave you at your last appointment help?" Dr. Chandler asked him.

"It made me feel like I was going to pass out. I felt better not taking it."

"I'll try you on another medication. Let me know how this one works." Dr. Chandler offered him a prescription. Jarrod did not accept the prescription Dr. Chandler handed him at the end of his appointment. He nonchalantly walked back to the car. Deandrea took the prescription, paid the bill and followed Jarrod to the car.

"Take me back to the church," was all he had to say once they got in the car.

"Jarrod, would you have gone if I told you about the appointment?" Deandrea asked while she drove them back to the church.

Jarrod did not answer.

"I could tell you were sick and you just kept going and going. If I say I love you, it means I will take care of you, even when you won't take care of yourself." Deandrea continued, "I could tell something was wrong. You were exhausted. Your face was ashen. You weren't sleeping. You were tense. On top of that, your blood pressure has been extremely high. It has been going on for a long time. Why didn't you tell me your medication made you sick? We could have taken care of this a long time ago."

Tiring of talking to herself, Deandrea closed her mouth and turned into the parking lot of the church. Jarrod jumped out of the car before it came to a complete stop and slammed the door. He disappeared behind the doors of the church.

For the next few days, Jarrod spoke very little to Deandrea. The night of his doctor's appointment, he slept in the guest room. Deandrea had his prescription filled. She secretly counted it every day. He refused to let her take his blood pressure. She had messed up this time.

Deandrea pulled into her driveway, tired from the exhausting day at the church. Jarrod stayed at home with the children and his mother was still in Snowhill at her house while Step visited from Ohio. Normally, she would not be concerned, but he did not go to church yesterday. For him not to show up at work two days in a row was strange for him and out of character. The atmosphere in their home for the past two weeks had been tense.

She sat in her car and prayed, "God, I want my husband back. I want my family back. I want my life back. I repent of everything I have ever done. Lord, please, give me my family back."

She opened the garage door and saw Jarrod's car parked inside. He was at home. She dreaded going inside. She entered the house through the mudroom and walked into their kitchen. Jarrod leaned against a counter drinking water from a bottle. The house was eerily quiet. Something was going on here.

Deandrea moved around the kitchen island and spotted several pieces of luggage sitting on the other side. It was more than he usually took when he traveled to preach. Panic filled her body. She fought to hold back tears. If he wanted to leave, he was not going to see her crying and begging him to stay.

"Where are you going?" she asked him. He lifted the water bottle to his lips and took a sip as if he did not hear her talking to him. "Why did you pack so much luggage?"

"This is not mine. It's yours."

Her eyes welled with tears. She looked around the room. She didn't see the twins. "Where are my children?" she yelled and rushed past him, searching from room to room, looking for them. "R. J., Drea . . . where are you?" she cried out. She returned to the kitchen where Jarrod stood in the same spot smiling as if he held the key to her panic. "What did you do with my children?"

"Calm down. Our children are at your mother's. Here, call her." He handed her the phone. "She will tell you she has them."

Deandrea punched in the number. "Mom, are the twins with you?"

"Yes, they are right here playing with your father. Jarrod asked me if I could keep them a few days until you came back from your trip."

"Trip?"

"Oh, honey, I wasn't supposed to say anything. Don't worry. The children will be fine."

Deandrea ended her call. Her heart was beating like she had just run the New York City Marathon.

"I owe you an apology," Jarrod began. "You knew I was sick and tried to get me help, and I got angry. I had a right to be angry. You tricked me. You should have told me we were going to see Dr. Chandler."

"Would you have gone?" Deandrea tried to slow her breathing.

"Probably not. I understand why you felt you had to trick me. You shouldn't have done it. But you saved my life. I didn't tell you I was sick because I didn't want you to be worried about me. I felt if I kept active, everything would be fine."

"Jarrod, I thought it was me. I imagined all types of things. You wouldn't talk to me. What was I to think?"

"I don't know what to say other than I apologize. That new medication works a lot better. I feel so much better.

"I have been so sick these past few months. There were days when I thought I wasn't going to make it. I had so much on my plate, and I neglected you and the children. I'm so sorry." He set the water bottle on the granite countertop and walked to Deandrea. "I resigned from the ministerial association."

Deandrea gasped. "Why?"

"I needed time for my family."

Deandrea could no longer hold back the tears, happy tears. They flowed down her cheeks.

"I'm sorry for all I've put you through these past few months. Forgive me," he whispered in her ear.

It was easy for Deandrea to forgive him. God had answered her prayers. God had given her back her husband. She noticed the luggage sitting next to the island. "Honey, why did you pack my bags?"

"Oh. I almost forgot. We're going on a trip."

"A trip? Where?"

"You'll see." He pulled Deandrea to him and kissed her. It felt just like the first time.

Deandrea peered out the window of the small private plane. The blue water of the Atlantic Ocean passed below. The water was so clear, she could see schools of fish swimming carefree in the water.

As the plane descended, Deandrea recognized the island airport. It was the same place Jarrod had proposed to her. The excitement was unbearable.

They exited the plane and got into a waiting car that took them to the same hotel they stayed in before. The lobby of the hotel had not changed in the years since their last stay. Jarrod had even arranged to have the same room.

Deandrea stood in their room peering out of the open window at the beautiful Caribbean landscape and feeling the gentle breeze coming off the ocean. Jarrod came behind her and wrapped his arms around her waist.

"Jarrod, you thought of everything."

"I wanted it to be special. I am truly sorry . . ."

"You've already apologized. Let's put that behind us and look to the future."

Jarrod kissed his wife, moving from her lips, to her cheek, then her neck. He lightly sucked her earlobe, and then began to whisper in her ear. "You exercise, I don't. Please don't hurt me," he jokingly said.

Deandrea and Jarrod did not leave the room for the next twenty-four hours. They were exhausted, having little sleep since arriving. They finally called room service to deliver a full meal of island favorites and fresh fruit. Jarrod crawled onto the bed, holding a slice of mango in his hand. He traced Deandrea's lips with the fruit. She licked the juice, then kissed him.

"I got you something. Wait right here." He walked into the other room and returned with a small package and handed it to her.

"What's this?" she asked.

"Open it and see."

Deandrea pulled the lavender ribbon on the package and lifted the top of the box. Inside sat a small sign with her name on it. She lifted it from the box and read the sign. DR. DEANDREA FULLER, PH.D., D.D. "What's this? I don't get it."

"Well, I remembered the day we were at Myrtle Beach and you told me why you became a psychologist. I took that away from you and forced you into my world. I realize you need that outlet. So I rented an office for you in town and applied for your business license. This is the sign that will hang on your door."

"You want me to open up my own practice again?" Deandrea sat up, holding the sheet across her chest. He had thought about her and her needs. It was the perfect gift. A week was not long enough to thank him for this one. "Where exactly is the office?"

"Well, that's the second part," he said. Deandrea didn't like the sound of his voice. He backed away from the bed. "It's two doors down from the hospital."

She could deal with that. "Which one, Memorial, St. Francis . . ."

"Snowhill."

"Snowhill? Don't you think I'll be more successful in Greenville?" she asked.

"I figured Greenville would be too far for you to drive every day."

What was he talking about? They lived in Greenville County. The traffic was bad. She would adjust. She didn't understand. Would she have to go to the church and her practice on the same day? That would be ridiculous.

Jarrod walked to his luggage and pulled out an envelope and extended it to her. "Take a look at this."

Deandrea opened the envelope and pulled out the deed to his parents' land. "I was thinking it's too far to drive back and forth every day from Snowhill. Our work is there. We should go ahead and move there. I've already talked to Mama and everybody about buying the land. We can build a house, and we'll be able to take care of Mama and the kids better if we didn't have that drive."

Deandrea's hands flew to her mouth. He had been thinking the same thing she had been thinking for months. She looked at the paper she still held in her hand. She spotted the selling price. "Is this a fair price?" she asked him.

"It's better than fair. I added extra to the appraisal. We should have a good return on our money within a couple of years with the way the town's growing."

Deandrea smiled. "Well, I guess we're moving to Snowhill." She dropped the paper onto the nightstand, then took her hand and caressed Jarrod's face. "I missed you," she said to him.

He took her in his arms, and she submitted to his embrace. "Well, baby, I'm back!"

30

Misha and Matthew sat in the lobby of family court awaiting the hearing concerning Courtney's adoption. Misha's leg shook nervously. She was more nervous than the day she got married. She had not gotten any sleep last night worrying about what was going to happen in court today. Matthew didn't get any sleep either. She could hear him praying well into the middle of the night. She had to trust and believe God had already worked everything out.

"I wonder what's taking that attorney so long to get here," Matthew's mother said to them.

Heckler's parents had been out of the country for months and had recently arrived, allowing them to finally schedule the hearing. Misha looked at every middle-aged white person, wondering if they were the ones who were objecting to Matthew adopting Courtney. She remembered that man had deep blue eyes. She looked for people with hauntingly deep blue eyes, but did not see anyone. No one seemed to notice her staring at them, inspecting every inch of their bodies, trying desperately to see the enemy working in one of them.

"Hello, everybody. Sorry I'm late. I was caught up in another hearing," their attorney, John Stone, said to them. He came highly recommended by Matthew's attorney. "We are going to go into a private conference room to discuss your case."

They followed him to the room that held a table and four brown wooden chairs. Misha took a seat in one of the chairs. She tried hard to keep her body from shaking. She never had to go to court for the rape, criminal or civil trials, because everything was settled out of court. But it felt as if this was the day to face it anew. It felt as if she was being raped all over again. Matthew sat next to her and wrapped his arm around her.

"As I explained to you in the office, the judge will hear the objection first," John said. "Then, if nothing goes wrong, he will hear the adoption. It should be pretty cut-and-dried unless these people come up with some unusual evidence. In that case, I will ask for a continuance so I can review the evidence. It shouldn't be a problem though."

That was the last thing any of them wanted to do. This case had gone on long enough. They wanted to finally get it over with. They sat around making small talk as they waited for their names to be called for the hearing. Finally, there was a knock on the door. A man entered the room and asked to speak with John privately. They met with a handshake and a pat on the back. They asked each other about their families and briefly spoke of the last time they played golf together. The two of them left the room, laughing and talking.

"What do you think that was about?" Matt, Sr., asked.

"It's probably one of his attorney friends. Probably heard they had a hearing at the same time," Matthew said.

"Are you paying him to socialize?" Matthew's mother huffed.

Everybody in the room was nervous. None of them really knew what to expect. Instead of assuring them the case will work in their favor, their attorney had left the room to talk to his friend about golf.

"I'm sure if we had anything to be concerned about, he would be in here preparing us. He said there was nothing to worry about." Matthew intervened on behalf of their attorney who was MIA.

The door opened, and John stepped back into the room. "Hey, everybody, that was Blake McCauley, the Hecklers' attorney. He said they want to drop the objection. Looks like the adoption will move forward."

"Praise God!" Misha shouted and leaped from her seat.

"Thank you, Jesus," Matthew said and embraced her.

A sense of relief filled the room. Misha hugged John. "Thank you. Thank you."

The sound of celebration filled the tiny conference room. Matthew hugged his mother and father, and then shook John's hand.

"Now we're still going to have to go to the hearing to let the judge know the case is dropped. He may ask you and them if you're in agreement. Understand?"

Misha nodded her head. Why wouldn't she agree to something as terrific as this? This is the best news she had heard all week. Now they could be a family. Matthew would officially be Courtney's father. They would ask the judge to change Courtney's name to Courtney Elizabeth Taylor. No longer would she be called Holloway. That part of her life would fade into her past without her ever having a faint memory of it.

After a few minutes their case was finally called, and they anxiously entered the courtroom.

"Judge, my clients have taken into consideration the circumstances surrounding the birth of their grandchild, and we move to have the objection to the adoption withdrawn, if it pleases the court," Attorney McCauley said as he stood behind a brown table in the courtroom.

Misha looked at the middle-aged white couple that sat next to Attorney McCauley, their arms locked with each other. Tears ran from their eyes. The man pulled a tissue from the box on the table and handed it to the lady who wiped her eyes. They were taking this harder than anyone else.

Misha searched their faces, trying to find an inkling of their son in them. It was as if God had erased the memory of him from her mind. She strained to see evil in them. There was something different about this couple. What was it?

After the hearing, the group stood outside the court-room waiting for John to give them final instructions and the next step of this process. Matthew was back, making people laugh with his silly jokes. Misha laughed as she listened to her husband's wild stories. This had been a tiring process, and they were all glad it was over.

One thing they had learned, though, was the need and importance of talking. Misha and Matthew's relationship had grown, and they were closer now than ever before. They had learned how to support each other during the tough times.

Misha saw the Hecklers move past her out of the corner of her eye. They were talking to their attorney. Mr. Heckler's hair was black with prominent gray streaks. His skin was burnt orange. Mrs. Heckler looked older than she actually was. Her skin held the same burnt orange hue. Her hair was sun-washed blond with gray streaks. Both of them were dressed rather conservatively, to say it mildly. They didn't look as if they had very much money. Ironically, Misha and Matthew would have paid them anything to get rid of them.

Mrs. Heckler wiped her eyes with the tissue in her hand. Misha's heart ached for them. Mrs. Heckler and Misha's eyes met. Misha could feel her sadness, like death. Misha turned away and placed her hand on her chest. The pain she felt for this woman was overbearing.

She tried to focus on Matthew's jokes, but she couldn't help but look at the people who just walked into her life. Misha had a funny feeling that even as they walked toward the door, they weren't going anywhere.

Days after the court hearing Misha still couldn't get the Hecklers out of her spirit. Try as she might, she just couldn't seem to shake how Mrs. Heckler's eyes pierced her soul. There had to be a deep loss to lose her only son and now her biological granddaughter. As a Christian, how could Misha let this go on? God changed bad situations and made them good. He had brought physical healing to her life, spiritual healing in her ministry and now emotional healing. How could she deny that same healing to someone else? Would it be a sin to withhold her blessing and testimony from others who may need it? How could she overcome if someone didn't testify? She pondered the trials of life while trying to keep Courtney from destroying the flowers that sat on the table beside them as she and Matthew waited in the waiting area of John's office.

"Okay, you guys can come in now." John directed them to enter into the large conference room. Misha's heart beat wildly in anticipation with what was about to happen. "Mr. and Mrs. Heckler . . ." John began "this is—"

"I'm Misha Taylor." Misha would not allow John to introduce them. This was something she had to do herself. "This is my husband, Matthew Taylor, and this beautiful young lady is my daughter, Courtney, your granddaughter."

31

The sound of the ocean waves beating against the sandy beach was exactly what Shante needed. She pulled her dark sunglasses out of her hair and placed them over her eyes. The glare of the sun bouncing off the sand was blinding. She sat trying to block out the sound of the people enjoying the beach and Misha's voice.

"This is the life," Misha said.

Shante didn't want to open her eyes for fear this was only a dream. No children, no husband, no congregants or fans; only a group of first ladies relaxing during their retreat.

"I wish Matthew was here," Misha said.

"You would have to ruin it, wouldn't you? You are always talking about your husband. Relax. Let him take care of the baby. I thought we taught you that last year at the first ladies' conference," Shante told her. Misha didn't see her wishing Max and the children were there.

"This is not like last year's conference. We were in Philadelphia, and it was cold. There were a lot of people around," Misha continued.

Shante longed for the days when Misha was shy and quiet. Now, she talked all the time, more than Dee. No one thought it could be possible. Shante tried to soak up the sun on this beautiful Hawaiian beach, and Misha's talking about husband, children and church, the three topics they had all hoped to avoid this week.

Their lives had changed since that chance meeting in Philadelphia last year. They arrived at the conference for different reasons but left changed people.

Camille had once again decided to join the women at the tail end of the conference just for some R&R and to spend time with her mother. She was basking in the sun with her large sunglasses shading her eyes from the early-morning sun, always the diva. She was all grown-up now with a husband and their own production company. They recently signed a couple of new Gospel artists to develop. Camille was making a conscious effort not to be so bossy and controlling. It was hard for her, but, she was learning.

Shante stretched out on her chaise trying to distract herself from Misha's constant chatter. She was thankful for all her blessings. She had two beautiful daughters, three wonderful sons, and an outstanding husband. She had learned to balance family, career and ministry. In finding balance, she found herself. Her home was happier. Her children were happy and no longer doing things to get her attention. Repentance and forgiveness came into their home and made her and Max's relationship better. Her home was no longer sick.

Misha was still talking. She had come out of her shell. She was no longer the shy, quiet young lady they met in the mall that day in Philadelphia. She learned to embrace her position as first lady and the wife of a famous entertainer. God healed her from her past, and she had a promising future as a stylist for many Gospel artists and ministers.

One never knows how God is going to move in their life. God had taken Misha's rape and developed an international outreach ministry with her baby's biological grandparents, who, Misha learned, were missionaries themselves. Now their church has a training center for people who desired to be missionaries. Who would have ever thought she would be able to allow these people to be a part of her life? It took God.

"Where's First Lady Edmunds with our drinks?" Misha asked.

"When are you going to call me Alicia?" she said as she approached, carrying a tray of drinks.

It was wonderful to have First Lady Edmunds at the retreat. She needed the break too. She and Deandrea had bonded over the year. Last year she was on the brink of suicide. This year she was full of life.

"Misha, when are you going to have another baby?" First Lady Edmunds asked Misha who had finally stopped talking.

"Y'all, it's hot out here." Deandrea walked toward the group and sat on the lone chaise lounge next to Shante. "How can y'all stand all this sun? I'm about to burn up," she complained.

No matter what was going on in her life, good or bad, the ladies came to realize that Deandrea was going to find something to complain about. They laughed at her. She was three months pregnant and looked six. Even with her second twin pregnancy, she insisted on coming on the trip. She was happy now. Getting back to her psychology practice, part-time, was good for her and had done wonders for her attitude.

Her seven thousand square foot house in Snowhill would be complete in time to welcome the twins. With the way she and Jarrod had been getting along lately, they needed that much space to welcome all the children that might show up in the future.

"Alicia, who's going to be your keynote speaker at the conference this year?" Misha asked.

"Well, Shante is speaking, of course. Dee, are you going to be able to sing again this year?"

"I plan to be there," Dee said. "Good thing the conference is in a few weeks. I don't think I'll be able to make it after that. But it shouldn't be so bad. It's not this hot in Philadelphia."

"Hey, ladies, enough shop talk. Let's sit back and relax," Shante said. She lifted her tall glass filled with a sweet tropical drink. "To our first ladies' retreat and all the ladies that wish they could be here," she said.

Misha, Deandrea, Camille and First Lady Edmunds lifted their glasses. When they agreed to this trip, they didn't know how good it would be for all of them. The scenery in Hawaii was breathtaking, and their spirits were relaxed and at peace.

Their group was so different. Camille, the sexy young diva, looked at life with great expectation. Misha, a woman with deep insight and wisdom, taught them how to overcome adversity. Deandrea, the career-minded, committed woman of God, taught them how important family was to ministry. First Lady Edmunds, the faithful one, had shown them how to bounce back after deep sorrow. As for Shante, well, she learned repentance and forgiveness. Each one of them had learned they could walk in front of, beside and behind their husbands without diminishing their husbands' manhood or their own womanhood.

Shante laid back, listening to the chatter of her friends, realizing they were so different but quite the same. They were wives, mothers, career women, ministers of God and the first ladies of their churches. They were happy, and there were no more Sunday morning blues in their lives. To God be the glory!

Reader Questions

1. What does the Sunday morning blues mean to you?
2. Shante, Misha and Deandrea were all first ladies of churches. Were they the traditional, stereotypical first ladies? Explain.
3. Is the role of the church first lady changing? If so, in what way?
4. Shante had a secret sin. Do you think this is common in the ministry, and should all secret sins be exposed?
5. Deandrea left her psychological practice and her life as she knew it to help Jarrod with his ministry. Do you feel she made the right decision?
6. Misha had the gift of prophetic vision. Should she tell everything she sees?
7. How could Misha's gift interfere with her and her husband's ministry?
8. Do you feel conferences are an effective way to minister? Please explain your answer.
9. Do you feel people should know all the challenges leaders of the church have within their own personal lives?
10. Can church leaders find balance in every area of their lives and still provide effective ministry to their congregants?

About The Author

K.T. Richey is the bestselling author of the *Lady Preacher* Series. K.T. is a former pastor and social worker. Her books have been featured in Black Expressions and are listed as Amazon.com Indigo love bestsellers. She has been nominated for author of the year by several book clubs. She is the recipient of several writing awards, including the L.G. McGuire Literary award in poetry. She holds a bachelor of arts degree in social studies and a master's degree in counseling.

K.T. Richey is a prolific speaker, popular with women's groups, churches and book clubs. In her spare time, she enjoys travel, photography and reading. She currently lives in Maryland.

To contact her for speaking engagements, book clubs, etc., go to www.ktrichey.com, www.facebook/ktrichey, or on Twitter @Author K T Richey.

UC HIS GLORY BOOK CLUB!

www.uchisglorybookclub.net

UC His Glory Book Club is the spirit-inspired brain-child of Joylynn Ross, Author and Acquisitions Editor of Urban Christian, and Kendra Norman-Bellamy, Author for Urban Christian. This is an online book club that hosts authors of Urban Christian. We welcome as members all men and women who have a passion for reading Christian-based fiction.

UC His Glory Book Club pledges our commitment to provide support, positive feedback, encouragement, and a forum whereby members can openly discuss and review the literary works of Urban Christian authors.

There is no membership fee associated with UC His Glory Book Club; however, we do ask that you support the authors through purchasing, encouraging, providing book reviews, and of course, your prayers. We also ask that you respect our beliefs and follow the guidelines of the book club. We hope to receive your valuable input, opinions, and reviews that build up, rather than tear down our authors.

What We Believe:

—We believe that Jesus is the Christ, Son of the Living God.

—We believe the Bible is the true, living Word of God.

—We believe all Urban Christian authors should use their God-given writing abilities to honor God and share the message of the written word God has given to each of them uniquely.

—We believe in supporting Urban Christian authors in their literary endeavors by reading, purchasing and sharing their titles with our online community.

—We believe that in everything we do in our literary arena should be done in a manner that will lead to God being glorified and honored.

We look forward to the online fellowship with you. Please visit us often at www.uchisglorybookclub.net.

Many Blessing to You!

Shelia E. Lipsey,
President, UC His Glory Book Club